Best Friends

and

Brothers

A Tale of the Mexican War

Farley Dunn

THREE SKILLET

BEST FRIENDS AND BROTHERS, Dunn, Farley L

First Edition

 THREE SKILLET

www.ThreeSkilletPublishing.com

Cover design by Farley L Dunn

This book may not be reproduced in whole or in part, by electronic process or any other means, without permission of the author.

ISBN: 978-1-943189-31-1

My Special Thanks to . . .

. . . my aunt, a genealogy guru, who spent weeks reviewing my research, providing me information, and pointing me in new directions. Without her, my ancestors would still be lost in the mists of time.

. . . and my nephew, in the Air Force at the time, who offered invaluable military expertise to hone my battle scenes. He spent hours with me pouring over my manuscript and providing real-life examples of how military actions sound and feel.

Best Friends

and

Brothers

Captain Benjamin Moore

c. 1846

Lieutenant Thomas Hammond

c. 1846

FOREWORD

This is a work of fiction, although many of the story elements are woven around historical events.

In 1846, the beginning of the War with Mexico ripped the North American continent in half, and the United States military mobilized on all fronts. In one of the largest Army deployments of the first half of the 19th century, Colonel Stephen W. Kearny (who was promoted to brigadier general during the westward drive) traveled from Kansas toward California with the Army of the West. Two brothers-in-law, Captain Benjamin D. Moore and Lieutenant Thomas C. Hammond, rode together into battle at Kearny's side.

Along the disputed Texas border, General Zachary Taylor, the future President of the United States, successfully led an offensive into Mexico via the Rio Grande. At the same time, on the western shores of the continent, Commodores John D. Sloat and Robert F. Stockton, along with Commander Samuel F. Du Pont, Captain John C. Fremont, Lieutenant Archibald Gillespie, and the well-known "Kit" Carson engaged the enemy on yet a third stage.

The eminently successful Army of the West traveled from Fort Leavenworth, Kansas, to San Pasqual near San Diego, California, in a bloodless campaign while claiming the area

i

encompassing Santa Fe as U.S. territory along the way. Then, in the Army of the West's first armed skirmish of the five-month trek, Captain Moore and Lieutenant Hammond, along with two dozen other officers and enlisted men, were killed by Mexican Lancers (accurately called Californios in the regional Spanish, or Californians by some in the West). By all eyewitness reports, Benjamin Moore went down first, and Thomas Hammond was mortally wounded in a valiant attempt to save his brother-in-law, who had been riven with sixteen willow lances. Moore died instantly, Hammond several hours later.

Fourteen years earlier, Abraham Lincoln and Benjamin Moore served concurrently in the Black Hawk War of 1832. There is evidence the young Lincoln helped bury the dead after the Battle of Stillman's Run on May 14 of that year.

Benjamin Moore transferred from the Navy to the Army in 1832, receiving an increase in rank. However, in this tale, the souvenir Navy sextant he carried with him afterward is no more than literary conjecture.

Jefferson Davis, mentioned in this story, was the future President of the Confederacy. He served at Jefferson Barracks with Matthew Duncan, Benjamin Moore, and Thomas Swords in 1833.

Thomas Duncan, Benjamin Moore's nephew, fought in the War with Mexico at Vera Cruz. Years before, at age 13, he served in the Black Hawk War as a member of the Illinois Mounted Volunteers. He rose to the rank of brevet brigadier general in the United States Army, although his permanent rank was lieutenant colonel. In 1866, when Duncan was commander of the 5th U.S. Cavalry, William "Buffalo Bill" Cody served as one of his scouts.

While a 1st Lieutenant, Major Thomas Swords was court-martialed in 1835 for attempting to provoke a duel with Captain Matthew Duncan, the elder half-brother of Benjamin Moore. Then Swords served alongside Benjamin Moore in the War with Mexico. In 1846, he raised the first American flag over Santa Fe. Almost two decades later, Thomas Swords was made brevet major general (13 March 1865), serving in the Civil War as quartermaster.

Thomas Hammond and Mary Ann Hughes Hammond were married on horseback in the winter of 1845. It is unclear from historical records whether the ceremony was clandestine or simply a creative method of consummating their vows.

Included in this tale is 1st Lieutenant Henry T. Ogden. He was reputed to quote Shakespeare by the hour to anyone who would listen. Filled with vigor, he needed his hands kept busy, and he found entertaining outlets to burn off his excess energy. Involved in much playing of pranks, he would often lecture the troops in a humorous vein, and was a favorite among both officers and men.

Susan Shelby Magoffin, a bride of 19 in 1846, traveled westward with her trader husband, Samuel Magoffin, meeting General Stephen W. Kearny as well as the future president, General Zachary Taylor. She found Taylor to be a nice man, even though she was disappointed to discover his manner of dress gave him an air of disarray. She chronicled her tales in a since published diary, making reference to Benjamin Moore, Thomas Hammond, and Thomas Swords, among others, using her own unique style of writing and punctuation. Although I have tried to mimic the style of her writing, the entries in this novel are my own.

As the Army of the West attempted to cross Pawnee Creek, a man named Hughes drowned in sight of two of his fellows. They were unable to pull him to safety. His death and burial are chronicled in accounts of the time by the Army's topographical engineers.

William Duncan, Benjamin Moore's cousin through his half-brothers, died at Bent's Fort exactly as described, never seeing one day of combat in the Mexican War. His brother, Theodore, was at his side during his illness, and then continued with Doniphan's Missouri Volunteers to Mexico. Theodore rose to the rank of captain by the time of the Civil War. In June of 1861, he was murdered while in camp with the Smithville Company. Shot in the mouth, the bullet had to be removed from the gristle of his neck. He died some days later. The "infernal scoundrel" who committed the deed was apprehended the next day and immediately shot to death.

Midshipman J. S. Bohrer was invalided home as referenced in this story on the *USS Constitution* in April of 1846 with a head wound received in Portsmouth. He had suffered periods of debilitating unconsciousness while aboard the ship. It is unknown what happened to him afterward.

Commander Samuel F. Du Pont waited a number of hours for a Spanish flag to be found before he raised the Stars and Stripes at San Diego. Although San Diego had been under Mexican Republic rule for 24 years, Du Pont felt it important to make the transition from Spanish rule to American conquest.

Lieutenant James W. Abert, one of the Army's topographical engineers, became seriously ill and was left at Bent's Fort. Lieutenant William H. Emory continued with the Army of the West, recording his observations for posterity.

The Mexican boy hunted and killed as sport by members of General Zachary Taylor's 1st Kentucky regiment is recorded in the annals of the Army, although the names I've given the guilty volunteers are my own. The men in question were never penalized for their horrendous misconduct.

After the conclusion of the events depicted in the final pages of this book, General Kearny and his troops limped into Los Angeles, and a new conflict erupted over whether Kearny or Captain Fremont would be the legitimate legal authority in the new territory. In August of 1847, Fremont was arrested by Kearny. Transported to Washington, D.C., for court-martial, he was convicted of mutiny, disobedience of a superior officer, and military misconduct. His sentence was quickly and quietly commuted by President James K. Polk, and Fremont resigned his commission to settle for a time in California near Yosemite. Unable to resist the siren call of the battlefield, Fremont later served as a major general in the American Civil War.

The War with Mexico officially concluded on February 2, 1848, with the signing of the Treaty of Guadalupe Hidalgo.

There are numerous historical facts in this tale not listed here. If you research them, you'll find conflicting sources about the war. I've had to pick and choose my version of events, and invent details where no information was available. Of course, I've made the lives of my characters my own.

I take pride that several of the characters referenced in this story are my direct forebears through the Duncan line. While Benjamin D. Moore (no connection to Benjamin Moore Paint stores founded in 1883 in Brooklyn, New York) and Thomas C. Hammond may not fall in my direct lineage, they are forever linked by marriage and blood to my ancestral name, and I feel justified in claiming them as family.

Farley L. Dunn

TIME LINE

May

May 17, 1844   Capt. Benjamin D. Moore
Lt. Thomas C. Hammond
Mary Ann Hughes

April

April 13, 1846   Lt. Thomas C. Hammond

May

May 10, 2009	Jon and Mary Ann McCreary
May 11, 1846	President James K. Polk
May 13, 1846	Lt. Thomas C. Hammond
May 14, 1846	Mary Ann Hammond
May 15, 1846	Christopher "Kit" Carson
May 16, 1846	Abraham Lincoln
May 16, 2009	SPC Matthew Duncan McCreary
May 16, 2009	Jon and Mary Ann McCreary
May 16, 2009	Mary Ann McCreary
	PVT Matthew Duncan McCreary
May 17, 2009	SPC Matthew Duncan McCreary
May 18, 1846	Mexico President Mariano Paredes
May 19, 1846	Susan Shelby Magoffin

July 26, 1846	Capt. Benjamin D. Moore
	Lt. Thomas C. Hammond
July 29, 1846	Commander Samuel F. Du Pont
July 30, 1846	Mary Ann Hammond

August

Aug. 2, 1846	Mary Todd Lincoln
Aug. 3, 2009	SPC Matthew Duncan McCreary
Aug. 5, 1846	Mexico President José Salas
Aug. 5, 2009	SPC Matthew Duncan McCreary
Aug. 6-15, 1846	Lt. William H. Emory
Aug. 16, 1846	Gen. Antonio de Santa Anna
Aug. 17, 1846	*Proclamation of California*
Aug. 18, 1846	Capt. Benjamin D. Moore
	Lt. Thomas C. Hammond
Aug. 19, 1846	Commodore Robert F. Stockton
	Brevet Capt. John C. Fremont
	Lt. Archibald Gillespie
Aug. 24, 2009	Jon and Mary Ann McCreary

September

Sept. 2, 1846	Susan Shelby Magoffin
Sept. 5, 1846	Lt. Christopher "Kit" Carson
Sept. 9, 2009	*Palm Beach Herald*
Sept. 14, 1846	Susan Shelby Magoffin
Sept. 16, 1846	*El Siglo XIX*
Sept. 25, 1846	Brig. Gen. Stephen W. Kearny
Sept. 28, 2009	Mary Ann McCreary
	SPC Matthew Duncan McCreary

October

November

December

Winter 2010

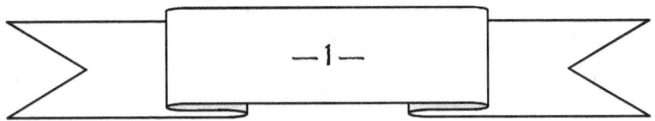

PLATTE CITY, MISSOURI
Home of Judge Matthew Hughes
MAY 17, 1844

"Ah, there you are, Mr. Hammond."

Captain Benjamin Moore called to his good friend, and he wore a wide smile on his face. A month before, President John Tyler had signed a Treaty of Annexation with the Republic of Texas, causing Mexico to sever diplomatic relations with the United States and raising threats of war. Fighting might erupt between the two countries eventually, but this night a rather more romantic campaign had been engaged. Ben was dressed in his most formal military gear, and his boots were black and shined. His hair was combed back with oil, and it glistened in the glow of a hundred candles.

His formal manner of speech was for this evening's events only, for he and Thomas Hammond were bonded by an uncommonly close friendship, indeed. At one another's side since their arrival, this was Thomas Hammond's first visit to the Hughes' household, and the good Benjamin Moore had insisted he not stray far until his sister-in-law could be found.

Thomas Hammond was also dressed to the nines, and he was enjoying his invitation to Judge Matthew Hughes' social gathering. Rather, he should say Mrs. Hughes' gathering, for the festivities had been hers to plan and in which to glory. Still. There was food aplenty, stuffed goose and ham, and root vegetables prepared in all manner of dishes. Meat pies were spread on the sideboards with generosity, and no shortage of drink could be found. And candles! Candles everywhere. More candles than could be counted—and oil lamps aplenty—lit the rooms of the Judge's airy residence. The household servants wore white aprons with matching caps on their heads.

As spacious as the Hughes' home was renowned to be, the festive atmosphere had expanded beyond the walls and spilled out the doors into the bricked courtyards surrounding the large building. Small, clipped lawns were installed with stone benches to provide seating for those who wished to converse privately. Of course, being outside, those areas were necessarily darkened in the deep of the evening, lit mostly by the fullness of the overhead moon. From several, laughter could be heard, both female as well as male. The soldiers from across the river, as well as numerous young ladies from Platte City, were present at the festivities, and all seemed to be finding abundant points of interest for their varied imaginations.

Three of the attendees had found very specific items of focus. Each other.

Thomas turned to see a beautiful girl standing at his

friend's side, and he flashed a broad smile. "Mr. Moore! How good to see you again on this festive evening!" He was barely able to tear his eyes from the girl. When his gaze did find his friend, he felt an unexpected warmth on his neck at the knowing look on Ben's face.

"And it's good to see you, Mr. Hammond!" Benjamin Moore's eyes crinkled in silent laughter, continuing their mirthful, clearly rehearsed conversation. After all, they had been together, or at least within sight of each other, since their arrival earlier that afternoon. This was no chance meeting.

There was a zealous lilt to their banter, for this conversation was solely for the sake of the young woman at Benjamin's side. The two friends had been among the very ones Mary Ann had earlier seen ride by, although she had remained hidden in among the lushness of the corn stalks in the field. Their banter at that time had been familiar and riotous, tending to the earthier side of bawdy. Currently, however, there was a pretty woman to impress.

"I see a personage of some beauty attached upon your arm, Mr. Moore. May I request an introduction?"

Thomas knew quite well who the girl was. She was, in fact, the very reason he'd acquiesced to this evening across the river. His closest friend, Benjamin, had raved about his sister-in-law's beauty and charm, and had, in fact, plotted and connived to ensure that Thomas was stationed at the fort when this date rolled around. Now Thomas could well understand why.

Just about that time, a small boy of approximately four years ran among the three and grabbed to Benjamin's legs.

"Papa!" He buried his face in the fabric of his father's

clothing, and wrapped his arms around the much-missed legs. "I'm hungry."

"Little Mattie, come up here." Benjamin pried the boy's arms loose and knelt to pick him up. "Let me introduce you to my dearest and best friend." He brushed the boy's long, curly hair from his face, and turned him to where he could see Thomas.

"Ah, this must be Matthew." Thomas held out a hand, and his smile was all warmth. "You must take after your mother, for you are a quite pretty child, so very unlike your father."

Mary Ann put her hand to her mouth and snickered, but Benjamin laughed and slapped his friend's shoulder with one hand.

"And who are you to talk, Thomas? What woman would have you?" Benjamin knew, though. That was why he had invited his friend here. He suspected Mary Ann would have Thomas without a moment's hesitation, if he understood his sister-in-law as well as he thought he did.

Mary Ann didn't need to suspect any such thing. From the moment she had glimpsed Benjamin's friend on the road, she had felt a stirring in her breast, and she had waited with bated breath for her brother-in-law to bring about their hoped-for introduction.

"Mattie and Benjamin," she turned to her nephew and his father, "I will be glad to entertain Mr. Hammond, if the two of you would enjoy visiting the meat pies. I requested Cook prepare the ham in my special way. You must partake of at least one slice each." She laughed and with a dainty hand pushed Benjamin away. When he made an exaggerated face of protest, Mary Ann brightly put him in his place. "Mr.

Hammond will not be lonesome without your presence, dear Benjamin. I can be quite good company, if I put my mind to it."

Benjamin laughed and leaned in to give her a kiss on the cheek. As he did, he whispered in her ear, "It's your beauty he's interested in, sweet Mary Ann. Not your mind."

She laughed again, and her eyes twinkled.

"Did I do good, Papa?" Four-year-old Matthew giggled as Benjamin carried him toward the sideboards groaning with their enormous quantities of food. His small eyes also twinkled with the trick they had just played on his father's friend, unaware that both his father's friend, Thomas, and his aunt, Mary Ann, had been in on the ploy.

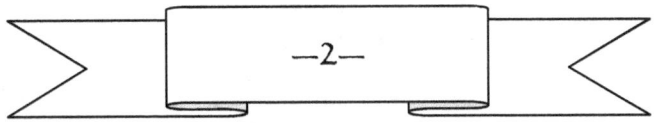

PERSONAL LETTER
Lieutenant Thomas C. Hammond
CARRIED BY ARMY POST

April 13, 1846

My Dearest Mary Ann,

War is upon us. This is a most dreadful time for a man to be a soldier, and yet you, my Sweet Wife, know the truest intent of my heart. The Army is my Mistress, and I long for battle, as do many of those who have seen the atrocities visited upon our brothers by the vile Mexicans. If we, as a nation, do not stand up to this tyranny, then where resides our Country in the grand scheme of the world? We might as well grovel at the foot of avarice and turn our backs on injustice. There are men in power, thank God, who feel this same way.

Now, to other matters. You always want to know of my days when we are apart. You should have seen us in formation the past day. In the morning when I arose, the sun washed the hills with freshness, but by the time we gathered on the field, the skies were gray. There we stood, the entire company upon the cleared meadow. The grasses were just out. (April came early this year, and thankful for that, I am. You know me better than I know myself, my Dearest Wife. I wish to walk upon grass, not wade in Winter's mud.) Standing upon the parade grounds, the wind turned, and it had to happen. Out of the skies came a splattering of drops, one we hoped would quickly desist. However, and you have my sincerest permission to laugh as you read this, my Dearest, for in an instant, the sky opened up, and it came a mighty drenching torrent. Then, before we could make a dash for the protection of our tents, the rain ended. The clouds broke aside, and the sun shone on our faces. We were all as drowned as rats stranded on a sinking ship, and still there we stood. In the sudden bright glare of the breaking sun, one of the men in the line, one that you do not know, began to laugh. From then on, there was no controlling our behavior.

I fear I have destroyed my breeches altogether. I was not the least in the wrestling that suddenly overtook the parade grounds, and I took down not a few of my fellow men. Within moments of my first attack on another of the Army men, a weakened seam gave its last exhaustive cry of resistance, and with a mighty tearing sound, it split in twain. Forgive me, Mary Ann, for my precise recounting of this tale, but you ought to have been there to see the ensuing events: I, dancing about with my drawers exposed between my legs, and all of us, to the man, covered in the final remnants of last Winter's mud. If an Indian war party had come swooping down from the hills, they would have thought us one of them and offered us horses and arrows.

I miss your laughter, my Mary Ann! I look forward to seeing you again. Even though I tease about my mistress, Mademoiselle Army, you know you are my only true love. You must be certain of that deep within your heart. Take care of our coming little one, for soon we shall be three, and do not let Sissy falter. She will allow distractions to pull her attentions away, if you are not firm. Remember, also, that the vegetable garden must be tended, if we are to have a Summer harvest. Plant the peppers along the Southern wall. They must have the sun, or they will provide a weak crop, as they did the year previous. Remember also, marigolds. Plant them among the tomatoes, and the insects will leave the seedlings alone. I do miss tomatoes during the depths of the cold season. At the end of the Summer, we must have enough to preserve at least a small portion. I shall be able to survive next Winter, if only I have tomatoes.

My Sincerest Regards to my Most Wonderful Wife, and may our Faith in God bring us together again, soon.

Your Loving Husband,

Lt. Thomas C. Hammond

United States Army

Post Scriptum – I have been horribly lax, for I have failed to substantiate my most vital news, dear Wife. My previously mentioned reference to the possibilities of war (which I must admit I find exceptionally welcome) has come to me through a trusted channel. The source is one which you know well.

You will remember our trip to Springfield during September last. On that warm September evening, we partook of wild turkey and sautéed greens with a family of our close acquaintance. Of course, it is Mr. Lincoln and his wife, Mary, of whom I write. You cannot help but be pleasantly reminded. We discussed our brother-in-law's elder sibling, Gov. Joseph Duncan, Jr. of Illinois, and our host spoke with pride of the "Long Nine" who endeavored to move the Illinois capital from Vandalia to its present-day location, as he was an instigator of this group. Gov. Duncan was still in office at the time and had signed the documents just before leaving his seat of power. We remarked afterward how surprised we were to learn our supper's host had served with our brother-in-law in the skirmish against Black Hawk some 14 yrs. past, and that Mr. Lincoln knew of Benjamin's sextant from his years in the Navy.

It seems Mr. Lincoln has no shortage of opinions on our upcoming conflict with Mexico. Undoubtedly, he believes we must support our President, but it is also Mr. Lincoln's firm certainty that Texas' claim to the land between the Nueces and the Rio Grande is tenuous, at best. Still, he sees war looming, and Mr. Lincoln has shown himself to be a visionary in such matters. I value his sentiments. I also trust his predictions will come true. Forgive me, Mary Ann, but I must be sincerely honest with you. I look forward to this war Mr. Lincoln claims to be inevitable.

My Love in All Things to my Treasured Wife until we are Together Again –Thomas.

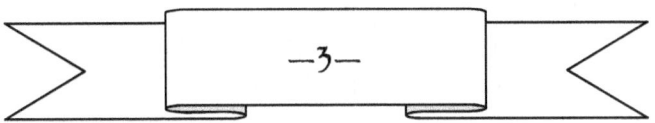

—3—

TABLE ROCK LAKE, MISSOURI
Jon and Mary Ann McCreary
MAY 10, 2009

"Why do you do all this?" Jon McCreary pointed to the overstuffed notebook in his wife's hands. Twenty years out of college, his blond hair was still full and luxurious. Taut skin gave him an athletic cast, although lines could be seen around his eyes, and he now sported a pair of reading glasses in his shirt pocket. The women who worked under him at McCreary's Printing and Shipping considered him quite handsome.

"What do you mean?" Mary Ann McCreary, his petite wife, didn't look up. Her attention was on the papers spread across the bed centered in the anonymous motel room. She absently worked the fingers on one hand through thick, strawberry blonde hair. A smattering of freckles tickled her nose and cheekbones. She could pass for thirty, although she was a decade older. The hints were there in the new shadows that haunted her eyes, ones she'd taken to using makeup to conceal. Some days she felt she looked fifty or more. The past year had done that to her.

"It's just history you carry around in there. After all, this is 2009, not the 1840s." He chuckled with forced amusement. He wanted his wife to laugh with him. Once she would have. Now? Since they'd received the news that had torn their world apart, he couldn't be sure, anymore.

The notebook seemed to contain everything. The cover was white with a clear, protective film overlapping the spine. The plastic sleeve wrapped around the front as well as the back of the thick volume. Just visible underneath Mary Ann's hand was a bright sheet of paper slipped inside the flexible sheath. It had once been straight, lined up with the notebook's edges, reflecting her organized and thorough mind. All the papers inside had been neatly ordered at one time. Then, their son Matthew Benjamin Duncan McCreary had gone to war to fight an unknown enemy, and nothing had been the same. Their lives had been left changed, and their world would never be as it had been before.

"Mom! Dad!" A familiar voice from two years before called its enthusiasm. The day was beautiful, the air smelled of summer, and the sun sparkled on the lake. It was a day for picnics, time spent at the shore waterskiing with favorite sons skimming the waves; or when there's just one, an only child surrounded by friends riding skis with the practiced skill of youth.

The point they were on jutted into the water, and the sound of waves slapping against the rocky beach surrounded them on three sides, bringing the flickering whitecaps right to them, no matter which way they looked. Missouri was always beautiful in summer, and that day more than ever.

High clouds ghosted the sky, and the grass was green, shimmering brilliantly in the sun. The rain had fallen all spring, and the Show Me State shouted the glory of all she claimed as beautiful. Come and play, she seemed to say, for everything is right with the world.

That day took a different turn, though. Matt, just eighteen, pulled up in his Jeep, flinging the door wide and leaping to the ground. He had his father's height with his mother's slender build and strawberry coloring. A new and unusual excitement painted his face bright, and he had a grin showing even, brilliant teeth. He ran up to them proud, sure of himself, and held out a manila envelope.

"Son," Jon called to him. "Have you forgotten what day this is? Your Uncle James is on his way with the boat. Did you overlook bringing a pair of trunks?" The boy had on tan chinos and a crisp white polo shirt. He was sharply dressed, but May in Missouri was for swim suits and tees.

Mary Ann frowned, suddenly cold against the heat of the day. The envelope concerned her, its flat, brown paper concealing what was inside; and then there was her son wearing dressy clothing on a watersports day. It didn't feel right.

"Matt, you do plan to ski today?" She asked her question partly because she loved to watch him ski, and she always had. However, another part of her wished for a distraction from the mysterious information in the brown envelope. It seemed too foreign somehow, too formal to be any good for this easy summer day.

Matt flashed a warm smile their direction, one that refused to be shunted aside. He had news to share. As his father took the envelope from his hand, he wrapped his arms around his mother. They were good arms, too, Duncan arms from her side of the family, arms that went with military men, wiry farmers, and eighteen-year-old boys who could do anything they wanted. Anything. From inside that brown paper, they learned Matthew had chosen war. He had brought his choice to them in his brown, paper envelope, already done and too late to be undone. He was eighteen already, and the choice was his, he told them, proud of his new independence.

In the motel room, with the air conditioner whirring softly in the background, Mary Ann sat with her cluttered notebook in hand, not noticing its disarray, and touched the letter from Lieutenant Thomas Hammond. The year was 1846, she noted with a certain sense of pride, as she stroked the date with her finger. The letter had been written over a century and a half earlier, and she had the original copy. It was yellowed with age, pulled from her great-grand-mother's attic just before the old farm had been turned into another sea of tract homes. The writing was faded in places, but the tears that had washed its surface hadn't completely wiped the ancient ink away. The time-eroded closing, an affectionate sentiment scrawled in old-fashioned longhand, was blotched at the end, perhaps a moment of sorrow gone awry, the revelation of emotions by that long-ago Mary Ann from over a century before. They were namesakes and sisters after a fashion. Cousins, really . . . or perhaps more distant than cousins. Married to cousins. Family, for sure. The connection ran in their blood.

Mary Ann Duncan McCreary looked at her husband for a moment. "It's my family, Jon. For no other reason than that. My family's what this notebook carries, my dear sweet

spouse, and without me, that's all they'll ever be. History."
She sent him a bright smile in apology, hoping to placate his
inquiry. Then it fell away as she continued, "When I read
what I've collected here, they're alive all over again." *Just
like when I reread all the e-mails Matt sent*, but she didn't
say that. Jon didn't especially like it when she reread their
son's e-mails. He told her she left him feeling isolated when
she became immersed in them. She turned despondent, and
that made him sad. She carried them everywhere on her
laptop, though. After they settled into their motel room each
night, she simply waited until Jon was asleep, and then she
pulled Matt's words from her computer, devouring them
once more, and for a time he lived again.

She let herself be drawn to that day at the lake, and it
was as if she were there all over again. It had been the start
of everything.

"Matthew, why? What makes you want to do this?"
Placing her hand on his chest and running her fingers against
the fabric of his shirt, the tautness underneath spoke of the
man he had become.

"Mom," and he grinned, as he grabbed her to swing her
around, his news bursting within him. "We're a family that
made this country strong. West Point. All those stories you
tell me all the time. How can I not want that?" He finally set
her down and smiled at her, his arms draped over her shoulders. He grinned and reached into his shirt pocket, pulling
out a sheaf of freshly printed business-size cards. Each one
was the same. "These have my e-mail address on them. I'm
planning to give these to everyone everywhere. Then they
can message me to find out everything I'm doing while I'm
gone."

Mary Ann smiled, knowing she should be proud. He would do just as he said. However, she would be equally proud of him for attending a university or raising chickens or marrying too young and having a family. It didn't take him joining the service for her to feel proud. The idea of Matthew in the military gave her another feeling, one that felt all too much like fear. Or perhaps dread was more it. Everyone in her genealogies died. Hadn't Matt ever paid attention to those parts of the stories? Lieutenant Thomas Hammond had died. His brother-in-law Captain Benjamin Moore also died. Boys who joined the army died. That was what the military did for its treasured sons. It put them in harm's way, and they gave their lives in return. She didn't say any of that, though. She smiled at him and brushed her hand against the smoothness of his cheek. He barely shaved, and now he was to become a soldier. He was young, still. Too young.

Just then a pair of orange and white trunks hit Matt in the chest, and he turned to his father with a grin. His eyes were bright, and his red hair and freckles caught in the sun. A dimple puckered his cheek, and he reached to pick up the trunks with a laugh.

"An extra pair, Son." His father winked. "They belong to one or the other of your friends. They've been with the ski gear since the last time we were out."

"Dad!" Matt laughed, holding the trunks to his waist. "These are big for me. I think these are Colin's. He couldn't find his the last time we were at his father's apartment. He had to wear a pair of his dad's."

"Put them on. You can wear them home and return them to Colin." Turning to glance over the lake, Jon tapped the envelope, and an expression passed across his face. Then, almost before it could be seen, it was gone. It was a look that whispered of an uncle killed in Vietnam, and a best friend who never returned from the Gulf. Jon had never spoken much of them, letting Mary Ann's tales of her family claim the boy's attentions during his formative years.

A bright yellow boat filled with teenagers roared by. A girl in a red bikini hung tightly to an inner tube as the rubber device skidded across the boat's wake. The rope ran to a tow bar that looped over the top of the craft. The crowd in the boat hooted and waved exuberantly to those on the shore.

"The skiing's great! Come on out, Matt!" The words drifted across the water as the yellow boat slowed to head away from land.

Matt and his dad looked to see a tall, slender boy in bright blue trunks holding to the tow bar and calling to them, one hand at his mouth. Then he pointed to the girl on the tube, grinning broadly, just as a spray of water obscured her from view. He waved as the boat shot away, the girl on the tube shrieking with glee.

"You know him?" This was a boy to whom Jon hadn't yet been introduced.

"From school, Dad. Brandon. He's a senior next year. Well, he's a senior now, I guess, since my class has already graduated. You see, though? There's no place to change." He made to fold the trunks up, but he looked longingly at the yellow boat that could still be seen flying across the water.

Jon shook his head. "There's the car, Matt. Everyone's busy having fun, not watching your wardrobe changes."

"Right, Dad." Matt rolled the trunks in his hand. He

hadn't given them back to his father or put them down, and his eyes kept glancing to the lake. A personal watercraft screamed past with a stream of water shooting high into the air. Matt grinned longingly.

Jon grasped the trunks and pulled them from his son's hands. Shaking them out, he smiled and pushed Matt's shoulder toward the car. When his son didn't take the hint, he opened the car door.

"I'll stand and block the girls' view, if that helps. You live for the lake, Matt. You need to do this for your mother, too. You'll be gone soon, and she needs you to be a kid again just for today." Jon pushed his son inside the car and turned to face the lake.

The boat of teenagers that had skimmed by before came flying across the water, aiming right for the point where Jon and Matt were located.

"Trunks on yet, Matt?" Jon rapped the hood of the car. "Isn't that Brittany, the girl you took to the prom?" He turned to see Matt climbing from the car, revealing his slender build in the oversize orange-and-white trunks. The boy had always worked hard to keep his weight up. Now it looked as if he wouldn't be able to keep his shorts up, either. Jon grinned.

"These are hopeless, Dad. I can't wear them. I just won't swim today." Matt's eyes were on the approaching boatload of his friends.

"Just yank the cords tighter, Son. You need to be out on that boat."

From just off the dock a new voice floated over the water, one about eighteen and filled with excitement.

"Mrs. McCreary, Brandon said he saw Matt out here

with you and your husband. Oh! There he is!"

"Hey, Brittany," Matt called out with undisguised pleasure. "Sorry about the trunks. They're Colin's. I, um, forgot mine." He laughed, pointing to the trunks.

"Hi, Matt! They look cute on you. I like skinny boyfriends. You can be my clown any day." She blew him a kiss and laughed, her twinkling eyes finding the humor in the situation. With his slim waist and baggy trunks, he did look endearing.

"Dad," Matt hissed in an aside. "Do Colin's trunks really look silly?" He waved weakly at Brittany.

"Just go have a good time, Son. Brittany likes you, not your baggy drawers. I didn't intend to embarrass you with them, you know. Just have fun today."

"You didn't intend to embarrass me? And yet I'm a clown?"

When his father threw an arm around him, patting him roughly on the cheek, Matt stumbled, a self-conscious grin shooting across his face.

"You're my son, and I love you. Even wearing Colin's trunks. Just have fun on the lake."

Matt made a face, pulling one leg of the trunks out to twice the size of his waist. "Okay, Dad. Wearing these is still going to be embarrassing."

"Good," Jon chuckled. "Trust me, when you're on some duty assignment halfway across the world, right now will be the memory that'll get you back home."

Years after his Uncle Joey's funeral, Jon had read the letters his uncle had written to his grandmother. It had been the kooky things he'd written home about, the quirky events that most people find embarrassing. He'd said those

19

memories were the ones that kept coming back to him, and he'd told his company the stories over and over just to keep them all sane. It had worked, too, until the day when a booby trap took his leg, and later, infection took his life.

"Go give your mother a hug, and don't stay all day." Jon pushed Matt Mary Ann's way.

As Matt hugged his mother and turned to run toward the water's edge, he swept Brittany in his arms, and his youthful legs bypassed the dock to splash his way to the waiting boat, his laughing voice greeting those onboard.

Jon tried valiantly to memorize the scene unfolding before him. For some reason, on that bright day, with sounds of laughter all around, all he could think of was his grandmother's voice as she placed Uncle Joey's letters back into the old shoebox where she always kept them: "If I'd only known I'd never see him again, I would have given him one more hug before he went off that final day."

The boat had been speeding away, though, and there was no opportunity for another hug. Now Jon and Mary Ann were on their way to California to pick up Matt's things. The news had been delivered. Missing in Action. So many men were missing in action, dead or imprisoned, and Mary Ann had been traumatized. His things were being delivered to Camp Pendleton near Los Angeles, and she insisted on being there to accept delivery herself.

However, when it came to boarding an airplane, all she'd been able to say was that Matt had taken a plane, and he hadn't come home. She wouldn't fly to California. Jon was taking some time off, letting his senior manager run things for a time, to allow him and Mary Ann to drive to California. They were in the car a few hours a day, permitting them time to stop at sights along the way. Overall he wasn't disappointed with the arrangement. He felt the time on the road was good for his wife.

He knew he also needed the opportunity to come to grips with their news. He did have one regret, though. He wished with all his heart that on that summer day when Matt had run for the boat, he'd called him back for one more hug. Now he never could. He knew he shouldn't blame himself for what had happened to his son, but at times he felt an overwhelming surge of accusation insisting that everything was his fault. Matt would have come home again if Jon had simply made the effort to give his son that final hug.

OFFICE OF THE PRESIDENT
James K. Polk
PRESIDENT OF THE UNITED STATES OF AMERICA

Washington, May 11, 1846.

To the Senate and the House of Representatives:

As you are aware, diplomatic intercourse between the United States and Mexico has reached a state of relations in which the long-continued and unredressed wrongs and injuries committed by the Mexican government have forced a suspension of the aforementioned intercourse.

Every measure has been attempted on the part of the United

States government to redress these wrongs, including repairing an envoy of the United States to Mexico with full powers to adjust every existing difference. This envoy was lately present on Mexican soil, with the full consideration and agreement of the Mexican government and bearing evidence of the most friendly deliberations, yet his mission was fruitless. The Mexican government refused to see him or listen to his overtures, and after a long-awaited series of threats, has at last set foot on our soil, and shed the blood of our fellow citizens.

It is now my duty to you to state in more detail the series of events that brought about that failure. On the 13th of October, 1845, in the most friendly terms, through our consul in Mexico, an inquiry was made of the Mexican government whether it would receive an envoy with all powers to resolve the dispute between the two governments. The Mexican minister, on the 15th of October, replied in the affirmative, requesting that our naval force at Vera Cruz be withdrawn to relieve the appearance of coercion in the negotiations. This was done immediately, and on the 10th of November, 1845, Mr. John Slidell, of Louisiana, was commissioned by me and entrusted with full powers to adjust both the matter of the boundary of Texas as well as that of the indemnification to our citizens, as the redress of wrongs to our countrymen blends insupportably with the question of boundary.

Mr. Slidell arrived at Vera Cruz on the 30th of November and was received with all courtesies by the government officials of that city. However, the Mexican government, over which General Herrera's Revolutionary Party presided, was by then instable. Although the government of General Herrera had shown itself sincerely desirous to receive Mr. Slidell, on the 30th of December, General Herrera resigned the presidency, and the supreme power of the Mexican government passed into military hands, yielding the office of president to General Paredes.

Under the date of the 1st of March, Mr. Slidell addressed a note to the Mexican minister of foreign relations asking to be received by General Paredes' government. The minister, in his reply under the date of the 12th of March, denied the application of Mr. Slidell, leaving our envoy nothing but to demand his passports and return to the United States.

Thus, the Government of Mexico, although in prior agreement to willingly receive our American envoy, has violated that agreement and refused a peaceful resolution to our difficulties. To reemphasize the full import of these events, not only was our envoy on Mexican soil with full powers to adjust every matter of difference, but the Mexican government refused any negotiation at all, and made no proposition of its own to resolve these matters.

Previously I have informed you that the positioning of Mexican forces for a threatened invasion of Texas had forced me to order an efficient military force to take a position between the Nueces and Del Norte. This force has remained at Corpus Christi, as I wished for assurance of the

Mexican government's intentions before calling for their withdrawal. Such a withdrawal will not happen at this time, for you may please be assured, this land is American soil, as I will explain.

By official act on December 19, 1836, the Congress of Texas had declared the Rio del Norte to be the boundary of that Republic. Our own Congress, by the act approved December 31, 1845, included the territory beyond the Nueces as part of our revenue system and appointed a revenue officer to reside therein. That soil was included into the act of annexation to the United States, and is now within one of our Congressional districts. There can be no stronger proof of our ownership of the land.

Now, after repeated posturing, Mexico has passed the aforementioned boundary of the United States and shed blood on what is clearly and unmistakably American soil. By her actions, she has proclaimed that hostilities have commenced, and that our two nations are now at war.

As a State of War in all manners conceivable now exists, and as the Mexican government has cast down every effort of our own government to prevent it, we are called upon by every measure of duty and patriotism to vindicate the honor, rights, and interests of our own United States.

August last, as a precautionary measure, General Taylor was authorized to accept volunteers, not from Texas only, but from the States of Louisiana, Alabama, Mississippi,

Tennessee, and Kentucky. Letters of instruction were drafted to each of the respective governors of those States. With the de facto State of War currently existing, General Taylor has called on the governor of Texas for four regiments of State troops, two to be mounted and two to serve on foot, and on the governor of Louisiana for four regiments of infantry.

To further this end, and to bring about a quick return to the peaceful state that once existed between the Country of Mexico and our own, I recommend firstly that the Congress recognize the existence of the war, secondly for measures to be presented with all authority to call into the public service a large body of volunteers, and thirdly that a liberal provision be made for the sustenance of said troops and also for providing the furnishing of supplies and munitions of war.

Be it also known that I wish to bring all matters in this conflict between Mexico and this Government to a speedy resolution, and I shall be prepared to renew negotiations whenever Mexico should notify this Government it is ready to do so.

James K. Polk

PRESIDENT OF THE
UNITED STATES OF AMERICA

PERSONAL LETTER
Lieutenant Thomas C. Hammond
CARRIED BY ARMY POST

May 13, 1846

My Dearest Mary Ann,

I have the most wonderful news, although wonderful for whom may be up to some discussion. However, it would be only to satisfy my own penchant for vanity, if I should tell you straightaway. So, I will put my news aside for now, with only a teasing morsel to tempt your appetite. You recall our dearest friend, Mr. Lincoln (although that term of affection may be unused by him with such abandon in regards to ourselves), with whom we dined September last, as he regaled us with stories of his childhood, charming us into bouts of uncontrollable laughter. I see you nod your head, Mary Ann, with an amused twinkle in your eye, for you enjoyed our discussions with Abe, as he insisted on being called. He told us stories of his youth in a log cabin, and of chopping wood for the family's fires. With his big hands, I have no doubt he was as proficient as he claimed. I remarked on it to you later that evening, as you will recollect.

More importantly, you will remember that I observed afterward, if he can overcome the rumors that he is an infidel, he may well go far. It is even said by some of my connections that he is in the forefront as the Whigs' choice for nomination for the U.S. House of Representatives. (Such may have already happened. I have not been privy to the results from the 1st of this month.) If so, he will surely win. He has a talent for words, and a charm that can easily convince the voting man to turn a blind eye to his opponent. He has been several times in the state legislature, if I am not mistaken, fortifying his chances for a higher office. If he makes Congressman, I fear (and it is a righteous, hopeful fear) that he will be President, someday. Our Country will be better for it.

Mr. Lincoln has sent me firm news. You may be put off when you hear it, but you will understand why it excites me so.

However, for the moment, I will speak of other things. Our brother-in-law, Benjamin, is one whom I look upon as a treasured friend, as you well know. I have had occasion to think of his boy, Mattie, whom I've come to treasure as my own. Our nephew was six this May 7 past. I do hope you made a point to see him on his b-day. Little Mattie has asked me about a sharpening stone for the knife I gave him this most recent Christmas. I left one for him in the hall cupboard. It is wrapped in a small scrap of tanned hide. I was remiss and do not think I mentioned it to you before my Company rode out for Maneuvers. Please give it to him, if you have not done so already.

Do not forget Ben's little Molly, either, my Dear Mary Ann. She also brings my emotions to bear. I am sure she has grown taller. Is she even more the image of your dear sister, Martha? I am filled with confidence that her dimples still shine when she laughs. I can see her even now as she follows Mattie around like a small puppy. I left a small doll for her.

27

You will find it in the cupboard adjoining the stone. I miss them both, and I long for our own child to arrive each time I am reminded of them.

You do remember Benjamin's references to his elder half-brother, Cpt. Matthew Duncan? Although he is now deceased, you are very good at recalling all the varied details of people's stories, and I am sure you have not forgotten him. I must admit, that after your sister Martha's passing, there are those who would say Benjamin's family is no longer yours. I disagree wholeheartedly. He may be forced to assume the tedious roll of lowly brother-in-law in accordance with the law, but in my heart, he is closer than a brother. I have told you this many times, my Mary Ann, and you know I mean it in all sincerity.

I wish to tell you of a new attachment to Col. Kearny's command. Just this month past, a Maj. Thomas Swords joined the company. I have not chanced to meet him as of yet, but by all reports, he seems most proud of his rank. For that reason, I believe his commission of maj. to be fresh to him. It is of interest to me that Maj. Swords served with Gen. Henry Leavenworth against the Indians, although I know that you, my Mary Ann, will be more interested in other details of my story.

Benjamin's elder half-brother served with Maj. Swords at Fort Leavenworth slightly more than a decade past, although Swords was merely a lieut. at the time. It seems there arose some 'Bad Blood' between them, and they had a severe falling out.

I have not learned the reasons for the 'Bad Blood,' but

it is most curious to me. To do no disservice to Maj. Swords, I have begun to entertain an earnest consideration that the good maj. may be the sort inclined to carry a grudge. If that should be the case, then both brother-in-law Benjamin, as well as Cpt. Duncan's son (if he serves in the United States Mounted Rifles as expected during this upcoming incursion), may well be ripe for Maj. Swords' barbs. It is well known within the officers' circles that Col. Kearny, the man who might lead us all into battle, and Maj. Swords are of the closest military associates. Pray that the col. does not overlook his duty, for we must have good superior officers to quell such atrocities.

Still, I must trust that Maj. Swords will be above the ghosts of his past, for to his credit I hear he can be a man of quick perception and quite dashing when he is with the ladies. I must be optimistic that Maj. Swords' dashing qualities are deeply engrained, so as to allow him to treat our brother-in-law with consideration, especially as Benjamin's rank of cpt. hardly exceeds that of maj. Otherwise, trouble could brew, as we will be on the advance for quite some time.

Have you come upon my news yet, dear Mary Ann? Without thinking, I have hinted at it numerous times. Now I fear I may as well tell you all. In my letter previous, I hinted at the possibility of war. You must be of good cheer, Mary Ann, when you read my newest words, and remember to plant the Summer squash and tend the peppers you planted along the Southern wall. You did plant them, I trust. You must keep the weeds back, or they will suffer greatly.

Minding such tasks will be the curative to keep your thoughts free of distress when you hear my news.

War is here, dear Mary Ann. Such is the news I have directly from Mr. Lincoln. Pres. Polk has already sent a message to the Congress asking that war be declared, as Mexico has already spilt the blood of Americans on American soil. You know we must respond, my dear Wife. As a Country we have no choice if we are to retain our proud standing against the tyrants that would bring our Great Land down. If your dear sister, Martha, were still alive, she would tell you so, and she would stand at your side, as she watched Benjamin and myself ride away to war. When that day comes, I shall gallop to battle with pride in my heart, if only I can see your handkerchief waving in the air, as you send your love. Your undying support will bolster my determination to crush the evil that attacks our Freedoms from every location possible.

Mary Ann, I know you have been worried about the nearness of our baby's birth. Have no fear. My things are packed, and no force under Heaven or on Earth will keep me from being at your side when God Above gifts us with this new life. Give me one short day, and I shall be with you. Meanwhile, insist that Sissy stay at your side day and night from the time you receive this letter, until I once again hold your hand.

As always, my Dear Mary Ann, without you, my life is forfeit. I would that you were at my side each step of my day. If our great Country did not have a dearth of good soldiers, I would throw my Commission to the wind and remain at your side eternally. Alas, my loyalty to my Country and my fellow soldiers will not allow me such a selfish indulgence. You surely understand.

My Sincerest Regards one final time before we meet again, my Most Wonderful Wife, and may our Faith in God bring us together again, soon.

Your Loving Husband,

Lt. Thomas C. Hammond

United States Army

PLATTE CITY, MISSOURI
Home of Judge Matthew Hughes
MAY 14, 1846

"Father?" Mary Ann Hammond leaned against the doorpost, holding her husband's letter in her hand, a flush across her cheeks. Her eyes were rimmed in tears. "Sister Martha has been brought to mind, and I find myself in a moment of sorrow."

The wood was thick and sturdy against her shoulder, and its touch reminded her of the years she had spent growing up in this substantial home. The memories were wrapped in private time spent with her sisters, as well as grand parties, also, great assemblages of soldiers from across the river showing up en masse at the Hughes' Platte City manse to mingle with the beautiful daughters of the Honorable Judge Hughes.

Today, however, the baby she carried firmly secured in her womb made her tired once again. Even in her weariness, she was quite beautiful, as were all her father's daughters. Her skin was pale, and her eyes warmed her face as if etched with the darkest of umber. Loose today, her hair fell in natural curls past her shoulders, casting her as too youthful to bear the child she obviously supported inside. Full lips that seemed as if they were perpetually ready to smile made everyone love her, especially the army men who traveled across the river to Mrs. Hughes' flamboyant soirées.

Mary Ann had caught one of those soldiers, just as her elder sister Martha had done a number of years before. Martha had married Captain Benjamin Moore, a younger half-brother of the Honorable Joseph Duncan. She had overheard her father telling a visiting general that the tall, swarthy governor with the piercing eyes and straight black hair had introduced the first bill providing for free education in Illinois when he was just a state senator. Only a man of the highest ideals would commit to so worthy a purpose, and for Captain Moore to be a blood relation to such a person had roused something akin to good-natured envy in Mary Ann's breast.

Martha was gone now. She had traveled with her treasured soldier on his military forays, as some soldiers' wives were wont to do, but she had not been of military constitution. Her normally sturdy health had suffered for it, and her exposure to the elements had taken its toll. When she had returned to Leavenworth, Benjamin had sent a post to

Platte City as quickly as a horseman could ride, and Mary Ann and her father had traveled to be at her side the very next morning.

However, within weeks, she had slipped from her earthly life to the Heavenly realms, leaving her infant daughter, her beloved Benjamin, and her three-year-old son behind to mourn her passing.

Now, though, Mary Ann's officer was away, and there was a baby wanting to see the light of the sun. Carrying the weight of this child brought beads of perspiration to her brow.

Judge Hughes sat at his desk, and at the sound of his daughter's voice, he looked up from his papers. A sturdy man gone to middle age, his coat was draped over the back of his chair, and he wore his cravat underneath his collar. The rumors of war had kept him preoccupied of late, but when he saw Mary Ann, he smiled, and then he noticed the moisture on her forehead and the paper in her hand. Exhaustion spilled across her features.

"My precious Mary Ann," the judge exclaimed as he pushed his chair back and drew to his feet. "You shouldn't be standing in the warmth of the afternoon. Here, come sit in this chair." He took her hand, and with a stern look, he pulled her from the door.

"Thank you, Father." She seated herself with the utmost care, adjusting her skirts around the enormous swelling that made her appear nearly three times her normal girth. Each time she seemed to find herself accustomed to her new shape, it enlarged once again, and she was more discomfited than ever before in her movements throughout the day. It was wearying, and she was ready for the baby inside her to scramble forth. However, she wasn't ready for it to show its little head until its father was at her side.

"You have something in your hand. Is it news from Thomas, pray tell?" Judge Hughes gently brushed the moist tendrils of hair from his daughter's temples as he knelt at her side. He loved this youngest daughter of his, and he always had. He refused to feel guilty that he cared for her more than her deceased sister even when they were both alive. He accepted that youngest daughters were like that for all fathers, loved more and deeper, simply because they were the youngest, and for no other reason.

"Here." Mary Ann handed him the letter as she closed her eyes against the sudden tiredness she felt in them. "He loves me dearly. He tells me so, as usual, and very elo- quently, also. However," and she gave a small laugh, "if it's possible, I feel certain his love for our brother-in-law sur- passes even that he feels for me." Missing Thomas was the true reason for her red eyes. She took a handkerchief from a pocket and dabbed at her forehead. "Oh, Father. I'm com- pletely weary of carrying two people around on limbs meant for one. I'm always excessively tired, and Sissy is off on another of her oh-so-important errands. Thomas says to tell her she cannot leave my side, but if he were here, he would realize the silliness of that instruction." She waved the letter at him. "Just read this, and you will see."

"He's on his way home, I trust?" Judge Hughes took the letter from his daughter's hands and ran his practiced eyes over the script written by his son-in-law's hand, catching the words telling of the upcoming war. He turned his eyes for a moment, not wanting his daughter to sense his moment of distress. He had expected events would come to this. Also, he knew of the 'Bad Blood,' as his son-in-law made reference. Judge Hughes had seen the court-martial from the 2nd of July, 1835. Benjamin Moore's elder half-brother, Captain Matthew Duncan, had served with Major Swords at Fort Leavenworth slightly more than a decade before, although Swords had been merely a lieutenant. It seems they had a severe falling out.

The first charge had been quite serious, insofar as 1st Lieutenant Swords had found the gall to send a challenge to Captain Duncan with the intention to fight a duel. Swords and two of his companions, Lieutenants Hamilton and Wheelock, had desired to discredit Captain Duncan and had challenged the man to said duel. Captain Duncan had refused to be called out, and for that he could be fully grateful, for Swords was later roundly cashiered.

More humorous, yet, had been the second charge in the court-martial. It seemed that 1st Lieutenant Swords then took it upon himself to upbraid and censure his good son-in-law's elder half-brother for not accepting the aforementioned challenge to fight said duel, decrying, "What sort of a captain Colonel Dodge has to depend on, to go out against the Indians!"

Such accusations had hurt Captain Duncan little in Judge Hughes' eyes. Before his Army days, Benjamin's elder half-brother had printed the first book in Illinois, *Pope's Digest*, and had begun publishing the first newspaper in Illinois. The paper was *The Illinois Herald*, Judge Hughes believed, although he recalled that after Captain Duncan sold it, the new proprietors renamed it the *Illinois Intelligencer* for their own purposes. He mentioned none of that to his daughter. Rather, he sent a smile her direction.

"A few days, he says, and the letter is dated the 13th of May." He looked at Mary Ann. "Perhaps even this night, or at the latest, on the morrow." He nodded at the news, even as he considered how his own wife would fare when she heard that war was imminent. Mrs. Hughes worried for her sons-in-law more than most. Pushing that thought away, he kept his expression neutral as he encouraged his most treasured offspring. "You should be pleased, my daughter."

She groaned, keeping her eyes closed. "I will be pleased when this protuberance is gone from my midsection." Her hand lay across her swollen belly, and she gave a deep sigh. Then she relented and opened her eyes to peer petulantly at the paternal tower of strength at her side.

"You are pleased that your soldier is coming home, my Mary Ann?" Her father smiled tentatively, hoping for her face to light in a smile of its own.

"Very, Father." A bright smile broke her dour expression, and in that small thing, she once again revealed the beauty she had carried since childhood.

Her father smiled back, this time without reservation, and he stood. "Then, my daughter, we must make preparations. I think a ham from the smokehouse might be just the thing, and I do know your Thomas likes my hams immensely."

She laughed as she patted the 'kerchief to her face one more time. "That he does, Father. He likes your hams almost as much as he likes me."

He winked at her. "Almost is all the difference in the world. Trust me. Be glad for almost."

"Ham, Father." She waved him away. "Go find Cook, and tell her we wish for ham. I think I will close my eyes and dream of my Thomas right here in the room with me."

The judge whispered, "You do that," as he reached to kiss his daughter, but by the time his lips touched her cheek, her eyes were closed, and her breathing had evened into the first moments of a well-deserved rest. He chuckled softly, "Yes, my Mary Ann, you do that."

He rose to find Cook and that blasted Sissy. She was a wicked girl, and the judge intended to give her a very firm piece of his mind. However, the ham came first, because, after all, one must have one's priorities in order, or life dissolves into anarchy, and what good would that do?

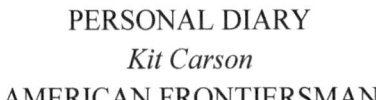

PERSONAL DIARY
Kit Carson
AMERICAN FRONTIERSMAN

Friday, May 15, 1846. Saturday previous, fellow trapper Basil Lajuenuesse was killed, as were 2 others of our party. I had made up my mind to speak to Fremont on the morrow about his lack of a watchman, but as we had seen no trouble, and in any case, I did not have the leadership of the Expedition, I felt I had no just cause for immediate alarm. Now I know the terrible realization that my friend Basil has paid the price for my lack of conviction. I can only console myself that an effort on my part to bring the matter to Fremont's attention was initiated, although it was regrettably forced aside by unforeseen circumstances. Such efforts I will relate now, for I wish to amelorate [sic] my own complicity in the matter of Basil's death.

Before our troubles had beset us, and upon realizing there was no watchman, I had gone to Fremont's quarters, seeing a light in his tent. When I called to him as I approached, he bade me enter, and I did so without qualm or hesitation, my concern about the watchman ready to spill from my mouth. Then, with a sweep of my eyes, I saw we were not alone. There, huddled in the candlelight with Fremont, was a man, Lt. Archibald Gillespie, who had arrived in camp with a dispatch containing a Correspondence only that day.

Seeing Fremont and Gillespie together at the light with their heads bent over the Correspondence, I bit back the harsh words I had brought with me. I do hold respect in my breast for Fremont, for I have been with him for nearly 4 years now, and this is our 3rd Survey Mission together, although this is no longer a Survey Mission by any credible means.

I did not know whether to welcome or despise this Gillespie, for he seemed to consider himself superior at first. His manner seemed proud, at the onset, and I felt much annoyed. Then, after hearing that our Expedition, commenced the Summer past, had successfully stirred up Patriotic Enthusiasm among the American settlers in California, Lt. Gillespie sang a different canary's tune. His simple dispatch proved itself to be from President Polk commending our Expedition and officially making us a Military Force.

I was mistaken to let such a moment distract me, yet that was exactly what I allowed. At the time, I felt I dared not correct Fremont's perceived lack of judgment in front of Gillespie, for I have learned that Fremont is a very jelous [sic] man where his standing among men is in question. I am sure it has to do with his Illegitimate birth, but it seems to me, if not to Fremont, he has remedied that quite nicely. His advantageous Marriage to the daughter of a United States Senator from Missouri certainly overshadows the debacal [sic] of his bawdy birth.

I now know I should have voiced my words no matter, but I did not. It saddens me that Basil is dead, but I have had my revenge. Twice, by my own hand. More than twice by others' efforts. I am also deeply indebted to Fremont for my very life.

The Indian Savages attacked us without warning or provocation. I had barely left Fremont's tent when I heard the 1st arrow fling itself past my head. We suffered several injuries as well the loss of 3 good men before the attackers were beaten back. One of the attackers, a Klamath Lake Native, did not escape, however, and in my rage, I smashed his face to a pulp. Afterwards, I regretted my lack of self-control, but it was all for Basil, in any case. When a good friend is speared undeservedly by an Indian's cruel arrow, Retribution must be made, no matter the Regrets that lie in store. I would want the same service done for me, if the hide were tanned on the opposite side.

The following day, the Indians tasted our wrath. Fremont gathered a party of willing participants, and in light of the Klamath native whom I'd so soundly pulverized the night before, we retaliated against an Indian fishing village named Dokdokwas. The entire place was completely destroyed, even to the women and the children. Fremont was in a fury as he ran the final Indians down, but he gave them no quarter, just as our peaceful encampment had been given no quarter the night just gone.

Afterward, as I drew my gun to shoot one of the last Klamath warriors from the village, he raised to fire a poison arrow at me. I felt no fear, as I am an Excellent Shot. Indeed, I can hit a target square at 100 paces. Still, I pulled the trigger, and I was wide-eyed with surprise when my gun misfired. I was certain Sudden Death would be my companion before the sun should set against the hills. It was not to be so. Fremont, to whom I now owe my life, charged from the trees and trampled the savage to his death.

So, 2 of the savages (and many more, in any case) paid for Basil's death at my hand. I am heartbroken at the loss of a friend, but I feel the debt has been fully and firmly compensated. Now, I can only hope that with a possible confrontation against the Mexicans looming over our heads, the resulting action will be as swift and decisive as our Retribution against these Indian Savages. I am sure that, if we are in God's Will, it shall be so.

Best Friends and Brothers

PERSONAL LETTER
Abraham Lincoln
SENT BY HIRED COACH

Saturday, May 16, 1846

Dear Mrs. Lincoln,

As always, my wife, I do miss your good companionship. However, you are quite aware of the travails of Public Service, and someone must do what needs to be done. As I received the Whig nomination for the U.S. Congress this May 1 just gone, at the present stage of this country's events, it seems it must be me. I have a stronger back than some, so I fear I cannot shirk this duty, even for the steadfastness of your arms.

I would remind you of the reception we gave for the Governor's relations September last. You will remember without my prodding overmuch how Lt. Hammond and his wife let peals of laughter echo from our hallowed walls as I reminisced of life in that log cabin from so many years ago. I should have thought such stories were now regularly recited at the bedsides of all good American children. (You certainly know I jest, Mary. It is that I have simply told the tales one hundred times too many.) Everyone enjoys my rendition of walking the young ones across the ceiling, leaving footprints there for another to clean away. I rather enjoyed the deed, myself. It was not so pleasurable when I was the one made to scrub the prints until they were gone.

I have initiated contact once again with Lt. Hammond, my wife. You do remember I had hoped to serve in the U.S.

Congress with his father, Gen. Robert Hammond, and would have, except that he was not reelected in '41. To lend credence to the Gen.'s standing, he was postmaster of Milton, Penn. in the years before his government service. Quite an astounding man to have for a father!

When I revisited references to serving alongside his brother-in-law during the Black Hawk incursion, Lt. Hammond was most inquisitive, asking me all manner of questions. It seems the good Lt. and his brother-in-law are quite close, and he wished to find news with which to tease him. Unmercifully, he said. That was indeed his exact word. I laughed, knowing he would do precisely that. I replied that I had only spoken to Lt. Moore (although his is now the rank of Captain) once or twice, and so would not be remembered by him. He had come up to see the events of the battle, serving with the Mounted Rangers while on leave from the Navy. He carried with him a sextant, however, one he had retained from his Navy days, and we had a discussion far into the night about its use. Alas, as far as your much-loved husband was involved, as I explained to the good Lt., I was to miss all the festivities of battle, except the burying of the dead at Stillman's Run. Then came the disasters of that summer, the loss of the election for the General Assembly, as well as the village store for which I worked going out of business. I was most joyous when that time was over and done.

My point, Mary? I do know you like me to get to the point, and I so often find my flow of words to be a most pleasant meandering path. Such must be the lawyer's tongue within my head. However, I will endeavor to do so now. When Lt. Hammond learned I had once served with his good brother-in-law, we began to converse of our current situation, and I shared with him the latest information. I am sure you know that I speak of Mexico. (I considered whether to involve you in my news, but when I remembered your interest in all things political, I told myself sternly that I could not inform one I socially know, only to leave my wife in the dark.)

Mrs. Lincoln, our American Institution is about to undergo turmoil. Already, the President has sent a request to the Congress to declare a formal State of War against the neighboring Country of Mexico. I have expected such for some time. You know I have said as much to you, and on more than one occasion.

It is from the annexation of Texas that our conflict arises. There is soil that is claimed by both the United States and Mexico, although for some ten years (or slightly less, as Texas was a republic unto itself from 1836 to 1845), it was soil solely disputed by Texas and Mexico, only. I feel Mexico has some right to her claims, and wish we could resolve this amicably. However, when we opened our country's borders, at the request of then Texas President Anson Jones, to include that of the Republic of Texas, we also annexed this conflict with our neighbors, who for so long have resided peacefully to the south.

There is one good thing that might come of this, Mrs. Lincoln. This war, and I believe the Congress will accede to the President's request, is a war that has indeed begun, for Gen. Taylor's army has already crossed the Rio Grande, taking the town of Matamoros unopposed. As disastrous as this news might seem, these events already in the making may yet divert attentions from two boils upon my potential

Career, ones that with little provocation could easily become open sores. With my nomination on the first of this month, by the Whig party, for Congress, there have been charges that I am an infidel, although you know I have never claimed to be such. Even so, I am drafting a rebuttal should it be needed in the upcoming months, for I hope to don the grand hat of a U.S. Congressman after the election this August 3. I would not that anything should come in the way. How would that be, Mrs. Lincoln, to be married to a real U.S. Congressman? Our lives could be worse. Think of it! I could be President someday, and do not pshaw that idea as you have pretended to do in the past. It could be possible, should events conspire to lead me down that road.

Second, I fear that my stance against the Institution of Slavery may hurt me in this election, if it should come out. Already there are those that think I am duplicitous, speaking of the depravity of slavery in my private conversations, yet refusing to stand up and be truly counted in the halls of Government.

I do not wish for War, but if it should be brought about by the machinations of those buffoons already in power, then I shall endeavor to avail myself of any of the War's more positive propensities, should they come to me with arms wide open. This war with Mexico might be as fine a distraction as we could manage to invent in order to make this election a success.

That does bring into mind my greatest fears, Mrs. Lincoln. Our country is already divided between those States determined to wrest the individual rights of life and liberty from those poor souls we call slaves, and those States stridently opposed to such atrocities against the human spirit. Can we count on this war with Mexico to draw our good Country together or to drive a stake into its heart? It causes me great bouts of dread, Mrs. Lincoln, and I only hope that in the future, I am given opportunity to mend this wound that threatens to wrest half our Country from us.

Say your prayers for me, my wife, and pray that there is a God that would give me strength and direction. If there is not a God above, then we are all lost.

Your Most Faithful Husband,

Abraham Lincoln

IRAQ
SPC Matthew McCreary
MAY 16, 2009

"Please, God. Be there."

The words were desperately whispered, but the response the boy got wasn't. Something hard slammed into the side of his head, and angry words screamed at him. That they were angry was obvious, but just what the words meant wasn't. The language wasn't one the boy had ever been presented the opportunity to learn. He fell to his knees, too tired from hunger to stand again.

Matthew Duncan McCreary had signed up to live the Glory of War, but instead, the Demons of War had snatched him by the cleanly shaven nape of the neck and tried to devour him. So far, he had been shaken violently and thrown into a dark cell. He assumed it was dark all the time, but with the blindfold that never came off, it was hard for him to tell. He could stand up, though, and there was a door of sorts, or at least he guessed it was a door, for it made a metallic, clanking sound whenever his captors came in or out of the "space" he was in.

He had no clothes. Even his tee shirt had been stripped off his chest and torn apart for his blindfold. His pants? They made up the knots that bound his wrists behind his back, or at least strips of them did. He felt lucky to have been left his undershorts.

At least the laceration on his shoulder no longer seeped when he moved.

He didn't know who was watching him. He never heard any feminine voices, leading him to think his captors were most likely men. Each time they beat him, he was relieved they left his genitals alone.

It was hot, though. It was always so hot, and he was constantly thirsty.

"God?" A strangely accented voice yelled the word at Matthew. The metal clattering came once again, as if the door had opened, and quickly, another voice was there, also yelling, "Not American God! Allah!"

Then a booted foot collided with the boy's side, and something cracked. Matthew fell onto his shoulder and instinctively screamed out in pain, "Dear God!"

"Shut up!" The second voice screeched its directive at him in almost unintelligible English, and with each word, a boot punctuated the tormentor's demand, each kick causing brilliant flashes of pain to lance through the near-naked boy on the floor. "Not God! Allah! Allah!"

Somewhere in the haze of his pain, Matthew remembered something, or at least he thought he did. Just after his transport had blown out from under him, and the sound of his dying buddies had ground to silence, a heavily accented female voice had whispered into his ear, "I must be quick. I am friend to Americans. Soldiers arrive soon with sound of blast. I felt for life in your friends, and only you live. You bleed much. I attempt to stop blood until your friends come. I pray to Allah you not die."

He had felt her hands on his body, and he'd looked into her dark eyes. Had she really been there? Had she really spoken to him? He didn't remember for sure. He was certain she hadn't asked his name, or told him hers. At least, he thought he was sure. He was so hot and thirsty that sometimes he wasn't certain of anything at all.

As he sank toward the welcome relief of unconsciousness, Matthew remembered a weekend when he had spent the day with his family at the lake. He hadn't intended to go out on the water, but his father had insisted he change into an orange-and-white swimsuit. Then his friends had pulled up in a boat, and Brittany was there. She was beautiful, the sun was hot, and the water was cool. He remembered his father's words. "Go give your mother a hug, and don't stay all day."

Matthew needed another hug. Dear God, he needed another hug even more than he needed water.

JOPLIN, MISSOURI
Near Midnight
MAY 16, 2009

"Look at this, Jon. I'd forgotten I have a copy of this letter from Abraham Lincoln to his wife. It's dated May 16th, 1846, 163 years ago to the day." Mary Ann McCreary gave a short laugh, glancing beside her to see her husband's eyes flagging, the lids barely open. "Am I losing you, Jon? Old Abe probably hadn't received the news yet that the Congress had already declared war three days before."

When he barely nodded, she closed her bedraggled binder and set the enormous collection of papers on the bedside table. Holding the letter carelessly between two fingers, she tapped the back of the sheet with the nail of her pinkie. Sighing, she murmured, "Mexico wouldn't declare war for another month, though." It was almost as if she laid blame with her words, although she couldn't have said against whom.

Using her free hand, she adjusted the reading glasses balanced on the end of her nose. The writing was almost like calligraphy, and while it was beautiful, it took a certain amount of practice to read it easily. Jon had never had the interest, but Mary Ann had always adored all things genealogical. Well, at least she had at one time. Now her research into her family's past had become more. An *obsession* was the word. She was obsessed with . . . no, she *devoured* the materials she had gathered over the years. She devoured them over and over.

Jon had told her she was using her records as an escape

mechanism, that it wasn't healthy. Matthew wasn't in her letters and newspaper articles or in all those diary entries from a century and a half earlier. He was in their hearts and in the photographs on the wall in the hallway. He was somewhere across the ocean, even if he was lost to them forever. He'd just told her that once, though, and she'd yelled back at him that he'd given up hope, and if hope was gone, then everything was gone.

In the silence following her outburst, she had turned from Jon and stared out the window to see a small black and white cat, more of a kitten, really, jump from the top of the fence into the yard. It walked across the grass for several feet, then it stopped and arched its back. Its slender tail flicked the air, and with a twist of its neck, a pink tongue began to lick at one leg. Unexpectedly, the small creature turned, leaped back to the fence, and was gone over the side. Life was simple for the cat, but it wasn't simple at all for the two people standing together in the room not really communicating with each other at the moment.

Then Mary Ann had felt Jon's arms around her, and his head had leaned over her shoulder. His cheek pressed against hers, and his breath was warm on her skin.

"I love you, Mary Ann, and you're right. Without hope, we have nothing. Whatever it takes to hold to that hope is what we must do."

She'd taken one of his hands and pressed it to her mouth, kissing it gently. Her eyes had also remained on the back yard for a time, wondering if the kitten would return, her hope that it would come back strong for a moment. It had been so full of youth and life, and she had needed to see that, even if it was no more than a small kitten that didn't belong in her yard.

Then, Jon had drawn her to him, turning her body to kiss her full on the lips, and she could tell he wanted her. He pulled her to the bed. After a time, when they were curled on the sheets together, she began to want him also. His touch and his attention were the only things that seemed to make her days bearable anymore. She sometimes pushed him away when the desperation threatened to overwhelm her, but she did need him. He knew how to ease the pain.

It was late as Mary Ann held the letter that had been penned so long ago by the relatively youthful Abraham Lincoln. He had been only thirty-seven and married for just three years. Yet, in all the pictures of him, it seemed he always looked so much older. She glanced at the letter then gave a sigh of resignation, oddly filled with disappointment in the man. Still, he had been a great leader, or so the history books said. He was, she knew, but this night, she didn't feel it. Laying the paper on her lap, she closed her eyes for a moment against the lamp's light.

It was quiet in the sterile motel room where she and Jon would plant their roots for only one night, even though they had spent hours on the road during the afternoon. She should be sleepy, she knew, but she never was. Tired? Always. However, sleepy and tired were not the same at all. Since receiving the message that Matthew was "Missing-in-Action," she could only sleep when she exhausted herself at the end of a very long day, and then only fitfully at that.

"He knew the war was about to start, and he did nothing to prevent it." Mary Ann whispered her words to Jon in amazement. "Men would die. *Sons* would die, and he saw the war as an opportunity to gain a seat in the Congress." She looked up with sudden tears blurring her vision. "One of the greatest men of all time, and he was willing to let women's *sons* die so he could advance his own political career."

She glanced at Jon, waiting for a response, knowing he tolerated her immersion in her history, but that he had no real interest in it. He hadn't criticized her for it after her strident outburst that day, and he did try to pay attention to her those times she focused on some newfound meaning in what she read. However, his interests were more practical, those of packing the luggage each morning, finding a good restaurant, or getting a good night's rest. She saw he was already asleep, and she smiled as she laid her copy of the letter aside.

"Abraham Lincoln was a good man, Jon, just like you. He was practical, too. He could see what he couldn't change, and he moved on past it, the way you have. Practical men keep the world functioning, and I shouldn't complain. Still, someone must maintain the hope, and that's why God made women, I guess."

She reached to him but didn't quite touch him as he lay sleeping. She did love Jon, more than he knew. However, she didn't want to wake him. This was the time of night when her heart missed her son the most, and it was the time when she had the privacy to bring him alive once again.

Slipping from the bed, Mary Ann wriggled her toes into her slippers. Reaching into her laptop bag, she pulled her computer free and carried it to the small table by the window. Opening the top, she pressed the power button and watched the screen as it began to glow. Soon Matthew would come alive for her once more, or at least a semblance of her son would be there with her. His words would wash across her screen, and in his stories, he would live for a time, if only in her thoughts.

Stroking the touch pad, she opened her e-mail reader and went to a folder labeled with Matthew's name. Clicking on it, a year of messages from her son flickered down the screen. Matthew was still breathing in her computer, and each time she reread one of his messages, he was whole and well, and that awful notification had never come. When Mary Ann laughed at the funny stories her son told about his buddies, Jon and she were no longer on their way to California to pick up Matthew's things, and her son could once again spend the day with them at the lake, testing the limits of Uncle James' latest boat.

Tonight, though, Matthew had just finished boot camp, and his deployment was far, far away. Tonight, with the click of a button, Mary Ann's son still lived.

IN THE QUIET OF THE NIGHT
The First E-mail
MAY 16, 2009

Matthew: Mary Ann:

From: Matthew Duncan   . . . Tomorrow would be
McCreary, Pvt.   the 17th. She raised one
Date: May 17, 2008   hand to her mouth and
To: Mary Ann McCreary   pressed her knuckle

Subject: I made it!

I'm here, Mom. Thank goodness Basic is over. It was great to see you and Dad at the ceremony. I can't believe it took so many months of waiting for a slot to open up, but it finally did, and here I am, a real American soldier.

The bus ride to my new base was rough. After riding the school bus all those years in grade school, you think I'd appreciate luxury. Nope. Seat time is seat time, no matter how thick the cushion.

At the station last night I got a snack from the vending machine, but before I could open it, my bus was called, and I had to grab my things and hustle to get onboard. I forgot my snack! That was a couple of dollars wasted.

against her teeth as her forehead twisted in sorrow. She glanced up at the clock. It was nearly midnight. Twenty minutes, and it would be the 17th all over again . . .

. . . "Oh, Matt!" Mary Ann barely breathed her words. After all, Jon was asleep, and while he wouldn't openly condemn her for burying herself in Matt's old e-mails, she knew how he thought. She didn't need his pitying looks and deep sighs . . .

. . . She thought of Matt at the bus station, and some poor homeless person finding his cupcakes, grateful for the snack someone had inadvertently left for him . . .

Oh, well. Maybe someone else was hungry, and I was supposed to leave it for them. They were those brown, iced cupcakes, the ones with the squiggle of white frosting on them. I never even opened the package. I hope they didn't just get thrown away.

The barracks here are huge. That's for you, Mom. Barracks. They don't call them barracks (try dorms), but it sounds like all those stories you used to tell me about my cousins from your genealogies, sleeping in Army barracks and eating in the mess hall, getting to know all the other enlisted men, and like Dad says, "Making memories." Yeah, right! He should come make some of these memories for himself.

Hey, four of the guys in my "barracks" are from

. . . Mary Ann reached to her touch pad and pushed the words to the top of the screen, soaking up each one as it disappeared from her view, anticipating the new ones that crawled into sight at the bottom . . .

. . . She laughed when she saw the word "barracks." That was an old term from all her stories, her genealogies . . .

. . . She remembered the day on the lake, that last one where Matt had gone off with Brittany on the boat. She'd overheard Jon's comment to him. "Making memories." She knew how much his father meant to Matt, although it often felt that she was the one holding them together . . .

Missouri. You might ask around and see if you know any of their families. Old Missouri, and all that.

Jeff's from Hannibal. He says he grew up not too far from where Mark Twain lived. I remember us going there when I was a kid. What was I, twelve? Maybe a little younger. Jeff thinks I look familiar, like he might have met me back then. Is that possible? We get along great, like we must have known one another before Army life. Oh, yeah, Jeff does have a last name. Strugger.

Macky Fredrickson is from Festus. He's almost an Illinois boy, although I guess Jeff lives just as close to the state line. Spitting distance, Uncle James would say. I don't think of Hannibal that way. It's Mark Twain, I suppose. He's so Missouri

. . . Old Missouri. That made Mary Ann smile. Matt seemed to think she knew everyone in the state. It was her genealogies, she knew. She talked of them so much she knew it must seem much that way . . .

. . . She remembered a boy from that visit, one Matt had invited back to their motel room . . .

. . . She knew a Strugger from her college days. Carole Pickney Strugger was why they'd gone on that trip to Hannibal in the first place. Carole had two sons. Jeffrey sounded right for the oldest, but Matt had said Jeff. However, since Carole's divorce, she and Mary Ann had fallen out of contact. Still, Mary Ann was sure she had Carole's that he could be in Illinois and still have a Missouri zip code.

The last two are Carroll O'Rear from Tuscumbia (had to ask him how to spell that) and Bubba Jenkins from Rockaway Beach. I've never heard of Tuscumbia, but it's up near Lake of the Ozarks, Carroll said. I think Rockaway Beach is near us. It seems like I've seen signs off 65 south of Springfield.

Anyway, that's my crew. I've met lots of other guys, and I like them well enough, but the ones from home are the best. Also, I thought I wouldn't say it, but I'm missing Missouri already. It's hot here in Texas.

One last thing, and I've saved it 'til last, because the guys are hanging on my back as I write this,

number somewhere. It had been over a year. Next week, perhaps, she would call, or write if she still had the address. It was time to check on Jeff Strugger and offer condolences, if he was indeed Carole's Jeffrey . . .

. . . When she read the name Macky, Mary Ann pushed the computer back for a moment, looking off into the darkness. Matt had brought Macky to meet them the first time they'd driven down after Basic. The boy had latched onto Jon as if he were the father Macky had been waiting on for his entire life. Jon and Macky had kept in touch ever since . . .

. . . Looking at her sleeping husband, Mary

acting like it's the junior varsity locker room (no wedgies yet, thank goodness), and I don't want anyone to see this.

Anyway, I sure hope Carroll's got a nickname. I can't imagine calling him Carroll for the next four years. It sounds too much like a girl's name. If not, I'm sure I'll get used to it. It's just that a good nickname would be nice.

They're keeping us really hopping, and we're tired all the time. I've given out lots of my "business" cards. The guys tease me about always having two or three in my pocket. I tell them I never leave home without them. I never know when I'll meet a pretty girl who wants to get to know me better! Ha, ha! Don't tell Brittney I said that. Anyway, I'm getting tons of new friends

Ann knew why she loved him so much. It was because of Macky. Oh, not Macky, not really. It was the way Jon had taken Macky on as a second son, keeping up the correspondence, making him feel a part of their family . . .

. . . Glancing at her computer, she noticed the screen had gone dark. Touching a key to bring up the display, Mary Ann saw Carroll's name. Of course, no one knew him as Carroll any longer, not after that fiasco with his sergeant. He was Cheeky, now, and he'd learned to love his new nickname. Now Cheeky even introduced himself to the new recruits that way . . .

. . . Mary Ann took a deep breath when she read

in my inbox. I'll send another e-mail to you when I get a chance.

Love,
Matthew

P.S. Tell Dad I'm making him proud, even though I'm still a slick sleeve.

about Rockaway Beach. Bob and Stridy Jenkins had been stalwart friends to them over the past year. They'd met them just after Basic when they'd gone down to see Matt. It broke Mary Ann's heart what had happened to Bubba . . .

She remembered Matt's promise of another e-mail. He'd sent them regularly, although not as many as she had hoped. She knew why, picturing Matt sitting around shirtless with his new friends, laughing and joking with those around him. How he'd loved making friends!

Thank God you sent more, Matt. They're keeping me sane. Thank God for all your e-mails. And Matt, your father's always been proud of you, and he never cared if you were a slick sleeve or not.

However, this e-mail was finished, and Mary Ann reached with her finger to close it out. She knew her eyes were red, and she was glad Jon didn't have to see. She wanted to be strong, and she tried. However, she needed her son to be alive for her. She couldn't accept that he was gone, although everyone told her what "Missing-in-Action" really meant. Have a funeral, they told her. You need closure. No, she needed her son back, and she would continue to believe he was still alive.

Then, in the darkness that overtook the room with the shutting of her computer, she smiled. For half an hour tonight, he had been. Matt had been alive and at his computer, sending her his love.

Dear God, she thought, I love him so much. You have to be there with him, wherever he is.

Then she let the tears flow down her face, and they dripped from her cheeks. Mary Ann missed her son more than anything in the world.

IRAQ
SPC Matthew McCreary
MAY 17, 2009

SPC Matthew McCreary held his hands to his chest. His thumbs throbbed with pain. One was broken, of that he was certain. The other? Maybe it simply hurt less. Broken, also? He couldn't be sure. Both were swollen beyond belief, and he could bend neither.

His shirt had long ago been stripped from him and used for a blindfold. For what purpose he didn't know, except that one of his captors had come into his cell, yelling in stilted, strangely accented English that Matthew was dead to the world. He must curse his American military and bow to Allah. Only his cooperation would allow them to feed him and provide needed medical care. Then, one of them had held him down while another had bent his thumbs back until they had snapped under the onslaught.

Matthew had screamed with the pain, immediately stifling his cries into the merest of whimpers when he realized that was exactly what they wanted. When his captors saw they would get no more from him, they began to kick him once again, violently, aiming for his kidneys. Matthew did all he knew to do. He curled into a ball and allowed himself to be drawn into another world, one of sunshine, warm water, and people who loved him.

"Brittany, throw me a life vest."

Matthew sat on the side of the boat, working his feet into one of the water skis. His hair was damp from his last dive into the lake, and his baggy suit clung to his legs like flypaper. However, a smile was on his face, and the sun was hot on his bare back. It was a perfect day to be out with his friends.

"Here, you." She grabbed one from under the front seat, but instead of throwing it to him, she stepped in front of him, holding it high over his head. With a laugh, she whispered, "Hold your hands in the air, Matthew." When he didn't respond, she reached to his chest and gave him a small shove, not enough to unbalance him, but enough to make him think she might.

"Hey!" He laughed, dropping his ski and grabbing at her waist. "I'm not ready to go in just yet. Do you intend for me to ski barefoot?" He could, he knew. He'd not planned to, though.

"If you want." The look on her face was impish, and she reached to give him another push on the chest.

However, before she could, he stood and threw his arms around her.

"If I go in, you go in." He pulled her tight, enjoying the feel of her skin and the smell of her hair. Laughing, he stepped on the gunwale and made to jump off.

"No, Matthew. Don't. I was only teasing." She began to

pound her open palms on his back. There was desperation in her words, but laughter, too. She was enjoying this as much as he was.

"I'm not teasing," he flung back. "It's about time you went in. Your hair's not even wet." He glanced at his friend, Brandon, at the wheel, only to see him feint toward them as if to push them both in the water. That decided Matthew, and with a burst of summer muscles, he leaped, pulling Brittany over the side with him. He heard her scream, but then they were in the water, sinking fast, Brittany's cries muffled with her drop into the drink.

In that moment, time seemed to stretch forever. The water was blissfully refreshing after the heat of the sun, and Matthew still held his girl in his arms. Underneath the surface of the lake, her hair floated around her head, giving her an angelic aura. The sun illuminated her skin, and it glowed like a mermaid at home in the sea. Matthew smiled at the girl in his arms, and she smiled back. Then, with a burst of their legs, they shot upwards, breaking into the sun, sinking back to the surface of the water to look at each other, their hair streaming water down their faces, and a flush of joy on their skin.

"Hey, chumps! Are we skiing or dogpaddling all afternoon? I don't know about you, but that's a new rope, and I want to put it to good use." Brandon leaned over and threw them the end of the ski rope, watching it splash within a foot of where they were. "C'mon. Grab it so I can pull you aboard. The afternoon's a wasting. You want to drive, Matthew?"

He did pull them in, but for the rest of the afternoon, what Matthew thought about most was Brittany in his arms, and the way he'd held a mermaid while underneath the surface of the sea.

When the beating was ended, and the boots finally left him alone, Matthew held his thumbs tightly to his bare chest as he lay curled up on the stone floor. The sweat on his skin reminded him of his day at the lake, and in the darkness of his cell, he was able to see Brittany's face as they floated underneath the surface of the water, an angel, his gift from God above. At least he tried to tell himself that, and it worked pretty well, right up to the moment when he passed out from the pain.

MEXICO CITY
President Mariano Paredes
NATIONAL PALACE

National Palace, Mexico City, 18 May, 1846.

To the Legislative Assembly and Corresponding Bodies, Etc. Etc. Etc.

Sirs:

To answer your questions, this country's armies have already begun to wrest our land back from those who would attempt to claim our soil by force.

Some seem to have forgotten our Grand Country's proud

history. Mexico stood in the face of the Spanish overlords, and with great vigor, she demanded her freedom. All she took is hers for always. The annexation of Texas by the Americans is a slap in the face of the glorious Annals of a Strong and Free Mexico. Such an action demands Mexico's Pride be assuaged without fear or reservation.

When that weakling, former President de Herrera, invited United States Envoy John Slidell to Vera Cruz December last, de Herrera showed intent to demean our Glorious Country once again. His actions were those of treason! As he has been deposed, and I am now President of the Republic of Mexico, this Gross Injustice has been righted. I rightly refused audience to Envoy Slidell and therewith cast him from our Country's Glorious Shores.

On 25 April of this year, 2,000 Mexican troops crossed the Rio Grande to force 70 American interlopers from Mexican soil. More forays were made for the same purpose at Palo Alto on 8 May and Resaca de la Palma on 9 May. The land Mexico wrested from Spain must remain within our National borders. The Pride of our Country demands it!

Within only a few short months, Mexico will once again occupy Texas, soil that is truly Mexican soil, and our Great Country will win this war that has been so wrongly foisted upon us. Without a single doubt, our Mexican generals will soon stand in New Orleans and Mobile. The United States will taste of our Furor, and it will leave them panting for

Mercy.

Do not doubt Mexico's ability to take back soil that is rightfully hers. Our standing army of 32,000 is 4 to 6 times the size of the U.S. forces. Furthermore, our Mexican troops are well armed, disciplined, and, above all, experienced in all manner of scenarios.

Logistics also stand in our favor. I do not wish to bore you with unnecessary details. However, the principal theater of war will be Texas, hundreds of miles from the populous areas of the United States. It is certain that the American abolitionists' objections to warring over a distant Texas that has permitted slaves within its borders will demoralize the United States, and I personally believe that when those subjected to the bondage of American servitude sense our Mexican army's pending arrival at their doorstep, our invading forces will find support in a massive slave uprising. How can it be otherwise?

At this time, a Manifesto of War is under draft, and by the end of this week will be available for your purveyance.

At your Eternal Convenience,

President Mariano Paredes

Best Friends and Brothers

PERSONAL DIARY
Susan Shelby Magoffin
MAY 1846

Tuesday 19th. Agreeable and punctual to his promise, Samuel has settled the accounts of the merchants here in Independence, and we are to travel West, before another month expires. Just before my faithful time-piece registered the hour of 10, he burst through my door. "Madame," he cried, much to my delight. "Pack up your valise, for before we are married for enough months to celebrate our Anniversary, you will know how it is to live a trader's life."

I leapt from my chair in my excitement, pushing its heavy, green brocade fabric away from me, and to my chagrin, it toppled right over, crashing my writing set to the floor. Samuel laughed heartily at me, as he retrieved the items from the carpet. "Be glad you keep your lids sealed, Mrs. Magoffin. If you are to be in the habit of spilling your things to your feet, you shall have no method of writing in your beloved journal, while we are in the wilds of Mexico. Who, then, would know the tales of your travels?"

My family tells me I have taken leave of my senses, and that Samuel will send me back to Independence in a fortnight. My dear Mother commenced to wag her kerchief at me, speaking to me in no uncertain terms, "Susan Shelby Magoffin, you do not know the terrors of the American West. If that Samuel carries you all the way to Chihuahua, you will likely die of snakebite or scorpion sting. Indians run rampant, also, as the Mexicans do not make the pretense of clearing them from their borders. If one knocks at your door, close it forthwith, and do not open it for the hardest pounding."

Her look was one of the utmost petulance, but I could not help but laugh at her. "Mother," I remarked, and not gently, "I am a grown woman, and married near eight months. I will not step on snakes, and each time I pick up a shoe, I will shake it out. If it will please you, I will not answer any knocks at my door unless my husband is by my side." I smirked at her with my most wicked look, but then I felt remorse in my breast. Mother had tears in her eyes, and I hadn't observed them. She was fearful for my safety, and her admonitions were those of a friend.

My dear, dear Mother. How I shall treasure that one memory as our Westward wagon pulled away from the bustle of Independence! Immediately I rushed to her and pulled her close. I brushed my hand against her hair, and I was aware that it is no longer the honey brown I so remember from youth. It is lined with streaks of a lighter color, one that tells of years of raising strong-willed children. I fear I must admit that I am one of them. Several (or more) of those streaks are, alas, due to my wild shenanigans. Perhaps, when I am gone to Mexico, my dear Mother will ease her travails with endeavors more suited to leisure and ease than I have provided for her. She will have the opportunity to dabble once more in her beds of flowers. I remember as a child helping her there. A little weeding now and again will certainly bring forth their best beauty.

However, I am not and have never been one to weed in gardens. I detest such activities, preferring to have some measure of Adventure in my days. Samuel tells me we will be in the Western Lands known as New Mexico for some time. I do so hope we have a little house in Santa Fe. I am looking forward to the true life of a married woman, with a household of my own to oversee (as long as I do not have to weed in a garden). It must needs be a mud house, or so Samuel tells me, for there are no other kinds built in Santa Fe, or at least none in which he will consider living. The mud walls, he tells me, keep out the Summer heat and the Winter cold, although I do not expect that we will have the opportunity to know the latter. We will be in Chihuahua by Winter, and Samuel tells me that the push of Winter's winds will not reach us so far South.

I fear I must put my writing aside for the evening, although I feel I have barely begun. I have had to stop and turn the wick on the lamp a second time, as the light from the day has faded sharply, and Samuel is sure to return before darkness overtakes us completely. However, my stomach is still agiddy [sic] with the thought of being gone for so long, away from the clutches of my family, even though I love them very much. It will be my first chance to be a proper married woman with no one peering over my shoulder to see if I have done everything rightly.

Oh, there. I believe I hear the cart approaching, for Samuel is bringing the first load of supplies for our journey. I must help him put them in the small room at the back, for I have promised. If Jane were awake, I would call to her, but she has been hard at work, for even in these moments of change, the house must remain orderly. Alas, so must our supplies. Samuel will want to sort them so that what we use will be in a proper fashion to be convenient and organized. He tells me that to move items to get at what we want will be a waste of our energies while on the journey. I am certain he is correct, although I am not certain that my arms and back will appreciate all he is doing, or at least not this night.

Still! How exciting!

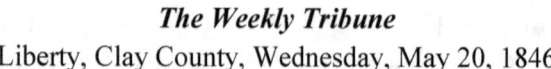

The Weekly Tribune
Liberty, Clay County, Wednesday, May 20, 1846

!!SPECIAL EDITION!!

Farmers, Shop Owners, and Wainwrights! We are being asked to print this Special Edition flyer solely for the benefit of the Army. Fort Leavenworth is abuzz with activity, and your help is needed. The Army is currently amassing supplies for an upcoming mobilization. Foodstuffs, wagons, and animals must be procured en masse. You can make good money for your surplus grains and machineries, if you should be so inclined as to wish to sell. Hogs-$8 ea. Cattle-10 cents lb. Butter-17 cents lb. Corn Meal-$2. Other prices available upon request. Payment options are Army script, paper dollars, or gold coin.

Send inquiries to this paper, Liberty, Clay County.

PERSONAL JOURNAL
Major Thomas Swords
QUARTERMASTER ASSIGNED TO KEARNY'S
COMMAND

Thursday, 21st May. It has been one month, exactly, since I had the good fortune to be assigned to Col. Kearny's regiment carrying the most eminent rank of major. Col. Kearny is a fine Episcopalian gentleman, and with my new assignment, on the Sunday last, I had the exceptional pleasure of being seated with he and his wife, during the Episcopalian worship service in the local chapel. Afterward, I begged Col. Kearny to introduce us, informing him that his darling wife seemed to be most charming.

When he brought her round, from her visitations with another of the attendees, a Mrs. Hammond (who seemed quite with child, indeed), she did charm me, in no uncertain way, while fluttering a lace handkerchief at her neck. I became convinced that her voice carried a lilt that seemed to hearken me to a man I met several years previous. In that moment, I determined to question the Col.'s wife, as to the nature of her family name. There was no doubt in my mind that she would find my query nonsensical, but I intended to pursue my end in spite of it.

However, by the beginning of my question (it had not yet been asked), our footsteps had attained the out-of-doors, and a small distraction pulled my thoughts away. Having felt free from the constraints of the chapel, I had reached in my vest for my smoking pouch. With a flourish, I withdrew my pouch and bowed, asking, 'Mrs. Kearny, will it offend you greatly if I have a smoke?' Then I withdrew a cornhusk as well as a sheet of perfumed cigarette paper, and I asked her to choose, if she didn't mind. 'The cornhusk will be more to my rough, military life, but for one so charming as you, I will certainly attempt to present myself in a more refined bearing, while in your presence.' I held each paper to my nose in turn, drawing in the specific aroma of both. I put on an air of exceptional discernment, as if I were a master of cigarette papers and choosing which was the better quality for purchase.

With my parody of manner, Mrs. Kearny was soon quite amused. She pulled a most dainty fan and opened it just in front of her lips. It was very clear she intended to keep her manner under control, but her eyes told the truth. She could scarce keep from laughter. Then, Col. Kearny came up to us, and he took his wife's elbow in his hand. 'My good Maj. Swords, my wife seems most excellently entertained. To with, will you deign to dine with us for Sunday lunch? Ah, I see you have your smoking pouch out. If you wish to partake, you most certainly have the opportunity, as we walk to our meal.'

Still, I had asked Mrs. Kearny, and I turned to her, bowing once more. 'With your permission, Mrs. Kearny. You were given first right of refusal.' She looked at the Col. and no longer tried to hide her mirth. Snapping her fan shut, her teeth shone in a bright smile, and her eyes once again reflected her amusement. With a singular motion, she touched her handkerchief to her eyes to dry the beginnings of tears. 'Feel free, Maj. Swords. Forgive my eyes, but I have not laughed so heartily in some time. I find your company quite enjoyable. I am pleased that Stephen has invited you to dine with us.'

It was during the most sumptuous meal of grilled trout and broiled chicken that I chanced to remember my question. As I passed the bowl of stewed greens to my right (for the serving girl had stepped from the room to retrieve another pitcher of the most excellent tea), I felt a moment of lag in the conversation, and threw my thoughts forth. I called to Mrs. Kearny, 'I seem to know one very much like you, my dear Mrs. Kearny.'

'Oh?' She placed her fork upon her dish, and she touched her lips with a small towel. 'What, may I ask, is her name, Maj. Swords? Perchance I might know her.'

'It is not a she.' I arranged my greens on my own dish, and when I finished, I turned my attention her direction. 'I met a man named Cpt. William Clark several years ago. It seems he was the Gov. of Missouri Territory at one time. You may have heard of him. His partner was Meriwether Lewis of the Lewis and Clark Expedition. Forgive me, but I have watched your mannerisms, and I have listened to your phraseology, and you remind me most intimately of the time I spent with Cpt. Clark. Have you perchance met him on occasion? He is a redheaded man of many talents, and he tells Indian stories that stretch the imagination, except that his records prove they are all fact.' When I paused in my narrative, the twinkle in her eye was back in quite a dramatic way.

'Why, Maj. Swords, my secret is now out.' I could see the Col. off to the side, and there was mirth on his lips. I did not know what I had said that had both the husband and wife in such an amused humor. When Mrs. Kearny continued, I then understood. 'The very Mr. Clark you speak of is my stepfather, and I have no doubt I carry many of his mannerisms and speech patterns. After all, we did live in the same household. Now, I have a question for you, Maj. Swords. You perchance saw me speaking with a pretty young lady, earlier. She is quite married, as we could all tell, and I do suspect there is a connection between she and you.'

'A connection?' I felt quite confused as to how the young woman and I could be connected. Still, the Col.'s wife had listened to my question with kind graciousness, and I would be inconsiderate not to do the same for her. 'I would like to hear this connection you speak of.' I smiled warmly when I said it, although I was certain it would prove to be false.

'Her name is Mary Ann Hammond. Her father is Judge Hughes. The Judge resides just across the river in Platte City. Have you heard of him?'

'Yes, ma'am,' I replied, for Judge Hughes is very well known. 'I do believe I attended a soiree there some time ago, but I do not know him personally, nor, I believe, would he be familiar with my name, if it were brought up to him.'

'Quite right.' Mrs. Kearny smiled, and she fluttered her fingers as if she should have known that. 'Mrs. Hammond's husband is stationed here. Lt. Thomas Hammond.'

'Hammond, you say,' I replied, taking a moment to recollect what I knew of the man, for I did recognize the name slightly. Then I brightened my expression in what I can only call a congenial appearance of high interest. 'The name of Lt. Hammond is somewhat familiar to me. He has a reputation as a young man with a future. He was at West Point, I believe, some three years ago.' Still, the name was only barely known to me, and I knew of no connection that drew us together, unless Mrs. Kearny intended a military one.

Col. Kearny spoke up at that time, and he reached to touch his wife's hand. 'See, Mary. I spoke to you of Maj. Swords. He has quite the head on his shoulders, and I could ask for no better in my command.' The Col.'s comment pleased me immensely. Still, his wife was not finished, I learned.

'Mrs. Hammond's sister expired some years ago, but the sister was married to a Cpt. Benjamin Moore, also stationed here, am I correct, Mr. Kearny?' I thought it most endearing the way Mrs. Kearny called her husband in such a formal fashion, and after having spoken his given name so easily outside the chapel. He nodded encouragingly, his action confirming her pronouncement in the most loving terms.

I smiled and inclined my head pleasantly, although I was reassured I personally knew none of those Mrs. Kearny mentioned, until she spoke of Cpt. Moore. My immediate recollection of the man was sketchy at best, however, although I hoped the specifics of the connection would become clear when I had a chance to ponder the relationship. Still, I spoke of what came to mind, wishing to maintain the conversation. 'I have not met with Cpt. Moore since my advancement in rank. Our mutual acquaintance is through our military careers, as I once served with him at Ft. Scott. However, we are not close associates, for you see, our military duties have not given us the opportunity to become better acquainted. It sorrows me to hear about Mrs. Hammond's sister.' I did not immediately think of Cpt. Moore's elder brother at that time, for their surnames are not the same. In fact, other than my vague recollection that the association had not been a congenial one, I felt only puzzlement at the references, for even still, I assumed no connection to my own person.

I continued in my words, for in the giving of my response, I did remember something of Cpt. Moore that had always made him seem queer to those around him. 'I saw once the sextant he carries with him from his Navy days. He brings it out when he wishes to impress those around him, his fellow officers, principally.' I attempted to keep my tone neutral but found an abrasive note rising as I spoke, one I have been told at various times borders on the element of sarcasm. I was surprised at an unexpected knot of rising irritation at the reference to Cpt. Moore which I had not thought to be in me.

Upon finishing my remark, a silence fell upon the meal, and I felt Col. Kearny's eye upon me. Glancing up, I saw him sitting with a raised eyebrow, and he gave a snort of disapproval. In that moment, I was immediately aware I had certainly suggested too much. My words had assuredly divulged a personal animosity toward Cpt. Moore, one unbefitting an officer of the U.S. Army.

Then, with fatherly good graces, and perhaps to smooth the moment for his wife's sake, Col. Kearny graciously admitted he had seen the sextant also, remarking that it was a useful tool when out on the open prairie, especially under a cloudless sky. By the Col.'s good manners, I was saved from my own foolishness.

Mrs. Kearny seemed unaware of the momentary tension, and she continued brightly, 'You, Mr. Kearny? You know of this? A sextant! I am much impressed.' Mrs. Kearny smiled, having the attention of all at the table by that time, although I still felt some confusion at the continued venue upon which we conversed. Still, it was a time of relaxation and ease, and I was in no hurry to be anywhere else. She went on, turning once again to me, 'I believe you were at Ft. Leavenworth with Cpt. Moore's elder half-brother, a Cpt. Matthew Duncan. It seems the both of you were in the Dragoons together, shortly before you joined Cpt. Sumner at Carlisle. See, Maj. Swords, I do keep up with my husband's business. Sadly, Cpt. Duncan is no longer with us. However, I thought you might feel inclined to seek out his son.'

I replied with as much forced good humor as I could muster, 'I did serve with a Cpt. Matthew Duncan.' My good mood was broken, however, as my previous relationship with Cpt. Duncan was hardly forgotten. Rather, it was a sore spot that still rankled. The connection with Cpt. Moore was also refreshed in my mind, for I now recalled the relationship, despite the differences in surnames. Even so, I smiled in the most pleasant manner I could contrive at Mrs. Kearny's presumption of conviviality between the two of us. 'I am unfamiliar with the late Cpt. Duncan's son, although at the time we served together, I do remember references to a family.'

'Of course, I am remiss. It's this nasty business with Mexico. Our own men are spread across the continent, and I am sure no one can keep up with anyone. Cpt. Duncan's son is with the U.S. Mounted Rifles at Jefferson Barracks, if memory serves me correct. I believe there is some talk, although I would not speak this in any company other than where it is proper, that they may soon be removed to Port Isabel. That is Texas, if you are unfamiliar with the location. Do you think there may be an adventure building in Vera

Cruz? Mr. Kearny, can they be on the way there already?' The Col. seemed to enjoy his dear wife's interest in all things military, for he was very indulgent in letting her speak. I noticed that he was mostly noncommittal with Mrs. Kearny's question, although he did reply that the Mounted Rifles were not underway just yet.

I believe I managed to contain any outward appearance of my growing irritation at the mention of Cpt. Duncan. However, as the discourse had grown more intimate, I had begun to desire to excuse myself. Yet, before I could, Mrs. Kearny gave me a proposition.

'Maj. Swords, I am confident you will wish to seek out the son of your old friend. His name is Thomas Duncan, a 1st Lt. I believe. If I am clear on his military accomplishments, he has quite a record of excellent service. Lt. Duncan served in the Black Hawk War when he was just 13. Imagine that! Why, it would not surprise me to see him become a general someday. Such a young man could surely benefit from your experience and encouragement.'

Mrs. Kearny seemed quite pleased with her encouragements to bring the young Lt. Duncan and myself together. Even so, in her ebullient and well-meaning enthusiasm, she had missed one very important facet of the events that had torn Cpt. Duncan and myself apart, resulting in my belated reunion with my regiment at Carlisle.

I was court-martialed for challenging Cpt. Duncan to a duel, one in which he refused to engage. It was only by my own good record (and the recommendation of the President) that my penalty was remitted, and I was allowed to return to duty, even receiving what some would perceive as a promotion, dare I brag on my own good name. However, I have no good memories of the time I spent under arrest, and if Lt. Hammond is related to Cpt. Duncan, as Cpt. Moore most certainly is, I do not see how I can help but feel animosity toward them both. I shall endeavor to act upright and above my feelings, but it shall be a trial such as I have never known.

Court-martialed! Such a black stain on a man's record can never be expunged, and it haunts me, still.

PERSONAL LETTER
Captain Benjamin D. Moore
NEVER INTENDED FOR DELIVERY

May 28, 1846

My Dearest Martha (Although You are no Longer At My Side),

The walls of my tent rustle with the breeze, and I keep the lamp trimmed low to avoid disturbing my fellow companions. They sleep, as I wish I could. If I thought they would tolerate my black humor, I would play a prank upon them, making them wish they had not slumbered while I remained awake. They are tired, as I should be, though.

We trained with exuberance this day. The ground has finally dried from the Spring rains, and we were able to tread upon truly firm soil for the first time in weeks. It is a very good thing to walk upon dry dirt after the Winter blizzards and the Spring deluges. Our muscles were becoming jelly, and our minds dens of iniquity. No more!

It seems the Mexicans are determined to draw our country into this disagreement over Texas. Our own Congress has already declared War. News has just arrived that Gen. Zachary Taylor has crossed the Rio Grande and taken Matamoros. Tampico has surely been blockaded by this time, and if reports I receive are correct, Vera Cruz will be next, if the blockade has not already been ordered. I cannot help but think that we will pull up stakes soon. Many of the men here are anxious to drive the Mexicans far from our precious homeland. They are right, you understand, and I am with them. We must protect that which is ours.

How hard we prepared this day! When we ride out (and be assured, we will), the Dragoons of which I am a part will be among the best-trained in all the Army. I know we did well, for my body is sore with the drills, and my eyes burn with exhaustion. Yet, how I wish my own could close so easily as those of my fellows!

On days such as today, with the sun warm against a brilliant sky, I remember working in the kitchen garden at your side, and my heart is filled with love for you once again. At such times, My Sweet Wife, I long for my days in the Navy. (I would not have any of my companions hear me say this. How they would glare at me when they thought I could not see!) In those wild bachelor days, your beauty remained a dream upon my most distant horizons, and I could only look forward to holding one as beautiful as you in my embrace. Damn this cursed Army existence that took you from me.

See? I have said it. I can see you purse your lips as you decide on how best to bring a retraction to bear on my coarseness. Ringing in my ears, I hear the words I've known you to say so many times to me, and you are right. Always you are right. The U.S. ship *Erie* was no more than the mistress of my youth. Commander Connor built my character, if not a friendship between the two of us, and for that you are grateful. I would not have found you, if not for my exchange from my Navy life to this one I now lead.

That long-ago day still remains fresh in my memory. You did admire my new Army uniform during my time at Ft. Leavenworth, you must confess. With anticipation, you first laid eyes upon me from your vantage point across the river. You must have, for my Dragoons arrived in high style. We wore our pride on our sleeves after our involvement in the Black Hawk incursion. I still feel unaccountably puffed up to remember how my company (under my eldest half-brother, the good Cpt. Duncan) was one of the first to respond, and I paraded myself shamelessly as a 1st Lt. (the first good thing I received in my exchange from the Navy). The defeat of Black Hawk at the battle of Bad Ax was a day of enormous pride for me.

Our son was born at Fort Gibson in Indian Territory, and for Matthew, I am forever grateful to you, my dear Martha. Our daughter, Mary, too, who was born during the time I commanded Fort Scott, fills my heart with love, for I have only to see her laughing face to envision you once again. The last time I chanced to hold our precious Molly in my arms, she so reminded me of you and your sweet smile, my darling, that I was almost overcome with grief, but could not shed my tears in fear that Mattie would notice and become alarmed.

You would be amazed at how much our son has grown.

79

He stands tall and proud with a military bearing as befits his heritage. On that day, as our small daughter clung to my neck, my glance fell upon young Mattie at his grandfather's side. I watched his lower lip quiver as a single tear escaped his eye. In that moment, I felt a sudden longing to keep them both at my side, although I knew such was an impossible wish. To ease the swelling tears I feared would erupt as I took my leave, I removed my sextant from my pack and allowed him to hold it in his hand. It seemed to calm his fears of loss, and to that end, I have left it with his grand-father to be given to him when he reaches his majority, if I do not come back from this accursed upcoming war.

Your words remind me how lucky I have been. I have taken my fortunes by the horns, and I have lived a good life. I have sailed the high seas, and I once commanded a good contingent of the finest Dragoons in the Country. How many men get to experience such a glorious existence?

Even so, my finest hours were spent with you, My Dear Wife. You do know that, Martha? Did I ever tell you those words? My longing for your company is what keeps my lamp glowing far into the night, and I try, to no availe [sic], to keep my tears from spotting the ink with which I write. My one regret comes when I remember that final Winter. You insisted you would be at my side as we traveled from Fort Gibson to Leavenworth. Exposure took you from me that March, and now, I am always glad when that fitful month is gone. Thank God for the warmth of May.

One bright ray in all the travails of my life is our brother-in-law, Thomas. How I enjoy his presence at my side! I am with him daily, and he makes me exceedingly glad, for he has become my dearest companion and friend. Your sister is a treasured one to have rescued him from a bachelor life. How lucky he is that she did so! He would have gone to the dogs for certain without her womanly touch. How I would have disliked having a cigar-smoking drunkard for a companion and friend! Despite his time at West Point, and his graduation from that hallowed institution just more than three years ago, Mary Ann has skillfully steered our brother-in-law down a better path, for which I shall be forever grateful.

I do believe that with my expressions of my emotions, my eyes have grown heavy, and I may be able to rest for a time. Also, the oil runs low in the lamp, and there is none to spare, as the new shipment has yet to arrive. Tomorrow, I am told, and if not, the day after. You, of all people, my dear Martha, understand the Army. Supply deliveries arrive at their own pace, dictated not by need, but rather by circumstance and convenience of those Back East.

I would advise you on the kitchen gardens, my Sweet Martha, but you are ever the capable one.

I continue to speak of you as though you are alive, for in my heart, you always will be. I will carry this letter next to my person, for it will remind me of you (and to hide my earlier remark about my desire to return to the Navy! No one shall be allowed to view it).

You are my Love Always,

Cpt. Benjamin D. Moore

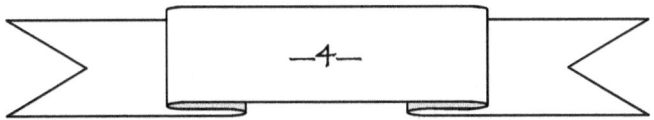

PERSONAL LETTER
Former Republic of Texas President Anson Jones
SENT BY PRIVATE COURIER

June 4, 1846

My Dearest Sister Almira,

I write to you, my dear Sister, for you are the only one with whom I have ever felt free to share my Black Moods. This is such a moment. I feel the skies above me have darkened, pressing my breath from me.

I feel I must explain what has brought this Blackness upon me. I hold a letter in my hand which rains terror upon my day. Please do not laugh in that cheerful way you do and tell me to look upon tomorrow as a brighter option. If I have brought blood upon the soil of my beloved Texas, and I suspect I have, I fear I shall not be able to live. There will be no brighter dawn for one such as I.

To buoy my spirit, I think of you, my dear Sister. In my

mind I see you at the sideboard, your dainty hand pulling a grape off the stem, gracefully placing it between your lips. You surely know of the particular event of which I speak. I do not remember the house, for as children, we often moved, hoping to better our circumstances, but I picture William and Ira as they run in, mud upon their boots, and you laugh, shooing them out the door. You do remember that day? You must. I had yet to be off to Bainbridge, and I still had hopes that my Moods would be vanquished with the change in scenery. Perhaps if I had become a printer as I had wished, it would have been so.

Instead, my life took me down a harder road, and I did not stand for what I wished I had. I gave up Texas too easily summer last, letting our fine Republic be absorbed into the greater country slowly swallowing this grand continent from shore to shore. It would seem to some that I pleaded for annexation. However, the truth is far different, for in my weakness, I caved to the demands of the people, rather than using my position as President to coerce a strong rebuttal against those in power with me. Now, it has been less than a year since my Letter of Assent to the Honorable Mr. Polk was placed in the hand of Mr. Kaufman, whom you will remember was then accredited as the esteemed Charge d'Affaires of Texas.

Ah, you do know that sorry tale already, for you have listened to it from my lips many times before. Even so, I fear I have wandered from my recounting of those events with which I strive to lift the shroud that lies upon my thoughts. Let me return.

Those brothers of mine, caught in their misdeed, gave you a look of dismay, and yet they called their love for you, still. I can hear their words, alive they were with the unassailable brightness of their youth. You have a touch of goodness about you, my dear Sister, and my brothers see it, as do I. How I wish I could fight my way through my Moods and find the good side of each moment as you manage to do! I fear my good wife, Mary, finds my Black Moods to be oppressive, often sending me to another room in which to mope in solitude. Only you, Almira, have understood how these Moods drain me, leaving no room for hope anywhere in my soul.

You have been most patient with me, dear Sister, for I have rambled, and I shall tell you what has brought me to my knees. Be prepared, for it is a terrible thing, perhaps even God's own reproof upon my head that the great Republic of Texas was allowed to falter in the end. Perhaps it is more precisely aimed at my own Dark Soul, for I took no stand when I should have stood with my shoulders back and my head tall.

War, Almira. I have said it, and it makes my hand quiver to see the word on this paper. The blood of innocent Texians shall be shed, and I shall be the cause. Can you forgive me, my Almira, as you forgave our brothers for tracking mud onto your floors? I had hoped for the possibility of an independent Texas, allied with England and France, for I fully anticipated annexation would bring about bloodshed. How could it be otherwise? It was why I labored to bring about a peaceful resolution that would guarantee the Republic's continued existence. Can it be only one year ago that I received word from the British minister that Mexico had agreed to a treaty guaranteeing peace and the permanent independence of Texas? How devastated I was when the

Texas Congress censured me for the boldness of my actions, stripping me of my powers! I had never known such shame and still feel it burn my face as I write these words to you.

At least Mary and I have had Barrington for solace. To walk her green fields and smell life in the soil I call home is peace of a sort. Sometimes my Black Mood is lifted when the wind blows through the treetops, and wisps of clouds lace the skies with a beauty that is never seen in Massachusetts. If only this stain of War could be wiped away, then I think I could at last find a measure of satisfaction in my life, and this Blackness that assails me would be gone forever.

You fully know my travails, Almira. Thank God for a Sister such as you. Please come to visit. It has already grown hot at Barrington, so bring your summer wear. Irregardless, your presence will be a treat that shall know no bounds.

> Your most Worshipful Brother,
> *(Ex-) President Anson Jones*
> *(Ex-) Republic of Texas*

P. S. My Sister, you see that I tease with you in my closing. I have found this one moment of lightness in my day. In doing so, I lay claim to an office that is mine no more (and one that did not want me at the end), in a country that no longer exists. Please laugh with me and share this with no one. Your Brother.

Best Friends and Brothers

PLATTE CITY, MISSOURI
Jon and Mary Ann McCreary
JUNE 4, 2009

"Did you know that, Jon?"

"What, Mary Ann?" He put his razor down and turned to where she was holding another of her artifacts from her notebook. There were many items and much information in her book that he was unaware of, but he loved her, and he had learned how to express an interest when needed. "You've found something new?"

"Anson Jones, the president of the Texas Republic. He had brokered a deal with Mexico for an independent Texas. The war never had to have happened. All those people killed, and it never needed happen. He was a broken man afterward."

"He committed suicide, didn't he?"

"Suicide?" Mary Ann frowned. "Are you sure, Jon?"

"1858. I didn't sleep through all my Texas history courses. I attended UNT in Denton, just north of Fort Worth and Dallas, if you remember. Of course, it was named NTSU then, North Texas State University. However, your Anson Jones was plagued with depression all his life. He lost a bid for the U.S. Senate in 1857, didn't receive a single vote in the balloting. He was shattered and shot himself with a pistol the next year in the old Capitol Hotel. It was in Houston, I believe, the seat of the former Republic of Texas." He looked very pleased. It wasn't often he knew something Mary Ann didn't.

"Oh, Jon. How terrible!" She looked away, her eyes stinging. It wasn't Anson Jones that made them burn, though. It was Matthew. It was Iraq. It was another death in another war that shouldn't have taken a life. Then she could hold the tears back no longer, and she felt the warmth flood her face. It was when Jon slid the folder and all her papers out of harm's way that she looked up.

"I love you, Mary Ann. Anson Jones chose his end, and it was a long time ago. Don't cry over that."

She sniffled and wiped her eyes. She smiled, all the while feeling it waver on her face. Her words were brittle as she let them escape her lips. "Matthew didn't choose his end." She looked quickly away, feeling the tears well up again. Then Jon's arms wrapped around her shoulders, and nothing more was said.

There was nothing left to be said, nothing that would change that horrible message that had been received those months ago. *We regret to inform you . . .* Nothing could undo that, and all Jon could do was hold Mary Ann as she let her grief rock her body once again.

FIVE DEAD, U.S. SOLDIER STILL MISSING IN IRAQI BOMB BLAST
Angelique de Rooij in Baghdad
The Guardian, Thursday 4 June 02.19 BST

As reported several weeks ago, the day following a coalition attack on a reported al-Qaeda command post, a chain of IEDs ripped through a convoy of coalition vehicles in central Baghdad, killing five soldiers. The first U.S. military Humvee took the initial damage in the blast as shop windows were blown out and the front of a two-storey building crashed to the ground directly onto the top of the Humvee.

Iraqis poured from the surrounding buildings in an attempt to pull supplies from the Humvee as sniper fire from the tops of neighboring buildings pinned down the coalition troops. One witness says an Iraqi woman attempted to administer aid to a stricken soldier, but under the hail of gunfire, she was forced to take shelter in an undamaged building.

As gunfire continued to rain down on the troops, Iraqi insurgents danced on the roof of the damaged Humvee chanting, "America is the enemy of God." Once the first furor subsided, coalition air support cleared the insurgents, effectively sealing the area. Only then were support personnel able to take a measure of the dead soldiers.

There were no survivors pulled from the mutilated Humvee. However, several witnesses pointed to a pool of blood, indicating a place where a wounded soldier had lain. As several of the troops were disfigured or dismembered, it was difficult to immediately assess just who was riding in the damaged Humvee. The U.S. military finally announced that one American soldier was unaccounted for.

Just yesterday, a key terror leader in Karbala, 50 miles south of Baghdad, went on television to present the U.S. with a bloody name tag torn from a shirt, claiming to have killed an American infidel. As the image of the blood-stained name tag filled the screen for nearly 15 minutes, a voiceover ranted repeatedly about the supremacy of Allah, frequently chanting, "Down with America."

In a surprising change of policy, American authorities have now admitted SPC Matthew McCreary may be the missing soldier who was seen being helped by the unknown Iraqi woman.

While it is now feared the insurgents may have killed SPC Matthew McCreary, coalition forces have initiated a search operation to locate the missing soldier. He is currently listed as Duty Status Whereabouts Unknown. No other details have been released.

The Associated Press contributed to this report.

IRAQ
SPC Matthew McCreary
JUNE 15, 2009

There was a coolness to the stone at Matthew's side, and as he drifted in and out of consciousness, delirious in the heat of the stifling darkness, he pressed his face to its roughness. Where his cheek was exposed just below the bottom of his blindfold, he felt the brush of feathers against his skin. Occasionally he realized it was the wisps of beard he had grown in the time since his capture, but other times, it was the touch of an angel brushing aside the tears that no longer flowed from his eyes.

He coughed, and pain knifed through his side. His rib was cracked, he knew, and no matter how gently he moved, it always found a way to torment him at the most inopportune times. His hands, too, were nearly useless, his thumbs swollen beyond belief.

Voices sounded somewhere in the distance, hollow against the darkness of his world. The reverberations of the unfamiliar words were garbled, spoken in a broken quickness that seemed melodic in their foreignness. The echoes seemed the lilting chants of monks in a cathedral, their praises rising to the vaulted peaks of the house of God, shimmering against the glittering expanses of stained glass and carved stone. Matthew smiled as he felt the pain in his side ease, and he let his naked body slip to the cool surface of the floor. Gently he stretched out. He was alone in his thoughts, and he was alone in the darkness. He was immersed in blissful solitude, and no one would bother him again, for angels were at his side, singing him to Heaven.

In another room in the prison, one without locks on the doors, the melodic voices continued their garbled conversations. They didn't speak with the words of angels, though. It was quite the opposite, for plans were being made, and none of them bode well for the American soldier lying beaten and bruised, locked in a dark and lonely cell.

***

FORT LEAVENWORTH, KANSAS
Army of the West
JUNE 25, 1846

"Major Swords, I have news."

The words were brisk in the bright morning sun, as a man in uniform astride a well-groomed equine approached. Clearly not Major Swords' equal in rank, the officious soldier seemed very young. Even so, his erect bearing and respectful manner indicated he was well on his way to better things. Today, though, he was at Major Swords' beck and call.

Thomas Swords turned, keeping his knees firmly on his mount's flanks. The light caught his eyes before he could dip the brim of his hat to block the rays from his face, and he blinked several times.

It was Thursday, June 25, and it had grown warm for late June, even in Kansas. With no rain for the past several weeks, the dust had begun to stir. By Saturday, Colonel Stephen Kearny hoped to have the military force under his command en route to Bent's Fort for an August arrival. If Swords could believe the commotion strewn across Fort Leavenworth, he was certain their departure would be timely, too.

However, before that day, Swords had other, more immediate fish to fry.

"Have you found them?" Swords asked. The newly-minted major looked back to the stirring dust. 17,000 regular Army and volunteer soldiers had mustered. The Army of the West, Kearny had named them. They were going west, too, all the way to California. The Mexicans needed a good trouncing, and Kearny was just the man to do it.

As he pondered the upcoming campaign, Swords smiled

in self-satisfaction. He was not yet forty and already a major. The thought was very gratifying. Other things were less so. He glanced at the man at his side, and he considered the job he had sent him to do. Find Moore and Hammond. Swords needed to see Moore's face to prove to himself that he was the same from a decade ago. The whole affair of serving alongside Captain Moore and Lieutenant Hammond rankled, scraping the scab from an old wound.

He reached absently into a pocket and pulled out his smoking pouch. He withdrew a cornhusk paper, unconsciously twirling it in a dramatic flourish, brushing it under his nose to draw in the aroma.

"Sir, Lieutenant Hammond is with his wife," his aide informed him. "He has a small child born little more than three weeks past. Captain Moore is with his men. I'm told he doesn't sleep well at night and sometimes takes his rest during times of inactivity."

"Captain Moore's men complain of this?" Swords frowned. Perhaps a reprimand might be in order, and hope made his chest swell with a deeply indrawn breath. If this were indeed the same man—and it seemed it might—to make this small measure of amends after all the years of suppressed anger would surely bring some degree of satisfaction.

Without taking his eyes from the activities boiling across the fields, Swords spread tobacco onto his paper and tamped it with one finger. He rolled it loosely and twisted the ends. He didn't light it, though, not here in front of this other man. When he was alone at another time, the inhalants would calm his anxiety. He could wait that long.

"No, sir." Turning also to the scene spread before them, the aide at Sword's side paused. When the major didn't seem to respond, except for a slight deepening of his frown, he offered further news. "Captain Moore is well-liked among the men. It seems he was a Navy man who once served on the *U.S. Erie*. His men tease him about it, and he takes it well, often playing pranks on them. It seems he was quite the jokester aboard his sailing vessel."

"Navy, you say." Swords took a deep breath and released it slowly, remembering an earlier conversation with Colonel Kearny and his wife. It was yet another assurance that this was the man he sought. A slight breeze ruffled his collar, and he caught the tang of smoke. A late breakfast fire, he guessed. Laxity. He must see to that.

"Yes, sir," the aide continued. "However, he's been with the Army for some time. He was already with the dragoons during the Blackhawk incident. Do you know of Congressman Lincoln?"

"The one from Illinois? Abraham Lincoln? I believe he has only ever served in the political arena at the state level." Swords snorted in derision. He had heard of this Lincoln and held no high opinion of his views on the upcoming war with Mexico. His remark made his denigrations clear, he felt assured.

"The same, sir, although there is talk he may soon be on his way to Washington."

"He doesn't refrain from expressing his poor opinion of our current conflict with Mexico."

"He feels Mexico's claims are valid, sir." The aide's tone made it clear he did not agree.

"Why do you mention Mr. Lincoln?"

"They served together, Captain Moore and the congressman. Against Black Hawk, although neither seems to have seen actual fighting. Captain Moore was on leave from the Navy and traveled without his commission, hoping to experience the foot soldier's life. Perhaps he may have even served as a spy in Whiteside's brigade, if such stories can be trusted. It seems there's a sextant the captain carries from his years in the Navy, and he makes certain everyone knows he and the congressman spent one night together, placing all the stars in the sky into their proper locations." The man laughed. "I don't know if I would brag of such a thing. It's not as if such a congressman will ever be important in the government of this country, not if he is unwilling to stand behind the policies of his betters."

"You're correct in that."

Still, with such a connection, an unwarranted reprimand would be out of the question. Another court-martial wasn't something Swords wished to contemplate. He did want to know more about Moore's relation, though. He seemed to recall Mrs. Kearny telling of the man having connections of his own, a judge for a father-in-law, it seemed.

He turned to the subordinate at his side. Surely this man would know if there was additional information of which he should be aware. Swords cleared his throat and motioned for the youthful aide to move closer.

"This Hammond. Has he also a Navy association?" *And*

does he maintain his own well-placed political connections?
God help us if he does! Swords didn't voice that question,
though. Such would reveal itself in good time, if it should
be the case.

"No, sir. West Point. Class of '42. Wet behind the ears,
still."

"That much I knew." He nodded absently, relieved, his
mind turning the situation. "The officer named Moore
fought against Black Hawk, though?" He heard the harshness of his annoyance revealing itself in his tone. A stone
had formed in his stomach, however, and he could hardly
care.

"That's what I'm told." The aide nodded, pursing his
lips. His eyes glanced to his superior, perplexed at the irritation present in the man's voice. It wasn't his to question,
though, and he kept his opinions stilled.

Swords cast his mind back. It had been a decade since
he'd seen Captain Moore, and he'd not known him then
except in passing, having engaged in a brief but heated discourse involving that accursed court-martial. Swords figured in his mind. If such was the case that Moore had fought
during the Black Hawk Incursion, he would certainly be
older than Hammond, but still possibly younger than
Swords. In addition to all else, that certainly suggested this
was surely the correct Captain Moore. Also, Swords felt the
age differences were not dissatisfactory. Over the years, he
had found it easier to intimidate younger men.

"Point me to Moore's tent." Swords smiled, once again
under control. He could be the gentleman, if the situation

required it. "I wish to see the man's face. He must certainly be a man of some excellence for his men to enjoy him so."

His words were far from his actual thoughts, but over the years, Thomas Swords had learned that to divide one's thoughts from one's speech was the way of a true gentleman. If his words matched his mind, he would be no better than many of the coarse volunteers who had joined the cause. It was the final results that counted the measure of the circumstance, and if speaking civilly helped him learn his adversaries well, then civil he would be, a man of upstanding manner in all things.

"Of course, sir." The aide glanced at Swords' dangling cigarette and indicated such with a motion of his head. "Would you care for a strike?" He reached into a pouch on his saddle and withdrew a locofoco, the common name for a friction match. He grinned broadly. "One of Mr. Phillips' inventions." The aide knew of the first small phosphorous matches that had been marketed in Germany a decade and a half earlier, but this one had been manufactured in the United States under a patent by Alonzo D. Phillips, a fact of which the aide persisted in sharing with anyone who would listen.

"Mr. Phillips from Massachusetts?" Swords raised an eyebrow in question. The name was familiar to him. Perhaps he would enjoy his smoke in front of this man, after all. When his aide nodded, Swords continued, "I've heard of him. Yes, I could care for a strike."

The wooden stick flared, the white phosphorous blinding both men for a moment. The horses jerked their heads in a quick moment of fear, then as quickly settled down. Swords smiled at that. Firm pressure of the knees and a good grasp of the reins could control any brute of the field. He leaned in to the locofoco, pulling on his cigarette, the acrid smoke filling his lungs.

"Wonderful invention," the aide commented genially. "Wouldn't you say so, sir?"

"Quite. Now, which way is Moore's tent?"

"Follow me, sir."

With a slight movement of the reins, and an almost imperceptible touch of one knee, the aide's horse started forward, dust kicking up around its feet.

Swords moved to follow, his body shifting naturally with the movement of the big animal. He had ridden horses all his life, and it could be seen in his casual ease and attention directed elsewhere. His eyes searched the activity building all around him. Somewhere out there was the brother of his nemesis, and yet in another place was the brother-in-law of the same. He would know them. He would befriend them, if he must. However, he would never like them, not if they claimed kinship to Matthew Duncan. A grudge held lightly was not a grudge at all. Major Thomas Swords didn't hold his grudges lightly, and he hadn't let this one go at all, even if it had been ten years and more since the deed had been done.

Acrid smoke drifted from under his hat, carried by the warm, summer breeze, his eyes smarting with the sting of the tobacco residue. A surge of appreciation for the aide's thoughtfulness filled him. He felt energized. Tobacco did that for Swords, fed him life. Thank God for green plants that could be put to such good use.

"Sir, watch that branch," his aide cautioned. "Just ahead by a tree, we'll cross a small creek. Mind your cues for a good transition, and we'll manage it fine." He slowed to give Sword's horse direction as they passed under a low-hanging limb.

"Thank you." Swords didn't feel any other response was needed. As a major, to converse too freely with a lowly aide, even one who had provided him with the convenience of an unexpected locofoco, could easily be seen as unseemly.

Anyway, he was already remembering that Sunday afternoon spent with Colonel Kearny and his wonderful wife. They had eaten grilled trout and broiled chicken aside stewed greens, and the day had been magnificent. Then, the dear Mrs. Kearny had mentioned Matthew Duncan, and all good humors had fled the table. He now felt obligated to call upon a third thorn in his side, Lieutenant Thomas Duncan, the son of his old enemy.

At least he wouldn't travel with either Moore or Hammond, nor this Thomas Duncan, thank God. Perhaps a letter of polite inquiry about the young Lieutenant Duncan's well-being would suffice, relieving him of that particular burden. Women, being the weaker of the two sexes, could so easily miss the mark. The colonel obviously cared for his wife deeply, though, and this would ensure Swords' place in Kearny's affections. For God and country, and especially as a gentleman, Swords intended to do this. Not even the sour taste of vengeance desired would allow him to stain his military standing with Kearny. No gentleman would permit such an atrocity.

Swords straightened his back as they came into the camp. When one lone man afoot turned and offered him a salute, Swords returned it with all the posturing any newly-minted major should show, and he never missed a beat as his body shifted to the cadence of the proud animal carrying him along the way.

As the two horses traversed the dusty tents, it was clear that not all the activities there were solely involved in pre-parations for the upcoming advancement. Rounding one tent, the clip-clop of their horses' hooves languid and repet-itive in the thick air, heavy smoke could be seen rising lazily from a recently extinguished fire. Major Swords frowned, remembering his earlier irritation. No one was nearby, how-ever, and he felt he must let the perceived infraction go, as his main thoughts were on the man for whom he searched. It would serve no good to allow distractions to alter his way now.

Then a loud voice pulled his attention from the remains of the fire. The speaker was some distance away, perhaps past three or four tents. His words were quite clear, however, as if the man were used to speaking before an audience. The cadence of the words seemed unusual, though, as if an oft-told tale were being repeated, albeit in a lilt not quite American.

"These words. Is this a political speech?" Swords turned to his aide, one eyebrow raised.

"No, sir." Laughter laced the response. "I know this

particular voice, and well. The man you hear is none other than 1st Lieutenant Ogden. Surely you know of him, sir. He is loved by all the men, and the officers, too. He's quoting Shakespeare."

"On the eve of departure?" Swords pursed his lips, then clicked his tongue against the roof of his mouth. Departure was in all likelihood two days away, possibly more if men were taking the time to harangue each other instead of preparing their things.

"Yes, sir. On the eve of departure and every other day, also. Lieutenant Ogden is quite brilliant, for he recites Shakespeare frequently. The men often press him until he lets it burst forth. Pranks, too. I hear Ogden is quite the playful officer among the ranks."

"You said as much of Captain Moore, also. We shall pass around this Ogden fellow in a moment, I suppose. We can pause here for a short time."

Swords grasped his cigarette, pulling it from his mouth, and absently held it away from his horse. He sighed, then squeezed the glowing tip, dropping it at his side once it remained dark. He brushed his fingers together rapidly to rid them of residue, before pulling the reins up to cradle them in his palm. The aide's remark about these officers being so well liked had worked a sudden and very unwelcome burr under his skin. An Army officer's duty should lead one to more efficient uses of one's time, such as pursuing dignity and self-control, not such base recreations as prankstering. Swords pushed aside the undercurrent of envy he also felt, assuring himself it was no such thing.

Restless to move on, his eyes turned back to the smoldering fire, a chorus of laughter at the orator's demonstration pulling them around once again.

"Ready?" He turned to his aide.

"I am afraid we shall not go around." The man at Swords' side nudged his animal forward. "In fact, there's our goal, if we're to find Captain Moore. That's his tent. I shouldn't be surprised if he and the good lieutenant aren't entertaining one another."

"I understood Captain Moore was resting, or so you indicated earlier."

"Not if Ogden has his way, I'm convinced. Perhaps the Shakespeare is his attempt to rouse the good captain. Shall we go see, Major?"

Swords gave a deep sigh, giving in as a gentleman must, although reluctantly. He adjusted his cap before replying, suddenly wishing he hadn't come this way at all. Still, he was here, and there was naught to be done about that.

"We shall. It is the gentlemanly thing to do. Carry on."

When the major drew close to the scene, he could finally see past the tents and into the unexpected crowd. He recalled the chorus of laughter overheard moments before. This was more than just one man waking another. This was a storyteller with an audience. Ogden lifted his arms with his words, his hands dancing with the sound of his voice, punctuating Shakespeare's montage of ribald humor with a ferocity that made the tale seem to leap to life. The men around him swayed and dipped with the movements of Ogden's body, their laughter coming as one, each face mirroring its neighbors in rapt attention or sudden dismay. It was clear the man was a natural, and that he had more than enough energy to burn.

However, Swords' horse snorted, and several men on the outskirts glanced his way. First one soldier scrambled to his feet, his hands brushing dead grass from his breeches. As he stood, his shoulders thrown back, and his hand becoming a salute, others also turned his way. With an additional scramble, there was a stirring of dust, and the powdered earth became more than the simple leavings of an early summer that had been hot and dry for far too long. A storm of magnitude arose with the shifting feet. Men at attention appeared out of the settling dust, and the man at the center was the lone orator, 1st Lieutenant Henry T. Ogden. His hand was to his cap, but his clothing showed signs of disarray, his storytelling having taken a toll on his sartorial perfection. However, in his bearing, there was no doubt that the man was a true United States military officer.

Swords returned the salute, his body remaining molded to his mount, his hand and arm alone snapping into position and as rapidly falling away.

"As you were, men." He leaned to his aide. "Moore. Do you see him?"

"In the red nightshirt, sir." The man nodded to a soldier, mid-thirtyish with a sturdy look, who was seated at the entrance to his tent, suspenders stretched over his shoulders, and a look of amusement on his face. His dark hair was thick and askew, jutting at angles from his head. The man called heartily to the Ogden fellow, his voice filled with companionship and enjoyment, voicing something Swords couldn't make out. Then they both laughed together, Ogden stepping to him and grasping an outstretched hand in an apparent excellent good humor.

The major reached to his pouch for another cornhusk, then he let his hand slip back to his side, irritated at the sight of the man. Studying him carefully, he considered whether this was the same person who had stood in Captain Duncan's defense those long years ago. The face was older, but he could be the one. Resentment washed over Swords that Moore, the brother of his old nemesis, if this were him, should be so well liked among his fellows. However, this wasn't the time to salve old wounds. Not now. Not here.

He turned to his aide as he spoke in a pinched voice, "I have what I came for. I've seen the man's face, and that's all I need." It was proof enough for the moment, anyway. If he felt further confirmation to be necessary, he could pursue the matter to a greater depth at a later time.

His aide caught the emotion permeating the words, and a frown creased his brow. He'd overheard whispered stories of old bad blood, that the major was one to hold a grudge longer than most, and of a decade old court-martial that had involved the major in a bad way. He wondered if this man they had come to find was the cause. Still, he knew he dared not cross his superior. He didn't desire to be subjected to the fate of his predecessor, to be publicly lambasted in front of the troops.

As Swords' horse moved away, the major let his thoughts ruminate on what he'd observed. More aptly, he ruminated on what he was sure he hadn't observed. Had Captain Moore stood to salute with the rest? Swords thought with that red shirt he would have noticed. However, there had been no red flash within the crowd. At least he hadn't thought so. He began to think he had dismissed the men too quickly. He should have waited a few moments before returning the salute, and then he would have known. Even so, he couldn't call back the moment, and a gentleman wouldn't even try.

Had Captain Moore stood or had he not? Much rested on that, even if the brother of his old adversary had no idea just whom he dealt with.

PERSONAL DIARY
Lieutenant Thomas C. Hammond
OFFICER ASSIGNED TO KEARNY'S COMMAND

Saturday, June 27, 1846. This has been the day of our departure. Col. Kearny led, glorious astride his mount, and in a storm of dust, the hooves of our horses led us toward our goal: victory over the Mexican beast.

I already miss my Mary Ann. I felt her tears as my own, when I handed her our newborn son. 'Mary Ann,' I consoled, 'Twill be but a short time until this conflict is finished. The Mexicans have no right to our land, and we shall best them with all diligence.' I kissed our son's head and whispered, 'I shall be here to watch your first steps. Also, I have counted the days 'til next May 22. We shall have a birthday celebration such as none has ever seen before.' My dear Wife laughed at that, assuring me she had spoken to my brother-in-law already. 'What?' I rose up, a mock expression of dismay on my face, determined to put on the most astonished countenance I could manage. 'And to what end may I ask, dear Mary Ann?' I could not keep the smile off my face, however, for I love her so.

'I begged him to watch over you and bring you home safely.'

'Nay, my Wife,' I replied. 'It is I who will have to watch over Benjamin. He is naught but an old man of 35, and his successes in all things military will surely lend him over-confidence. He will force my hand, and I will find it most necessary to intervene when he strays.' By this time, I had Mary Ann in stitches, for I could not stop my overly dramatic gestures from escaping my hands, and I felt forced to take poor Thomas from her as a foil for my game. I began talking to him as to Benjamin. 'I am fresh from West Point, dear Benjamin. You are an old, old man with many years of experience. However, you must heed my words if you wish to find success against the big, bad Mexican forces. After all, we must save the Texians and bring California into the U.S. of A.'

Mary Ann leaned her head against my shoulder, her voice low, and the remains of her tears apparent in her words. 'Do not make Benjamin so very old, my dear Thomas. My precious departed sister, Martha, would not have married such an old man. Besides, little Matthew is only six. His father should not be such a weary creature.' She brushed little Thomas' head before continuing, 'Will Maj. Swords travel with you?' She knows of the bad blood between Maj. Swords and our dear brother-in-law (the cause of which to me is wholly unknown) and accepts it as unavoidable, although she wishes it weren't so. 'If so, surely Cpt. Johnson can lend a mediating hand. Benjamin has mentioned he will be traveling at your side.'

I lifted her face, her eyes red rimmed. I was saddened to see her sorrowful, yet in the same moment it made my heart soar. Her eyes spoke her love for me, even if her voice could not declare it aloud. I attempted to reassure her. 'The good Maj. Swords is quartermaster, dear Mary Ann. I fear he'll be far too indisposed to find this a convenient time to go gallivanting about the countryside to chase the Mexicans down.'

'You know him, then?' Her eyes searched my face, as if she also feared for my well-being.

I laughed. 'Only by reputation. I am yet to know his face, although I'm certain we shall meet soon. Still, even then our duties will undoubtedly carry our paths different directions. He must remain behind, for someone must sort out the baggage and the wagons, as well as the mules, food supplies, and weapons. I understand that he, only yesterday, with his aide to accompany him, took leave to personally speak to farmers about ongoing shipments of supplies, early spring vegetables and the like, if any should be up, and root vegetables from the farmers' cellars, if not. If I'm not mistaken, various stock traders have already met with him at auction sales to pick up mules.' I must have laughed, then, for Mary Ann took little Tommie from me, telling me to go on, that I seemed to find excessive joy in parading my knowledge of Maj. Swords' activities. 'It's not privy information,' I explained. 'All the local blacksmiths and wheelwrights have been preparing our wagons for some time. After all,' I quizzed her, with some mirth, 'from where might the good quartermaster get our supplies? A notice in the local papers? Yes,' I cried, without waiting for her to respond. 'From local merchants? Of course, after much ferocious negotiating, I am certain.' I winked, before going on. 'Have there been consignments arriving from the East? Certainly, my good Wife, but if so, from where? St. Louis? Chicago?' By this time, she was in a right good humor with laughter on her face, and it drove me to added jabs of fancy. 'All and more. Maj. Swords has been very busy sorting it all out, I daresay, whether he has managed to pay with government script, or he has been forced to procure gold, or sometimes even paper money to close the deal. I am certain the good Maj. will be far too preoccupied to chase down such a poor target for revenge as our beloved brother-in-law. I should not worry overmuch, dear Mary Ann.' I smiled brightly, and then to divert the talk from such matters as an old conflict between two experienced army men, with a teasing bow, I whispered dramatically, 'I do believe there may even be live cattle to supplement the officers' diet. We will appreciate that, if our shooters fail to get adequate wild game.'

'Stop, Thomas.' Mary Ann laughed at my parading of pretend knowledge. 'You'd not be able to subsist on just deer, antelope, or wild turkey for this entire campaign. You will require a good meal of beef at least once a week, if you wish to keep your trim.' She patted my stomach to show me her words were only those of teasing. 'You shall be grateful for your live cattle.'

'And for you,' I whispered. At that, my dear Mary Ann,

who knows me too well, reached to me with her free hand and wiped some errant grains of dust from my lapel. She understands my military bearing and my need for all details to be in place. I am proud to be an officer, and none shall trivialize the honor of such an estate. Then I released my Mary Ann to Father Hughes, mounted my beast, and joined the dust of the multitudes.

In that 11 o'clock hour, as we made our way from Ft. Leavenworth, even overwhelmed as I was with the sorrow of our parting, I gave thanks to God. The day was an auspicious one for embarking on such a journey. The sun was high in the sky, and a light cloud now and again hung over the landscape. The prairie land seemed to many in our company to have been cultivated by the hand of the Heavenly Father, himself. The rolling landscape underneath its contrast of sun and cloud seemed a charming entrancement, beautiful for the eye to behold.

At 8 miles out from the Fort, a large butte presented itself. It was quite impressive, and how I wished Mary Ann had been with me to see it. By this time, I had located Benjamin and Cpt. Johnson, and we rode three abreast. I pointed out the butte to them, and Benjamin remarked on the fine forests of timber that draped across the valley, reaching almost to the top of the protruding earth. 'That would build a fine home or two,' he commented dryly. Cpt. Johnson patted his steed's neck, muttering, 'I wouldn't want to be the one that cuts it down. Give me a horse and a good general, any day.' Such is God's honest truth. For our good country to prosper, we must have those who work with timber and such, but the same is said that we must also have those who work with swords and guns. I will choose the latter, for such, I feel, is my calling, even if it takes me from those I love.

There were one or two problems we encountered upon commencing the initial stages of our journey. I was discomfited to see more than enough scatterings of the Volunteers: a broken wagon in one place, tinware and castoff camp kettles in another. The American West is already become the American East, and such is not said as a compliment. Not far from the beautiful campus of West Point, there are avenues where life is hard, and the scenes are much as I have described here, although there, the castoffs are often of the human variety.

After 13 miles of pleasant travel, we found an enclosed piece of ground. We had expected to locate water nearby, and it seemed God's hand continued upon us. The water is cold and clear. This evening, the sky turned to clouds, and we are driven into our tents by a plentiful shower of rain. My brother-in-law is procuring an evening meal for us, and I await his return. It seems especially lonely without the wail of a small child. How quickly I have grown used to the presence of the small son Mary Ann so valiantly provided. I would turn to my brother-in-law for comfort, but I know his heart is as heavy for his own Matthew and little Mary. I will not bother him for such.

However, and I am gleeful for this, I can prank him as he has pranked me in the past. I do believe he will not immediately notice if I fold the sheets of his cot in a shortened manner, for he has shortened mine on occasion many times. I will have to wait until we retire for dear Benjamin to see my attempts at joviality, but I am sure the surprise will take his mind from his children, and that is all I intend for it to do.

Outside the tent flap (for I have it raised for a little air) I see the whirling flight of a turkey buzzard. There were many earlier, and I hope nothing has died. We have a long journey ahead of us, and a turkey buzzard overhead seems not a good omen to me.

Now, to Benjamin's cot. May I do well.

PERSONAL DIARY
Kit Carson
AMERICAN FRONTIERSMAN

Sunday, June 28, 1846. 3 men are dead at my hand. I would have liked to arrest them and have them held in irons, but Fremont was adamant they should be executed. He said to me, 'I have no use for prisoners, Mr. Carson. Do your Duty.' When I showed I would do otherwise, he yelled his demand to me, 'Mr. Carson, your Duty!' I have expressed my regret to Mr. O'Farrell but do not feel readily absolved. It would seem that in repayment for my life, Fremont will require such service of me almost daily, as this has not been the first such ocurence [sic]. I will narrate the tale such as it unfolded.

Some several weeks ago, as I recount the time, a flag with the image of a pig-like bear was raised over a fortified Adobe home on the North side of Sonoma's plaza. I have not seen it. Neither has Fremont, although he has had a hand in precipitating the insurrection. Many have claimed it as the Bear Flag, intending to portray a revolt against Mexico. It

111

seems a most unusual choice for a symbol of revolt. However, the man responsible for its construction is well-known to be the nephew of Abraham and Mrs. Lincoln, the outspoken state congressman from Illinois, and allowing for that lends some credence to its design. Surely such a man would not deign to capriciousness in such a symbolic manner. Todd, I believe to be his name. William Todd.

It was this flag that was the cause of the Disturbance, initially, or so I feel assured. General Vallejo wished for cooperation with the American conquest of California, as he was certain Mexico was unprepared to govern such a large and verdant land. (It was the General's house where the flag was first raised.) Various American Nationals rallied at the sight of the flag, and soon many Californios were given no quarter. Fremont imprisoned José de los Santos Barreyesa, the alcalde of Sonoma (to settle the dust of dissent, he claimed). I fear it was to exact revenge for some yet to be ascertained misdeed against American authority.

The 3 men who will breathe no more had traveled San Francisco Bay, landing near San Quentin. Their claim was to visit the alcalde in the prison. One was the alcalde's father, prominent landowner José de los Reyes Barreyesa, accompanied by 19 yr.-old twin sons of Francisco de Haro, alcalde of the Presidio of San Francisco. These were important men, I felt, ones who could support the American assumption of Government in this wild and beautiful land. Still, Fremont is my general, and I must do as he says. I drew my gun, and it made my heart glad to see the young men stand tall with no fear in their eyes as I took aim. Were it not for Fremont's gaze upon me, I might have let my arm waver, hoping they would run, for in truth, I regretted the deed. I did not falter, though, for I had 2 of our company assigned to assist me, and the men fell one at a time. I am certain I hit them squarely in the heart, and they did not suffer overmuch. The elder man grew faint when the young men lay upon the ground, and I had to yell to him to *stand tall*. I would not shoot a man upon his knees. Finally, he did as I asked, and I was fair with him, ending his life quickly and without malice.

In the heat of battle, men always face the final moments of their lives at another's hand. However, it is tragic when young men must die so cruelly as these brothers have done, without the feel of steel within their grasp. I fear I shall dream sour dreams this night. I shall endevor [sic] to remember that one's duty done is never held as an onus upon one's soul. It will be a Grand and Glorious Thing, and our Country will stand Proud, when this land has been relieved of the Mexicans who claim it as their own.

How I miss my sweet Josefa, not yet 4 years my wife, and my darling daughter Adeline, nearly 10 years old! Soon this Cruelty and Mongering shall be over, and I shall see them again.

If I am in God's Will, I am sure it will be so.

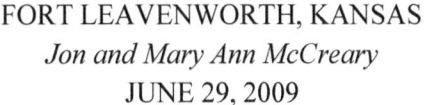

FORT LEAVENWORTH, KANSAS
Jon and Mary Ann McCreary
JUNE 29, 2009

"We didn't make it, did we, Jon?" Mary Ann McCreary squinted her eyes against the brilliant Kansas sun, one hand shading her face. They had allowed ten days to reach California, and here they were, still in Kansas. "Even Dorothy made better time than we have. I guess the good Lord knew what was coming and slowed us down." She stepped forward into what had become a stiffening breeze, a strand of hair blowing into her face. She didn't move it. She didn't have the energy. She was barely in control of her emotions, and she refused to let herself cry, not here in public, not in front of Jon. Not after rereading Matthew's latest e-mail message.

"No, we didn't." Jon reached for her arm, a flicker of a frown appearing on his face when he saw her flinch, his expression smoothing as quickly as the breeze ruffled his collar. He knew what she meant. They had left their home for California back in April, and now it was almost July. Their ten-day drive had turned into months, and Jon didn't regret their extended time on the road. The distraction had been good for Mary Ann.

"Fort Leavenworth. There it is, right in front of us. Would our cousins have really ridden away if they'd known they wouldn't return? Would Thomas Hammond have really left his wife and their three-week-old baby if he'd realized he'd held them for the very last time?" She reached and wiped at one eye. It had become a fight to keep the tears at bay. She turned to her husband, her voice suddenly hard. "Did Benjamin Moore have a death wish? Had he given up on life after his wife's demise? Tell me that, Jon. Did they not care?"

Jon sighed, and he pulled Mary Ann to him, her body finally giving in to his arms. He looked off to the old fort. The day had grown hot, already, and it was probably much

the same as it had been a century and a half before. Not care?
No, it was because they did care. Matthew had taught him
that.

He whispered, his face pressed next to Mary Ann's
sweet-smelling hair, "They were part of the military. It was
their job—"

Pulling roughly away, Mary Ann spat her response,
"Their job! They had *families.* Benjamin left a son with his
in-laws. The boy couldn't have been more than five or six.
Could you do that, leave your son behind to go off and get
killed? He left a daughter, too, even younger." She wrapped
her arms around herself, glad for the heat and the wind. It
would keep her eyes dried. Her anger, less real than she
intended to reveal, would keep Jon from bringing up her
computer and Matthew's old e-mails, the ones she pretended
he'd just sent each time she reread them.

Her notebook was what had slowed them down, that and
the fact that when they made it to California to retrieve
Matthew's things, it would mean that all the hints and
suggestions, the "missing" and "unknown" words, could so
easily turn into death and a funeral. Instead, she had found
small minutiae in her letters and news clippings that simply
must be researched out. They had stayed an extra night in
one small town to visit a local historical site, only to have it
turn into three days. Then they had found a county records
office that had provided a new lead into the events surrounding those long-ago relations. For two days, they'd pushed it
all away, staying in St. Louis, even riding to the top of the
Gateway Arch. For those few precious hours, Mary Ann had
been alive again, and the reason for their trip to California
had been only a mist on the distant horizon.

Then had come the belated news report from *The Guardian*, seen in a coffee shop when Mary Ann had turned on her computer to view the latest on the war. There had been Matthew's name in bold black-and-white, and it had been a knife thrust through her heart. "Missing-in-Action" had suddenly become something much darker, sinister, even.

In a flurry of phone calls and e-mails, of "How could you not have notified us?" and "We tried, Mrs. McCreary. You have our sincerest sympathies," the realities of life had come crashing back around them. She should accept some of the blame, she knew, for not keeping her cell phone on. However, too many condolences and explanations for hers and Jon's extended absence had forced her to keep it off except when making a call. E-mails would have to do, she'd told those who did get through.

Now, all hope was gone. The bloody name tag. There was no doubt that it was Matthew's. Even the State Department had admitted that. They had encouraged her that his body hadn't been recovered, so there was still a possibility he was only a prisoner.

The arrogant, pompous fools on the other end of the phone had revealed their thoughts otherwise, though, with their false cadences and mechanical phrases. If not, why would they have told her they planned a memorial ceremony for those killed in the convoy, and she and her husband were encouraged to attend? Weren't memorial ceremonies for soldiers who were already dead?

Deep within her chest, something wouldn't let go of Mary Ann's heart. Perhaps it was a mother's love for her only son. She knew she had more than enough of that to spare. It was more than just love, though. She somehow knew with an unwavering certainty that Matthew was still alive. He had to be. He simply had to be.

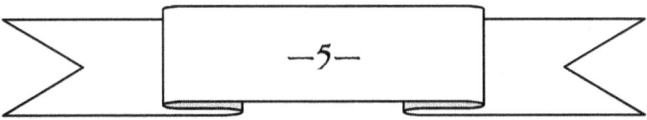

—5—

PERSONAL DIARY
Susan Shelby Magoffin
JULY 1846

Thursday 2nd. Strange and unusual though it is, the first day
of July has come and gone. I had thought to find it momen-
tous, having looked forward to its arrival for the entirety of
the previous month, but such was not to be the case. When
I mentioned it to Samuel at the break of dawn, he laughed
and gave me a tender kiss on the cheek. "Tell me, Mrs.
Magoffin. Why should that concern you?" I told him he has
been a trader far too long, traveling outside the confines of
the greatest Country in the world. I must admit I laughed at
myself after a time, for I quickly realized it was silly of me
to expect all the World to make plans to celebrate our distinctly American Holiday as their own. I am just so used to
seeing colorful bunting displayed from every available surface, flags hung from the eaves, and bands practicing in the
most patriotic fashion for days before the Fourth actually
arrives. It has always been my favorite Holiday. (After

Christmas, of course—who could not adore that day with all the presents one receives?) I think of the Fourth as the harbinger of Summer, although to tell the truth, as we travel this dusty trail, it's clear that Summer has already claimed this land. At least the walls of my carriage keep the midday heat at bay.

Yesterday, as the Mexican servants assembled our tent, I let Ring out to run. It is too much for a greyhound to remain in a carriage all day, even a Rockaway, for his legs need to exercise. He has more energy than any creature I know. As I was resting in the shade, Jane called to me, asking if I needed water. She had been asked to fetch some by a fellow trader (a man known to Samuel but not to me) just arrived from Kansas. His name, I later learned, is Sam Townsend, although his full given name must be the same as my husband's. I do hope no confusion develops from the likeness. He called to Samuel from his cart, one filled with bolts of cloth as well as kitchenware and several earthen pots, telling us the world we left behind was changing, and did we wish to know the state of things? We took our leave to cross the dusty field and see what news he brought. It seems that officers and their armies may soon be coming our way.

"Mr. Townsend," I asked him pointedly, "do you not think both Mexico, as well as the United States, want peace with equal vigor?" I was very proud of my question, for it seemed as one which my dear PaPa might ask. Mother wouldn't care. If she were to hear me ask such a question, yet another gray hair would appear in her curls, and I would know (with only the smallest remorse, I must admit) that I was the one who had caused it to be there.

"My dear lady (I was charmed to be called a lady in this

land so far from home, so long as he does not desire for me to pull weeds!), I fear the wish for peace is long past. Have you heard of Zachary Taylor? He is a Bvt. Brig. Gen. with the U.S. Army. I have on very good authority that he commanded a skirmish with the Mexicans at Fort Texas little more than one month ago. It was quite an affair, I am told, routing the Mexicans thoroughly."

"Fort Texas?" my dear Samuel questioned, a puzzled look on his face.

Mr. Townsend laughed, and it was one of embarrassed good humor. "Fort Brown, now, for it has been renamed for a man who was killed there. Near Point Isabel. The battle itself was at a field called 'Resaca de la Palma.' "

Samuel laughed, as much in recognition of Mr. Townsend's words as anything, I think. "I do know Point Isabel. This Zachary Taylor, also. You should meet him someday, Mrs. Magoffin."

I agreed that I would probably enjoy that very much. I was sure he would be dashing and most charming. However, I wished to know if this conflict would affect Samuel and I in any way, and I pointedly asked as such. We are on our way to Santa Fe, and I do not wish to become embroiled in matters that might hurt my unborn child.

"Why, yes, Mrs. Magoffin." Mr. Townsend tipped his hat to me, which I found amusing. It was a very old hat, one that had clearly seen more days in the backwoods than on a civilized street, I'm sure. "As you will recall, I'm traveling from Kansas. There's a fort there just over the river from Platte City."

I told him I knew of it, Fort Leavenworth, and to go on.

"The armies are already amassing, my dear lady. If the

weather holds, they may even join you in Santa Fe before the middle of the next month. They are to be commanded by a Col. Kearny. Have you heard of him?"

I replied that both Col. Kearny, as well as *Gen.* Taylor, were both well-known to me, and if the Army were indeed coming to Santa Fe, I would trust to meet them both. I near trembled, though, for to meet two such famous people was almost too much to bear. I so wished in that instant to entertain them in a home of my own. Wouldn't my sisters be so very envious?

We said our salutations to Mr. Townsend, and he thanked Jane for kindly offering him a drink of water. She returned to her Dearborn, and within moments we were back about our business. Even so, I could barely focus my thoughts. I knew Ring was still running around madly, and the tent was being rapidly erected. Jane would soon be outfitting the bed with fresh linens, and it was to be supper within the hour. However, I could only think of one thing. The Army is headed to Santa Fe. What good fortune it is for Samuel and I to be there when they arrive!

Now, I have the shade in which to wait. It's good that there are no gardens in this countryside to weed, and none at all outside my carriage. I am so giddy with anticipation for more news, that I should pull every green plant from the soil, if I should be forced to touch a one.

I think I shall withdraw a fresh paper from my store, for I have not written Mother in a week or more. We have chanced upon the Army express, and they have promised to carry it East for me. My inkwells are freshly replenished, and Samuel has promised me more should I need them. As I write, I shall try not to gloat at my news too strongly. Then

I shall certainly find cause to take a stroll, if only Jane can find time from her duties to accompany me.

I cannot believe the wonderful news that has been brought our way! Life in Santa Fe will be more than I ever imagined!

PACIFIC COAST OFF CALIFORNIA
July 2, 1846
USS SAVANNAH

"Look at him up there." Seaman Emanuel Laff murmured the words as he glanced at Commodore John D. Sloat perched on the bridge of the *USS Savannah*. The blue waters of the Pacific stretched as far west as could be seen, and it seemed the skies overhead were no more than an extension of the sea. To the east lay the rugged land of California. The great man towering above Laff stood regally with his eyeglass and watched the sloops *USS Cyane* and *USS Levant* come into view.

Laff himself was far from regal in his appearance. He carried a swarthy complexion, one that still bore marks from a childhood disease. His dark hair stood on end, continually at odds with his attempts to keep it under control. However, he had a quick smile, and he used it often, making friends easily aboard his ship.

Clouds filled much of the sky close to the shore, but overhead it was clear. The slap of water against the hull told of their speed, for the *USS Savannah's* sails were full. The sound of seamen pulling the ropes and lines, the birds overhead crying out their songs of land ahead, and the chill of the ocean breeze spoke of the adventure of sailing. The cannons visible on the upcoming ships told of the reason they were here. Two great countries were colliding, and only one could rise victorious in the end.

Laff recalled a moment months before with Midshipman J.S. Bohrer, a close friend who had been invalided home on the *Constitution* in April. Laff had been heartsick to see him sail away. Still, before his friend was injured, his enthusiasm for battle was quick to be spoken. He had decried that there was too much slack time aboard ship when at sail, and when a chance for a stroke of victory was offered, it should be taken. Laff was inclined, when his not-so-slack duties aboard ship provided him enough time for the concept to bother him, to agree. This day, in the bright sun, with a few leisure moments on his hands, it felt a good time to speak those sentiments.

"Mr. Sloat should take action, if we want to claim California as our own. It's only two mornings until our Independence Day. That should be his opportunity, and he should take it." Laff repeated Bohrer's oft-expressed thoughts as he turned to catch the eye of the fellow at his side.

"Ho, now. I should speak that softly. Commodore Sloat is quite respected. He'll step to action when matters require it." The reply was pleasant enough, if somewhat brisk. "You do know that for some years, he was in charge of the Portsmouth Navy Yard. That speaks highly of him, if I do say so. I believe he first intends to go ashore to make a formal call on the port officials upon our arrival. Perhaps then he will take the town."

Henry Gleason, a midshipman, was with Laff onboard the frigate, *USS Savannah*, Commodore Sloat's command vessel. Gleason tended to portliness, although in all fairness, no one could yet call him fat. However, exacerbating the issue, the breadth of his face tended to portray an additional air of undeserved girth. His forehead was outsized, and it seemed he would have a bald pate before too many more seasons fled the calendar. Gleason privately agreed with Laff, for he also felt Sloat was somewhat overly cautious. However, he knew that complaints went up the ladder, not down. He would make no negative remarks to Laff.

"Still, look at what Commodore Thomas Jones did back in '42. He took Monterey without bloodshed. There was no resistance at all," Laff groused. "We should just take California, for Mexico has no power to keep it from us, and it cannot stand alone. Mr. Sloat should just do it."

"Patience, Laff. Remember also that in '42, there was no declared war, and Commodore Jones had to return the territory to Mexico, along with all the weapons he had confiscated. That's also the reason Commodore Sloat is now in command of the Pacific Squadron. He doesn't wish a repeat of such buffoonery. Now, you might watch to whom you express your opinions after this. Some officers aboard this ship might not look so kindly on your sentiments."

As the discourse faded to the simple sounds of water slapping against the hull and the cry of seabirds on wing, Gleason pressed his lips together in a manner that seemed very serious and official to him. However, the wish for quicker action was felt by more than simply he or Raff. Commodore Jones might have been rash in '42, but unless Sloat got on the ball, Gleason suspected Laff might easily see a new commodore over the Pacific Squadron—as well as Laff's lowly personage—before too much additional water slipped beneath the stern.

AT THE PUEBLO OF SONOMA
William B. Ide
THE CALIFORNIA REPUBLIC'S FIRST AND ONLY PRESIDENT

July 3, 1846. The morrow will be the day we make our most important stand. It will by all measure be a morning with auspicious tones, for we have planned it as such. I am ready to move without delay, for since the capture of Mexican Commandante Mariano Guadalupe Vallejo some weeks back, frustration has haunted the back of my thoughts. My fear has been compounded by the presence of Captain Fremont during the previous week. I would not that our efforts have been for nothing. No more, though, not after the sun breaks this night asunder.

Back East, celebrations for the American holiday of Independence will assuredly be at hand, for I am certain many will partake of the opportunity to rejoice in the birthday of the great United States of America. Yet, the questions in my mind remain to tantalize me. When news of what we do this day reaches those on the eastern edges of this grand continent, will our own stroke for freedom be seen as a glorious break from tyranny, or as the pathetic scrabbling of malcontents? Only time will tell, for either we will be damned as inciters of war or revered as fellows in a struggle for freedom. To hell with it, though. Mexico has ruled—unwisely and harshly—over this land for too many years. It is time to take arms against the tyrant. On the morrow, California will truly be seen to stand as a free nation. Mexico's harsh grip will have been cast aside, and the California Republic will be proclaimed united forever under the Bear Flag.

In my most private times, however, I wish our families were not at our sides. The Mexican generals do not retreat to far Mexico City so easily, and I fear much bloodshed will be left running across our thresholds. I can only pray it does not run from my own Susan's veins, or from the arms of those sweet children among us. However, my dear wife stands behind me in this endeavor, and for that I am utmost grateful. I know in this late hour that our lives can no longer be the same, and while I am filled with anticipation and excitement, deep down I also know a knot of foreboding. Even so, it is that very foreboding that will be my strength when the sun rises and it comes time for our deed to be done, I feel most certain.

No matter the price we pay, there is one thing of which I have become certain. Life without freedom is not life at all. The tyranny of Mexico must not be allowed to continue. May God help us in all that we do, for it is certain that no Mexican will.

A Tale of the Mexican War

MEXICO CITY
President Mariano Paredes y Arrillaga
UNIFIED MEXICAN CONGRESSIONAL ASSEMBLY

Congressional Assembly, Mexico City, 7 July, 1846.

To President Polk, the United States Government and All
Corresponding Bodies, Etc. Etc. Etc,

Sirs:

By unanimous approval of both the Senate and the Chamber
of Deputies, and with the full support of the War Ministry
of the Mexican government,

And recognizing that an unresolved State of Tension now
exists between the Mexican government and the United
States government,

And in light of attempts both great and small to ameliorate
the Hostilities already incurred,

And in light of Mexican nationals having been provoked and
unwillingly involved in unwarranted hostilities leading to
their untimely deaths,

And in light of the refusal of the return of Mexico's rightful property, including the parcel of land known in some Assemblies as the Nueces Strip,

And in light of the blatant annexation of Texas by the United States government, despite repeated warnings by the Mexican government that such designs would precipitate the direst of reprisals,

And in light of John C. Frémont entering the Mexican lands of California under false pretenses, building a fort and raising the U.S. flag at Galivan Peak, and inciting U.S. Nationals to 'play the Texas game' by declaring independence from Mexico,

And in light of John Slidell's offensive and ill thought out gambit to buy Mexican land, which the Mexican government was not and is not inclined to negotiate for or willing to cede for any amount of money,

And in light of General Taylor's refusal to submit to Mexican demands to withdraw his forces to the Nueces River, and instead, commencing to construct a fort on the banks of the Rio Grande River opposite the Mexican city of Matamoros, Tamaulipas, and thereby inciting a conflict between Mexican forces under General Mariano Arista and a U.S. patrol found scouting on Mexican territory,

It is now a matter of common knowledge that no amount of Negotiation between our Countries will resolve the Disagreements that have brought our two Nations to blows.

In addition, it is also clear to all concerned that there is now no recourse but to admit that a State of War has existed for some time between our two Countries, and in the light of such evidence, it is with due determination that an Official State of War is now Declared by the Government of the Republic of Mexico against the Government of the United States of America.

Be it known to all who read this Manifest that Mexico has Endeavored to Resolve these many Issues without Bloodshed and with Negotiation where possible, and that this Declaration is a Matter of Last Resort and Desperation,

For we hope that these Differences can still be settled agreeably, with Civility and Honor, before our two Countries find themselves irrevocably enmeshed in this State of War that may inevitably bring them both to their knees. I come to you

President Mariano Paredes y Arrillaga

For the Unified Mexican Congressional Assembly
And With All Due Diligence,
Representing the Mexican Ministry of War

Best Friends and Brothers

NEAR THE LITTLE ARKANSAS RIVER
Army of the West
JULY 9, 1846

"Morning to you, Ben." Thomas Hammond hiked his boot onto a wagon wheel, and pulling a soft, well-worn cloth deftly and mysteriously from an unseen pocket, deposited a measure of spit on it. With one raised eyebrow, he targeted a small smear of muddy soil and wiped it clean.

"Humph!" Benjamin sat on his haunches and snorted. Off some distance to one side, a tent flap opened, and a partially dressed soldier peered through. His hair was rumpled, and sweat stains dotted his undershirt. Many of the other tents had already been broken down, as the sun was by now brightening the horizon. The smoke of campfires clouded the air, and the wind offered little respite from the gnats and flies that circled the camp incessantly. It had been a long night, and Ben had dreamed of his beloved Martha as she had come to him in the dark. It had brought one of his melancholic moods over him, and his head throbbed with tremors. He had barely managed his baleful growl in reply and wished to be left alone.

Thomas laughed as he brushed unseen dust from one lapel. "It's to be like that for today, is it? I see I shall have to cheer you up." He tugged at his coat, his demeanor that of one who feels the need to keep up his military appearance.

Ben tightened his lips. Reaching to his feet, he casually scooped up a measure of damp earth and tossed it onto his friend's freshly cleaned boot.

131

"Hey!" Thomas jumped back with a frown. "I'll have you know I awoke early this morning for no other reason than to polish these boots. Now you've undone it all." His eyes gleamed, though, and he winked at his brother-in-law.

"The rigors of the trail today will do you worse, my friend." Ben ran a hand over his unruly hair. "We are on a tour, not giving a military parade for the ladies."

"Ah! Speaking of the ladies, where is that pretty Indian girl I saw pushing herself at you last night?" Thomas squatted, and once again, the cloth was out and wiping the soil from his boots. He glanced up, and it was clear he meant to get a rise out of his friend. He laughed when the other man's face began to turn red. "Was there more to her attentions than met the eye?"

Ben stood with a sigh, and he turned to look over the preparations going on all over the camp. The day before they had seen numerous buffalo skulls beside the trail, and a small stream they had crossed had been identified as the Little Arkansas River. It had been hot and humid. Today, heavy clouds had already begun to form along the horizon, meaning a good chance of additional showers at some point during the day. At least the rains sometimes kept the masses of flies at bay.

"We're getting a late start on this daybreak. Look at Slaughter over there just now coming out of his tent. We're only a month out, and already we're growing lax." Ben's voice was tired and filled with gravel.

"Lax? Ben?" Thomas stepped up behind him, placing one hand on the older man's shoulder. "This morning's mood is not just about laxity, that I know. I'm sorry I teased you about the Indian girl. I know there was nothing there. Is that what's bothering you?"

"See the prairie dog holes?" Ben pointed off in the distance, ignoring the other man's entreaties. "I think the rain yesterday flooded them out. I haven't seen a one this morning. I met with Lieutenant Abert, the topographical engineer, this morning. I told you about him. Well, he tells me that's purslane we see growing all along the creek. It makes a fine vegetable for eating."

"Not if you ask me," Thomas guffawed. "Out with it, Ben. What has you so dry and humorless? The rain yesterday? It looks as though there'll be more today." The humidity spoke as much, and men could be seen mopping sweat from their faces.

"Martha." Ben paused. "I dreamt of her during the night. When I do, I miss her terribly. You know how I get."

"Then I'm twice sorry I teased you about the Indian girl. If I weren't a married man, though, I would have her for myself." He laughed and jerked away when Ben's elbow caught him in the ribs. "I only tease, Ben. If you write to Mary Ann of my words, I'll deny every one."

"I should write, and perhaps she could find her a man who would be faithful to her, instead of one who chases after every Indian girl who crosses his path."

He did let a chuckle escape, and for that reason, Thomas knew his friend was coming out of his mood. He was glad of it, too.

"You do feel better. I can tell. You know how much my sister-in-law loved you."

"And she would be with me still, if I had insisted she not suffer through the winter in conditions only a soldier should endure. I sometimes feel responsible for my own loss, and my children's, too."

"Regrets cannot undo the past," Thomas intoned very seriously, so much so that it was clear he was being overly dramatic. "However, the present circumstance is always with us, and our present circumstance is soon to be upon our horses. Care to join me, Captain Moore?"

"What would I do without you, my friend?" Ben grasped Thomas' forearm and squeezed it tightly. "I will be glad to join you, Lieutenant Hammond."

"Then we are off! And if the rains come our way, may they drive these damnable flies from our faces."

Even as he said the words, one especially large one buzzed near Thomas' eye, and he reached to brush it away. It caught on his sleeve, and to his dismay, left a brown smear when he flicked it off. For a moment, he stood looking at it, a comical expression of utter disbelief on his face.

"Right you are, there," and a laugh finally broke from Benjamin Moore's chest as he slapped Thomas on the shoulder before marching off to find his mount.

RATON, NEW MEXICO
Waiting for a Watch Battery
JULY 11, 2009

Matthew:	Mary Ann:
From: Matthew Duncan McCreary, PFC Date: July 11, 2008	Mary Ann rubbed her arms. Even in summer, it was cool in Raton. Off in

Best Friends and Brothers

To: Mary Ann McCreary
Subject: Missing Home

It's not like I thought it would be, Mom. We make forays into the mountains, but it's not like at home. These mountains have a sniper behind every rock. I try to keep my head down, though.

Got any chicken and dumplings you can send my way? All the guys here would appreciate it. I'd be the toast of the camp. You might add some of your cherry pie in the package. I'd have to eat most of it, but I'd share a few of the cherries with my friends. We're tired of all the MREs, pouring water into the bag, turning it twice, and letting it heat. The food's not bad, seriously, but it's not quite the same when it comes out of a bag, and whatever it is, you eat it with a spoon. Just one bite of

the distance, a haze obscured the farthest mountains, and lush grass surrounded swaths of colorful wildflowers. The smell of mountain pine trees hung in the air. Tomorrow Jon hoped to make it to Santa Fe, but Mary Ann wanted to enjoy the freshness of the mountains while she could. Santa Fe projected a level of civilization she wasn't quite ready to face.

She set her computer on the chair beside her, imagining the world her son must have lived in so far away. She couldn't do it, though. It was hot coming through Oklahoma and the Texas Panhandle, but surely nothing compared to those far deserts on the other side of the globe. Instead, she reached for her tea, and she swirled the ice inside before taking a sip.

brisket hot off the smoker. Just one bite!

Remember how I never liked to shower as a kid? What was I thinking? I'd give anything for a shower every day with as much soap and water as I want. We have to drink all our water here, as much as we can get down. We can't waste it on showers, although some days I really want to.

Dust. There's dust everywhere. It's in my shoes, in my bunk, and in my teeth. It gets in my shorts, and there's no escape from it. We even see it floating in the water when we hold it to the light.

Jeff's here with me. Remember the guy I told you about from Hannibal? Jeff Strugger? We're bunking together. Somehow, that's better than being here alone.

No, Matthew, she thought. Nothing's like we thought it would be, including our family. You were to always be mine, my wonderful son, someone to grow up, someone to give me grandchildren, someone to be there for me in my old age. You weren't supposed to put yourself in harm's way, to risk your life the way you did.

She laughed when she thought of his request for chicken and dumplings. She remembered her grandmother's homemade dish, and she also remembered chewing it carefully just in case her grandmother hadn't gotten out all the bones. How Matt's friends would berate him over that!

The dust? There had been many wash days when she'd shaken out her son's small jeans, only to

Something happened the other day. I can't give you many details, but it scared me. I was riding in the back of a Humvee, couldn't see squat, and suddenly the driver just speeded up. We hit something. I know, because I felt it as we bounced over it. I understand what they've told us. If anyone doesn't yield to one of our transports, no one stops. If we stop, we're dead. The enemy will send out little kids rigged with bombs, just hoping we'll stop to help them. I just prayed it wasn't a kid. No one wanted to look and see, well, except for one of the guys. His name is Frogger, a guy I made friends with after I gave him one of my business cards. He always wants to see. It scares me sometimes.

Life here doesn't mean the same as it does back in the have dust coat the laundry room. Still, she was sure it was different when it was forced on you, instead of chasing it down because it was something you wanted to do.

She was glad about Jeff. Mary Ann had written to Carole after rereading Matt's e-mail back in May, relieved to find her letter had been forwarded through a friend who knew Carole's new address. Carole had called. The divorce had been brutal for her, and she had run to California. She told her that yes, it was her Jeffrey. He'd run off to the military in an attempt to escape from his father's abandonment. Wasn't that like a man, to run away when life got tough? Now he was gone forever. How could he have done that to her? Mary Ann had thought of how far Carole

States. I had one guy who was shipping out the day I arrived tell me that they should just nuke the whole place, let it return to desert. I didn't know how he could say that, and I hope I never feel that way. I'm starting to understand, though, and I've not been here that long. Understanding and feeling that way are two different things to me, and I hope it stays that way.

Hey, my CO's on his way. I've got to get this wrapped up. They want us to use the computers they've set up, but here they try to monitor what we say. It doesn't matter, though. I'm cool with it. I can usually e-mail out whenever I want. When I get home, I can share the rest, although I don't think you'll want to know it all.

I miss Dad. I still remember that day at the lake. Ask him

had run, but she let that go unsaid.

Mary Ann watched two small children playing across the street for a time. Jon was inside looking for a new battery for his watch, and knowing Jon, it might be a while. She had time, and the children, a boy and a girl, seemed to enjoy each other's company, spinning one another on a red and blue merry-go-round. Then, they must have had a disagreement, because the boy jumped off and started violently spinning the merry-go-round, in spite of the girl's cries to stop. After a time, she lost her hold and slid off onto the ground. Her crying must have gotten through to the boy, because he knelt at her side and eventually reached a hand to help her stand. When she showed him her elbow, he studied to buy some flowers and drop them off at Brittany's house for me. Make them daisies. Somehow that just seems right to me.

Mom, I know Dad's not so much into spending time on the computer. However, do this for me. Over dinner one night, make sure you read him my e-mail.

Gotta go. My CO's here. I'm hitting send now.

Love,
Matthew

it a minute, then leaned to give it a kiss. The girl laughed, and they were off again, the best of friends.

No, Mary Ann thought, like a knife in her chest, life doesn't carry the same value all over the world. Here, right here in New Mexico, in your mother's heart, life carries a great deal of value. I'd give anything to have you here with me, my son. In my heart, I don't feel that you're gone. I can't. I have to believe you'll be back with us.

Mary Ann saw Jon walking out of the shop, and she raised her hand to wave. He smiled, and she reached to close her computer, aware that he wouldn't openly criticize her for rereading Matthew's e-mails. Still, his disapproval would be there, nonetheless. Jon dealt with things and moved on. Mary Ann had never had that talent. She was Matthew's mother. She firmly believed it was a mother's job to believe in her son, even when everyone around her told her he was dead. She would know in her heart, wouldn't she? She would know if he was gone, and she didn't believe that could possibly be true.

HARTLEY'S MERCANTILE
Platte City, Missouri
JULY 13, 1846

"Sissy, honey, I have your things ready." Mary Hartley-Buford, the proprietress of Hartley's Mercantile, stepped from the back room and called into the shadowy interior of the building. A bustling, self-assured widow woman of late middle age, she moved with ease amongst her wares. Her hair was pulled back in a knot at the nape of her neck, and without looking closely, the gray would go mostly unnoticed. The crinkles around her eyes lent her an air of constant amusement.

The shelves were lined with all manner of goods and sundry items for sale. Bolts of cloth were high along two walls, and the shiny bodies of canned tins lined one shelf at waist level. Occasional snatches of home-canned fruits and vegetables were gathered in prominent locations, easy for the eyes to see and the pocketbook to purchase. Several wooden barrels sat close to the door between the building's only two windows. They were covered, but inside were usually round, plump salted pickles and sausages.

There were also several large sacks of flour and corn meal, although Mrs. Hartley-Buford would be the one to measure what her customers might need from those. A person could buy anything he or she required in Hartley's Mercantile, including a limited supply of basic clothing necessities. Of course, anything that needed to be special ordered was easy to get, also. Tools, farm equipment, or even the latest hat from New York. It simply required a week, or perhaps a month or two, for the order to be filled.

"Mrs. Hartley-Buford, it sure be hot outside. Do you think the heat ever going to break?"

The voice called from the hardware section, and Mrs. Hartley-Buford stepped from behind the counter to find Sissy holding a small measuring tin. The girl was wiry, and except for her vividly colorful cotton dress, she could easily blend into the aisle's deeper shadows. She carried the look of someone to whom hard work was no stranger. Her eyes were bright when they looked up.

Mrs. Hartley-Buford smiled. "Do you like that, Sissy? It holds one cup. Here, look on the side. It has marks stamped into it to show a quarter cup, a half, and this one is for three-quarters of a cup. You can see them from both the inside and the outside, and they can never wear off. What do you think of that? I have one just like it I use all the time."

"What 'bout measuring spring water, Mrs. Hartley-Buford? Do you think it be good for that?" Sissy peered at the rim where the bottom was attached. The metal on the side was rolled underneath and pressed into a tight seam.

"Certainly, Sissy. I use mine for measuring milk, also. When I finish, it washes right up."

"Don't it leak none, though?" She pointed to the seam. "My papa had one something like this back at home, and it leak plenty. Drip all over, if we leave it sitting too long."

Mrs. Hartley-Buford placed a thick, comforting hand on Sissy's thin arm, her skin pale against Sissy's dark. She patted the arm in reassurance. "I've used mine for months already, Sissy. It's never leaked a drop. Are you interested in this one?"

"I doan know, Mrs. Hartley-Buford. I might have to ask Mrs. Hammond. It ain' my money, after all, that I be spending." She held the cup without returning it to the shelf, though, and longing was in her eyes.

"I have two of those cups here in the store, Sissy." Mrs. Hartley-Buford turned to head back to the counter, calling over her shoulder, "You don't need to worry. I expect I won't sell both of them today." She had a smile on her face. She might sell this one if she worked it right. "Just don't wait too long. Mr. Barker was in just the other day, and he said he needed a new measuring tin for his flour bin. One cup was just the right size, he said."

"Mrs. Hartley-Buford, me, too. I need just 'bout one cup size."

The proprietress glanced back to see Sissy with the cup still in her hand, and she smiled wider. "Sissy, if you think Mrs. Hammond might be interested, you just take that right on home and try it out for a day. Let Mrs. Hammond measure up some milk with it. You might let it set out for a bit, if you want, to show her it doesn't leak. If she wants it, you can bring the money in next week when you pick up your regular order. If not, just wash it up and bring it back in. I have it on very good word that you are an excellent housekeeper, and I have no doubt you'll return it as clean as it is now."

Actually, Mrs. Hartley-Buford had no doubt that once Sissy got the cup out the door, the money was what she would see next week. Only once before had she lost money doing this. A short time back, a man name of Todd had come through on his way to California. William Todd, she believed he'd called himself. Mrs. Hartley-Buford had thought him a cousin of one of the Lincolns up north a ways, and to her, that made him trustworthy. He'd taken off, though, never paying for the steel knife and fork set she'd entrusted him with, but it had been a small loss.

Sissy was local, however. She had nowhere to disappear to except the Judge's place just outside of Platte City proper. Anyone could find her there. Besides, Sissy might be taken to flights of fancy, but she didn't have a dishonest bone in her body.

There was one other reason why Mrs. Hartley-Buford didn't worry. She could just put it on Mrs. Hammond's bill, if necessary. Mrs. Hartley-Buford would get her money, but she had to get the cup out the door, first.

"Sissy, can I put that cup in the sack for you?" Mrs. Hartley-Buford made to unroll the top of the brown paper sack into which she'd packed all Sissy's goods. "Sissy, dear?"

"I doan know, Mrs. Hartley-Buford. It ain' my money, after all."

"And you have not spent any of Mrs. Hammond's money just by putting the cup in this sack." She held her hand out for the tin measuring cup. "If Mrs. Hammond doesn't want it, simply return it, and you still haven't spent any of Mrs. Hammond's money. Now, hand me the cup."

"If you insist, Mrs. Hartley-Buford. I guess what you say make sense. After all, I doan want to spend any of Mrs. Hammond's money without her knowing 'bout it."

"You are a good girl, Sissy." Mrs. Hartley-Buford reclosed the top of the sack with the tin cup inside. "Now, Sissy, how is Mrs. Hammond's baby doing? He must be seven, eight weeks now. Is that about right? I bet he cries up a storm at night. Is he nursing all right?"

"He doing fine, Mrs. Hartley-Buford. He doan cry all that much. When he do, I just give him a bit of peppermint to suck on, and he quiet down right fast. You doan worry 'bout that baby none. I take good care of him." Sissy's eyes were on the bag, though, and her tin cup inside.

"I wasn't worrying, Sissy. I was just asking. Are you and Mrs. Hammond in town for the summer?"

She knew they were. She had seen them walking along the street. It was good to have a finger on what was going on, though, and as proprietress of the mercantile store, all news filtered through her. Asking was her way of gleaning new information that she could pass along, if appropriate, as well as the permission to do so. It wouldn't do to gossip. After all, sharing the news of people's comings and goings had to be accomplished somehow. Not everyone in the world lived in a city with a newspaper, like those folks in Liberty over in Clay County. Some people had to share news by word of mouth, and Mrs. Hartley-Buford didn't intend to gossip.

"We have been, Mrs. Hartley-Buford. 'Cept the garden done gone dry, and we might take up at the Judge's place in a week or two. I get you your money for your cup, though. Doan you worry none 'bout that."

"I'm not worried, Sissy. I'm just asking." Mrs. Hartley-Buford wrapped the package with string and tied it up neatly. Then she slid it across to Sissy. "There you go, Sissy. Say hello to that boy's momma. I intend to stop and see her before you head out for Judge Hughes' place. You tell her that." She reached into a jar at her side and pulled out a peppermint. Then she pulled out a second. "One for the baby, Sissy, and one for you. You remember to tell Mrs. Hammond I plan to come by." She held out the mints, smiling when they were quickly snatched up.

"I will, Mrs. Hartley-Buford. You bet I will." Sissy was gone with her words, her hand running across the brown paper at the top of the package. Her cheek could be seen already sucking one of the candies.

Mrs. Hartley-Buford smiled at her retreating back. That was a sale that wouldn't come back to haunt her.

She reached to a folded newspaper at her side. It was *The Weekly Tribune* from Liberty, just over in Clay County. The date on the front showed Saturday, July 11, 1846. It was now Monday, and that meant it was only two days old. It had just come in that morning, and she opened it to the first page. She looked at it for a moment, and a frown grew across her forehead. Her eyes danced along the words, and it was clear she didn't like what she saw. Glancing out the door, she searched for Sissy, thinking to call her back. Mary Ann Hughes Hammond would want to hear this news, but the girl was nowhere to be seen. Mrs. Hartley-Buford took a deep breath and held it for a moment before letting it out in a great sigh.

"War. It's finally here. Poor, poor, Mary Ann. You dear child. I just hope that nice man you married comes back to you alive. War is hard, and I know that myself." She glanced at the band on her finger, the one she'd been given by Mr. Buford so many years ago. He'd not come home. No, that devil of an Indian, Black Hawk, had stirred up trouble, and her man had been left dead in a dry creek, his heart pierced by an arrow.

A noise at the door caught Mrs. Hartley-Buford's

145

attention, and she slipped the paper aside to greet Mrs. Idella Shanksky as she walked in the door. She smiled as she called to her. Mrs. Shanksky had ordered new curtains from Back East, and how fortunate she was! They'd come in only that morning.

However, the headline could still be seen shouting its news. "Mexico Declares War on July 7." A second headline, one down lower in a slightly smaller type, read, "U.S. Troops Already on the March."

Mrs. Hammond's good lieutenant of a husband was on the march, was what Mrs. Hartley-Buford had been thinking. Mrs. Hammond's brother-in-law, too, that nice Captain Moore. They were both on the march, and Godspeed them back home once again.

PERSONAL LETTER
Lieutenant Thomas C. Hammond
CARRIED BY ARMY POST

July 15, 1846

My Dearest Mary Ann,

I feel remiss, my Precious Love, and I feel I have let you down. You know I try to write every chance I get, for there is a regular post system to ferry mail back and forth. However, at times, it seems the Devil, himself, conspires to tangle my days with events of horror and travail. I will speak more of that later, my Dear Wife.

Best Friends and Brothers

In the first words I write upon this page, I wish to let you know how much I treasure each letter I have received from you. They are a wealth more valuable than jewels or gold, and I reread each and every one. I carry them next to my heart, and if my fellow officers should accuse me of an expanding chest, perhaps blaming it upon too much meat at the evening meal, I will tell them that I have dined upon the love of a beautiful woman, and know, my Wife, that I speak only of you. I think of you daily, and I only wish to hold you once again in my arms.

Our son, how is he, my Mary Ann? He was so small when I left you, and I fear I will not know him when I return. It is clear to me that I will mean nothing to him. You must read my letters to him, for it is entirely possible that he will absorb some of my character from the words I write, and he will indeed know me when I stand once more at my family's side.

Our brother-in-law has turned my trick back upon me. You may remember my plans to sheet his cot in a shortened fashion. My game was wonderfully played out, for we spoke of many things far into the night, and only when our eyes could remain open no longer did we deign to find our cots and rest. I pretended I needed help with my boots and coat, for I wanted to be already within my linens when Benjamin retired to his. I moaned and called for help, claiming a bunion upon my toe. Yet, when my friend pulled upon my boot, I curled my toes to where the item would not be removed from my feet. I made him tug for a full 5 minutes. I was certain he would curse me and leave me to my own devices, but alas, I was wrong. Benjamin braced his feet, and I began to fear he would break the bones of my toes, for he tugged excessively hard. I had to cover my mouth and pretend moans of increasing pain as I relaxed the grip of my toes, otherwise, he would have known I was only pretending. You see, I could no longer control the laughter boiling up within me.

I so much enjoyed his huffing and puffing, and the riotous expressions on his face, that I pretended the same with the second boot, but by that time, he had figured out to brace against the legs of the cot, and he had the boot off in no time. It was not without some entertainment to me, though, and I found it well worth the effort.

I did pull him aside as I removed my clothing, my Dear Wife, for I claimed he had hurt my feet, and I could not undress properly unless he held my arm. Oh, what a good man I have found for a friend! He did as I asked, and there was not a word of complaint. I was fast in my bed before Benjamin had removed even one stitch of his clothing.

I could not help but watch him in anticipation as he prepared for his own slumber. For you see, Mary Ann, I knew what was to come. Our dear Benjamin loves to throw himself into his bed in a great, mighty swoop, and that was when I would see all my efforts come to fruition.

The end of the game played itself out more excellently than I could have imagined. Oh, you should have seen it as it happened! Ben prepared himself for the night—a warm one, to be for certain—and with a great yawn, he doused the light. I heard his cot creak as he shifted the coverings, knowing he would quickly fling himself into the bedclothes. I only hoped my eyes would adjust to the darkness hurriedly enough to allow me to view at least a small portion of the spectacle. We did have a small moon, after all, and there was some light outside the tent.

Picture what I describe to you, my Mary Ann. You must put little Tommie down before you read this next part, for you will laugh so hard, you will not be able to hold to him. The tent was in darkness, and all that could be heard was the riotous sound of crickets ringing in the night. I expected a giant exclamation of surprise when Ben's feet would not reach the end of his bed, but instead, his cot creaked mightily, and in that moment, a sound as of a barking seal filled the tent. This huffing went on for some minutes, as apparently Ben thought his feet had gotten caught in a hole in his linens, and he tried unsuccessfully to untangle them. He kept pushing with his legs, and the cloth simply would not give. Then, there was a great tearing sound, and I sat up in dismay, fearful that I had been the cause of something disastrous. And so it was, my Dear Mary Ann. Our treasured brother-in-law had put his foot completely through the bedclothes! Suddenly, he leaped from the bed with a loud commotion, greatly entangled and hopping around until he fell directly upon my own cot, and I still in it! Of course, I leaped up, or at least I attempted to do so, but it was a fruitless endeavor. You see, Ben was lying across me. I could flail my arms, though, and I did so without thought of rhyme or reason, and that, my Dear Wife, is why our tent came down upon the two of us in the dead of the night. Thank goodness for the moon, for we had to reassemble the lines and redrive the stakes in the muggy darkness, and that was not enjoyable, except that I told Ben what I had done, and he wasn't upset in the least. In fact, he clasped me on the shoulder, and told me in the most sincere tone, that he could think of no better man to become entangled with in a falling tent than his own brother-in-law. I consider it a great compliment, for I feel the same about him.

There has been a long-term consequence brought about by my prankstering, however. It would seem that our brother-in-law has felt a little revenge might be in order. At first, I considered his demand that I repair his damaged bedding as my only penalty, and that was a relief to my soul. Yet, I have found on repeated occasions that my own cot has turned up sheeted in the same shortened manner, requiring me to arise in the dark of the night to strip it bare and remake it by touch. I have gotten quite good at it, if I do say so myself. As I reassemble the linens, from time to time, I seem to hear laughter coming from the other side of the tent, although our brother-in-law denies with utmost sincerity any such participation in any act so degrading to his sense of honor. Still, I am plotting a way to even the score, and I am sure I will have something in mind before too many days have passed.

At this time, I return to my opening statement, and I shall explain why I have seemed to feel the Devil at our doorstep. I had occasion to be frightened for Benjamin, most frightened, just two days past, my Dear Love. Before you read on, know that he is well, and no harm has come to him. No, the danger he faced was in my mind only, and I have not told him a word of it, for now I feel very silly in my reaction. For, you see, we had come upon Pawnee Creek just the other day, and due to excessive rains that must have fallen far upstream, it was swollen beyond its normal capacity. Our supply wagons could not cross due to the force of the swirling waters, and it was decided we would have to build a raft of logs.

As we were readying our tools, three men (I did not see them at the time) decided on their own to test the waters. They quickly found the rushing eddies were no laughing matter, for the currents were far too forceful for any human to master. One man slipped into the waters, and before his friends could reach for him, he was gone. Their cries for help aroused the rest of us from our endeavors, and those of us readying our tools immediately ran to the scene, only to see the man go under the final time.

When we frantically quizzed the other two men on the identity of the one in the water, they could only cry, "It is Hughes! It is Hughes!"

When I heard those words, my Mary Ann, I thought of you, and of your dear sister so lately gone from this world. Hughes! How could I not think of your family? And, for some reason, my mind played with those whom I love most, and this Hughes became Benjamin to me.

I am aware how this sounds, my Dear Wife, and yet it happened just the same. Perhaps it was because both Benjamin and myself have each married such a beautiful Hughes girl, or perhaps, because at a distance, the bobbing head of the drowning man made me think of Benjamin, I do not know. I was only aware that my friend was not at my side, and I was suddenly convinced he was sinking to his death in the swollen river. In that moment, I knew I had lost him, and I was frantic. I yelled for a rope, and in my madness, I ran along the riverbank, knowing that I must save this man, even at risk of my own life. However, it would have been useless, even if it had been Benjamin, for the man was already out of sight. I was most grateful, although only afterwards, that several of my companions (Cpt. Johnson, most especially, for he was at my side, and he saw my lack of self-control most clearly) pulled me back from the edge of the raging water, for I would have gone in. As I fought the arms that held me, I could not understand why no one had jumped in to save the drowning man, still thinking it was Benjamin who had gone under. I must have left numerous bruises on not a few arms and legs, I fought so fiercely.

I understand now that if someone had dived in to rescue him, the water would have simply taken another to his death as well. It was only when I saw Benjamin come running that my heart was returned to my control, and I could breathe calmly once again. I clasped his hand with one of mine, and I drew him to me to throw my arm around his shoulder in a brotherly hug. I know tears must have been on my face. All I could say to him was, "You still live, Ben. Thank God you still live."

Of course Ben laughed at me, for he knew nothing of the drowning man, and I laughed at myself, also, for I was embarrassed at my reaction to this drowning man's name. How I could have become so confused, I do not understand. I do know one thing most clearly, however. If such should ever occur to threaten my dear brother-in-law's life, I will not hesitate to jump with both feet to save him, even should the river of circumstance carry us together to our deaths. Forgive me, Mary Ann, but you must know how much I have grown to care for this friend of mine. It is, I suppose, the way of men who have become companions in war, and although our company has not fired a single shot in this campaign upon which we endeavor, it is a war, still, and I cannot describe it as any other thing.

To discuss brighter matters, this evening we completed our raft, and there is talk of making our crossing in the morning. I believe our new construction will easily bear upwards of 1,000 lbs., and that is without it being excessively loaded. I feel most proud of what we accomplished.

During the day, several of our men caught various specimens of a large white crane, and they are to be a fine and glorious supper for a number of us. Because I worked so diligently on the raft, I have been invited to partake. So, Mrs. Hammond, you might imagine me this evening at a grand table with the finest of linens, for I shall dine upon the most exquisite of dishes as this day draws to a close. Under the setting sun, I shall feast upon braised crane, and the flesh shall strengthen my body. I shall be able to fly to you in my dreams, telling you of the thoughts of love I carry within my heart.

Write to me often, my Dear Mary Ann, for there is little I treasure more greatly than the letters from you which I carry next to my heart.

My Sincerest Regards to my Most Wonderful Wife, and may our Faith in God bring us together again, soon.

Your Loving Husband,

Lt. Thomas C. Hammond

United States Army

OFFICIAL JOURNAL
Lieutenant James W. Abert
TOPOGRAPHICAL ENGINEER ASSIGNED TO
KEARNY'S COMMAND

Monday, July 20: I have not written for several days, as I have felt some illness upon me. I shall attempt to right that in this sitting. We are now upon the prairie, and it rightly deserves to be called the Great Desert. There is grass of a short and wiry nature, and cactus abounds everywhere. Three wild horses were seen in the distance not long after setting out this morning, a bay, a roan, and a black. I would have thought to see mustangs; however, these were large, fine animals. Their wildness was extreme, and it was clear that no man has ever ridden upon their backs.

Our crossing of the river last Thursday was achieved without serious incident. Thankfully, a rope was stretched across to prevent the loss of our raft in case the cable should break. At one point, the rope did give way, but the knots upon it prevented the noose from slipping all the way off, and it held. Many of the horses entered the water willingly, but others seemed put off by the swirling eddies and had to be coerced into entering the pulsating madness. Although the level had dropped by 2 feet, much slippery mud had been deposited, and the Volunteers camping by the regular ford lost several animals in the crossing. By 11 o'clock, our passage was complete, and all our goods were to the other side.

Also, the man who drowned was buried. Upon his retrieval from the flood, his clothes had been delivered to Lt. Emory. His friends sent for them after they had dug a grave in the earth. Capt. Johnson stepped up, commenting favorably on the man's dedication to his fellows, and by nightfall, he was entombed in the earth. "Requiescat in pace."

About 11 o'clock Col. Donithon [sic] arrived. He spoke to Lt. Peck and myself, and we were invited to attend Col. Kearny. The Col. wished to know of the road to Bent's Fort by the way of the Smoky Hill Fork. We spoke of its length and the hardships one endures along that path, and he was forced to decide against that route.

We pressed on about 3 o'clock following a tributary of Pawnee Creek. We soon came upon the road and traveled until about 10 at night. We found a supply of bois de vache and kindled a cheerful fire. Skylarks abounded, and before much time had passed, the cooling weather had many of the men calling for blankets. We discovered we were in the midst of prairie dogs, and there was little grass for our horses. I believe the temperature fell to near 60° F.

On Saturday, we came upon a very large herd of buffalo not 300 yds. from where we had camped. There was no doubt they saw us, but the wind forced our scent away, and they seemed undisturbed. Occasionally one would cast a sinister glance our way. In spite of my illness, I made an attempt to sketch one or two. My sickness quickly overcame me, though, and I was forced to put my sketchpad away.

We determined we were on the upper route as some had long suspected, and to avoid another night as we had just spent, we determined to move to the army's main column. Once we found the road, we located Maj. Clark's battalion of artillery.

Yesterday, after only 11 miles in the Arkansas bottom (by Maj. Clark's odometer), we reached Jackson's Grove. The loss of a linchpin obliged us to stop for an hour. Our men manufactured one from a picket, and we were soon off again.

I was interested to know the precise location where Capt. Cooke captured the Texians in 1843. Col. Kearney [sic] detailed Lt. Love of the Dragoons to assist me. He pointed out a large grove that stretched for a quarter mile along the riverbank. That evening, I felt it necessary to have some of our animals' shoes adjusted. I made my way to Col. Kearney's [sic] encampment, thinking it to be only 4 miles, whereas it was 8. The Col. suggested I remain for the night, and I acquiesced. I am grateful I did, for it seems that he has now become very ill. He rides in the instrument wagon, for it is light and has good springs. The other wagons, made after the plan of the Santa Fe wagon, are too rough to carry an invalid without advancing his ill condition.

We covered a distance of 31½ miles this day. The sun was most intense, and many men dismounted and walked to rest. Several men were seized with sickness, and vomiting has become rampant. The footsteps of the guard now keep me awake, and the conversation of our French boys continually breaks the silence of the night.

Maj. C and Capt. W were called upon this afternoon to have a hind axletree made.

OFFICE OF THE NAVY
George Bancroft
UNITED STATES GOVERNMENT

Order No. 243456

Effective date: July 23, 1846
Reassignment location: Norfolk Navy Yard
Last permanent duty location: Commodore, Pacific Squadron
Reporting date: October 15, 1846

June 12, 1846

Commodore John D. Sloat
United States Navy, Pacific Squadron

Dear Commodore Sloat:

You are hereby relieved of command of the Pacific Squadron, and on the date assigned, will report for further orders at the Norfolk Navy Yard. Your achievements at the Battle of Monterey are a credit to your record. Your meritorious contributions to the defense of California are greatly appreciated.

Your command will be assumed by Commodore Stockton without delay.

Sincerely,

George Bancroft

United States Secretary of the Navy

PACIFIC COAST OFF CALIFORNIA
July 25, 1846
USS SAVANNAH

"This Fremont. He's a brevet captain of the United States Topographical Engineers." Aboard the *USS Savannah*, surrounded by the deep blue waters off California's Pacific coastline, newly appointed Commodore Robert F. Stockton pursed his lips. A gaunt man with thick hair, muttonchops, and a flowing moustache, his appearance carried presence. "I believe he's the same man also dubbed Pathfinder of the West."

"Yes, sir. I understand he has a man by the name of Lieutenant Gillespie in his party. He's the tall, dark-haired Marine who spoke briefly with you earlier. Also, there is a 'Kit' Carson in his group."

"I know this Kit Carson. He has a reputation that precedes him." Stockton laughed in an amused way. "How many others are there altogether?" He moved several papers on his desk, finally placing them in one orderly stack. Onboard the *USS Savannah*, room was tight, and he was still organizing his things. He capped his inkwell before continuing. "Do you think we should accommodate them all?"

There had been discussion of assigning each man a rank in the military, although the thought had received less than unanimous applause.

"There are about two hundred, altogether, I'm told, plus Fremont and Gillespie. I believe they know the land, and they've been instrumental in swaying the mood of the Californians in favor of conquest. Some are quite rough, but we could do worse. All? Yes, I would suggest so, sir."

"Then it's done. Bring them aboard the *Cyane*. Gillespie will have to be second in command under Fremont. What were they called before?" Stockton looked for an answer from his second.

"The old Bear Flag Army, sir."

"Such a label will never do. What about the California Battalion of Mounted Riflemen? That's much better." Without waiting for a response, he went on, "We sail for San Diego on 25 July. Make sure they are ready."

"Yes, sir. Will there be anything else, sir?"

"Not this morning. You may go."

"Thank you, sir."

Stockton watched the man depart, then he stood and stepped to the window. He rested one hand on the beam above his head, the gentle rocking of the vessel vaguely reassuring. He reached and adjusted the opening of the glass panes, grateful for the cool sea breeze wafting inside. It carried a smell that spoke of the freshness of clean ocean water, and it made Stockton proud to be what he was. He caught sight of a number of frigate birds circling, their wingtips fluttering in the breeze. Soon enough there would be other, less peaceful sights and smells forcing their way past this glass. Not today, however.

Even so, Stockton couldn't wait. Sloat had been too fearful of making a mistake, of turning out like Jones, who had mistakenly taken California and been forced to return it. Not Stockton. He would make a difference. He would help win this war, making damned sure the Mexicans were defeated in his little part of it.

PERSONAL DIARY
Susan Shelby Magoffin
JULY 1846

Sunday 26th. We spent last night encamped some fifteen miles from Bent's Fort. It was quite a cool evening, and I helped Jane string a rope to dry our things. Some items were still damp when we awoke, so I suppose there must have been some sort of dew during the night. It is of a good thing that Samuel and I were in our tent, and we knew nothing of it. Still, Jane has had to pack the clothing damp, and I am not sure it will be good for the fabric. I have told her she must shake them out as soon as we arrive, for they must not be allowed to mildew. There is no easy way to replace them in this desolate place.

We approached the Fort under full light, today. It was

some four miles away, I did suppose, when I first saw it. It was at that place where we first viewed the soldiers' encampment, and it was a sight most novel. I attempted to count the numbers of tents, and came up with perhaps fifty, and maybe more. They formed a ring interspersed with a wagon or two, and on occasion, a shade made of tree limbs. Many soldiers were idle, quite a few stretched out under the shade, although some were laying out clothes to dry in the sun or watering the horses, &c. &c.

As we approached the encampment, a sentinel of no large height, yet filled with pomp and dignity, marched up, his musket held against his shoulder. "Where go you?" he called to us in his most serious voice. I would have laughed, if I hadn't seen the stern look upon his face. Still, we informed him of our destination, and after he reported to the sergeant at arms, with no supplementary ceremony, we were given permission to pass. When a little time had elapsed in additional travel, we were able to enter the Fort with no further ado.

I have held some concerns within my heart which I hope can be addressed now that we have arrived. We are told that we will find a Dr. Masure within the Fort. I trust he will be in residence, for during my inauspicious July 4 "celebrations," I received a dire injury, not to myself, I believe, but to the one who so recently came to share my existence. Thank goodness, after the accident at Ash Creek, that my carriage suffered little harm, but I was quite ill for some time afterward, and I am quite confident the life I once carried has been aborted from me. How hard it is to think of all the women who give birth, and in a matter of hours, stand and wash their babes in a pan of lukewarm water before suckling it at their breast! It breaks my heart to think of it, for such a duty was to have been mine. That chance for Motherhood has been taken from me, and it has made the past week of our journey very difficult indeed.

Samuel has been told that we will be forced to wait until the Army arrives, if we wish to continue to Santa Fe. The passage is no longer considered safe. It does not seem that our passage has been especially safe up to this point, not for the little one that so lately travelled within me.

I have asked Jane to check our things from this morning, and she promised she would see that they are spread to dry. My driver has dressed down my horse, and our bed has been moved to a space within the fort. A number of private apartments were to be had, and Samuel procured one with several rooms. The noise from the Activities within the fort is atrocious, but even so, I rest upon my pillow, for I know of no other way to dispel this longing in my heart for the child I came so near to holding in my arms.

For all that Samuel has promised me a proper house when we reach Santa Fe, I have heard tell there are no proper houses in that distant city. Instead, all is desolation and houses made of mud. However, if it is to be mine, I am of a thought that any dwelling Samuel provides will be considered a fairytale castle worthy of my abode. How I long to be there now, for I have dreamed of Santa Fe, and it is in that place where I will truly become the mistress of my own home.

NEAR BENT'S FORT
Army of the West
JULY 26, 1846

"This person is your cousin?" Thomas Hammond stood at his brother-in-law's side. A short distance in front of them was a cot, and on it lay a very ill man. "The messenger who came to you knew this?"

"Our cousin, Thomas." Ben emphasized the word *our* as he clasped Thomas' arm in a firm grasp before quickly releasing it. "The one lying down, his name is William Duncan, and we come from the same stock. His father, William, Sr., is my cousin through my elder half-brothers. There's his younger brother, Theodore." He called to a man with narrow shoulders and even narrower hips, "Theodore! I've come to check on William."

The young man, no more than nineteen, if that, turned and quickly stepped to him, a bright smile on his face. His eyebrows seemed to reach toward each other in a permanent scowl, but his eyes gleamed with the discovery of a recognized relation. It was a likeable face that seemed open and approachable.

"Why, it's old Ben. You did get my message. How do you do, sir?" He looked at Thomas. "And who might this be?"

"Thomas Hammond, my brother-in-law."

"Through Martha." Theodore's face darkened, and for a moment he glanced at his brother lying on his cot. Then he turned back with pursed lips. "I'm sorry about your wife, cousin. Your son, how old is he now?"

"Old enough to be precocious," Ben laughed. "He's with his grandparents."

"Old Judge Hughes?" Theodore chuckled as he looked at the ground and kicked at a dirt clod. "I hear the judge sired only beautiful daughters." He glanced up impishly. "And a gawky son. Do you dare entrust your boy to a man who rears only gawky sons?"

Ben punched him on the shoulder. "He should have a go at you, Theodore. He would have you in line before many months passed."

"How is your elder brother, the governor?" Theodore had that impish look again. "You cannot get him to solve all the world's issues? I believe he knows that smancy con-gressman, Mr. Lincoln. Surely they can work out this little matter with Mexico. Then we can all go home."

"My brother is no longer governor. If you haven't heard, he left that office, passing several years back. In addition, at this point, Mr. Lincoln has never been more than a local statesman in Illinois, I seem to recall." The news of his brother's death had been mourned long ago, and he could surely shift the question of the *smancy congressman* to his brother-in-law. Ben turned to the man at his side with a grin. "Well, Thomas? I believe you know Mr. Lincoln better than I. I am not certain at all that Illinois could solve this war issue all by itself, even with Mr. Lincoln's considerable skills. Where is your answer to that question? Is he as fine as everyone claims?"

"I have no answers." Thomas raised both his hands, his

expression noncommittal and his palms out, to fend off this inquiry. "I'm just a simple soldier. I was away at West Point, remember. I carry no politics in my heart, and I have no agenda. It's all I can do to keep my boots polished and my sabre clean. When Colonel Kearny says to fight, I'll prime my rifle and give it my best." He chuckled, relieved to have so easily dodged a possible sinkhole of dissention.

"As will we all," Theodore echoed.

"You are here with the Missouri Volunteers?" Ben questioned.

"My brother and I joined to do our part for the war. It seems he will not be continuing, though." His face clouded, for the subject was dear to his heart. He and William had joined to be together, not to be separated. It seemed they might have no choice, now. "His fever does seem to have broken, in any case. Still, I'm concerned about the rising it has left on his jaw. It's certainly odd."

"Let's go talk to him. He's well enough to speak, if his fever's broken, yes?" Benjamin thrust his hand around his cousin's neck, and he gave it a quick squeeze. "Otherwise, we will leave him in peace."

"No. My brother would think me negligent should I allow him to miss a favored cousin. If I let you go without speaking with him, I'll never live it down. Remain here a moment, and I will see how he is at the present time. His strength comes and goes." With a skip to his step, one that told of youth and enthusiasm, Theodore darted away, nimbly dropping to his brother's side.

"He seems a fine brother, this Theodore." Thomas nodded the boy's direction. Idly he reached a hand to adjust the lay of his collar, for it had risen, catching on his chin when he turned his head. "To volunteer to risk one's life in this war takes a fortitude many young men cannot claim."

"I have always thought of my cousins as having such courage." Ben pursed his lips, his eyes on the two men, one kneeling at the other's side. He had always wanted that of them, anyway, and to find them here seemed a good accounting of their moral fiber.

Thomas unconsciously brushed at a dusty place on his breeches, then looked off to see a carriage approaching the encampment. Following was a virtual caravan of wagons and carts, including a great, slender dog running free. A driver pulled the carriage up short when a stunted sentry pompously offered a challenge.

"I see we have visitors of the finest caliber to observe our fortuitous volunteers as they gather," Thomas chuckled. "I hope they think us a fine army."

"We are a fine army, or at least we are fine officers." Ben tapped his friend's shoulder and pointed off to a circle of tents down the hill. A number of men were lounging half clothed in the shade of several branches, and items were spread to dry in the sun. "There, I'm not so sure." He grinned and winked.

His remark held substance, in spite of the wink. Some volunteers, not being military trained, of course, behaved in an atrocious manner. Stories had begun to filter northward from troops in Texas of abhorrent deeds flagrantly committed by immoral volunteers, often with few reprisals by the military's upper echelon. The volunteers with the Army of the West had exhibited better manners, thankfully, if measurable only by degree.

"Your cousin, the one sick." Thomas made to divert his brother-in-law's attention with his abrupt change of topic, as he wanted to know more about this newly met man. The enlisted troops and rowdy volunteers were old news. "Do you know him well? I mean, his mannerisms? What's he like?"

"Oh, William is quite a character." Ben laughed. Theodore was still at his brother's side, and he had taken a damp cloth to his brother's forehead. It seemed there would be no lack of time to tell much of what he knew. "I'm not surprised to find him here. He's from Clay County, and if you recall, that's very near Platte City—"

"I know Clay County. I've spent time in Liberty," Thomas broke in. "It's little more than half a day from Leavenworth. We should get together with this branch of your family when the war's over, since he lives so near. Perhaps when I write Mary Ann, I will see if, by chance, her father is aware of his family. Tell me more, Ben."

"I will, if you'll leave me uninterrupted. Besides, he's part of your family, just as you are part of mine, brother-in-law. The key word is *brother*, you must remember." There was a smile suppressed on Ben's face. He meant the gibe as a friendly roust of his companion's stoppage of his tale. "My cousin, William, is a wrestler. Well, and a runner, and anything else physical. I've seen the young men who travel with our army, the volunteers especially, running and jumping during the evenings. Now that I've seen that my cousin is with us, I realize it must have been he I watched much of the time." He coughed in an embarrassed fashion, as if reluctant to reveal his next parcel of information, and he gave a little chuckle. "William was never one to let another best him. As boys, I tried once, and only once, to take him down. He was younger than me, but I could not. He fought like a mountain cat, forcing my legs from under me, twisting my arms until I cried for mercy."

"You?" Thomas laughed. "I cannot imagine you crying for mercy."

"And you have not wrestled my cousin, William." Ben slapped Thomas' arm, pointing to Theodore. He was motioning for them to come over. "It seems my cousin will not let his illness best him, either. Follow me."

"Ben," William spoke, and a labored smile grew on his face. "I have not chanced to see you in some years. You do wear the Army fine upon your shoulders." He took a deep breath, and it was plain it sapped all his energy just to converse. "Theo tells me your companion is your brother-in-law. Thomas, he says. I would shake, but as you can see, I am quite incapacitated." He laid his head back and inhaled a deep breath. "I'm tired of this illness, and now my jaw pains me. I hear I'm to find relief at Bent. Do you think it might be possible?" He chuckled, but it was weak and fell off quickly.

"I should think Bent is just the place." Ben knelt and grasped his cousin's hand. "I understand we cannot be more than two or three days from our arrival. I hear they have an excellent doctor there, and I'm sure he will know just how to bring you back to health. Then we shall wrestle again, and this time, it is you who shall cry for mercy."

"You have not forgotten that summer we were together

as boys, have you? You always did have the best of memories, cousin. We should have lived closer, so as to know each other better. However, if you truly want to best me, perhaps you should wrestle me now. Otherwise, I shall never quit until I have you flat on the ground."

William began to cough, and Ben stood, releasing his hand to his brother.

"Thank you for taking time to inquire about my brother." Theodore stood also, and he turned. "Walk with me a moment."

"Is there something we can do, Theodore?" Ben grasped his forearm as they walked, pulling him to his side.

"Only that my brother's jaw concerns me greatly. I fear it's serious, and I don't know what to do. I'm afraid to express my concerns to William. He has endured enough, already."

"We cannot be more than several miles from the fort," Thomas reassured him. "We saw a carriage just a bit ago, and it will likely be there before nightfall. Your brother will find his relief soon."

"Ah, you are probably correct." Theodore smiled and looked back at William lying on the cot, one arm thrown back over his head. "He will be the old William soon enough, and then what a wrestling match we shall have!" He reached and gave Ben a clap on the arm, then turned to offer his hand to Thomas, shaking it firmly when it was taken. "I know you have duties, and it was kind of you to spend your valuable minutes boosting William's morale. I cannot tell you what it has done for his spirit." Then Theodore was off again, his youth carrying his feet swiftly back to his brother.

"He will be fine, do you think?" Thomas turned to Benjamin.

Ben thought of Martha, his poor wife, gone from him in a fever, and he wasn't sure. He replied with a smile, although it didn't carry into his eyes as his most deeply felt expressions were wont to do.

"We have the time that God chooses to give unto us, Thomas. I've lived long enough to carry my years heavily upon my shoulders. Sometimes I feel them as an unbearable weight. I no longer claim the audacity to answer that question."

"Perhaps I should wrestle you to the ground and see how many years you have weighing on you. I might be the cause for you to cry mercy for a second time in your life." Thomas grinned.

"Mercy?" Ben, the teasing having lifted his spirits, grabbed his brother-in-law's arm and twisted it behind his back. "Only my cousin has ever given me cause to cry for mercy. Shall I show you why?" He made as if to throw Thomas to the ground.

"No, Ben!" Thomas was in full laughter by this point. "You mustn't! I give! Mercy!"

"You are no challenge." Ben released his friend and pushed him away. "You should make me earn my victory, and then it would be worth the effort."

"I wish to remain an officer of the United States Army," Thomas smirked. "To do so requires dignity."

"And a clean uniform?" Ben raised his eyebrows at the gibe.

Thomas laughed. "Yes, Ben, and a clean uniform." He

reached to brush a dusting of soil from one boot.

"Ha!" Ben laughed. "My Martha would have laughed at you, so prim and proper. You are a true West Point man, Thomas."

"What matters is that Mary Ann didn't laugh, my friend. She didn't laugh at all. She married me, instead." He shot a superior look toward the man at his side. He fondly remembered his and Mary Ann's wedding day, impromptu though it was, as they sat astride twin horses, and were married in the field. It had been most unusual, rather less than what Judge and Mrs. Hughes had desired, but not unwelcome in its final outcome.

"That's true. She certainly did. I was never sure of her taste in the opposite gender, and now the proof walks beside me. She has no taste at all."

However, he laughed, and he threw an arm around his brother-in-law, for indeed, they were more like brothers than brothers-in-law ever could be.

As the two officers marched off across the field, side-to-side, the sunlight caught against the grass at their feet, illuminating motes of dust and small flying creatures that stirred in their wake. Among the enlisted men, several soldiers could be heard calling to one another, and off in the distance, someone was quoting Shakespeare. Smoke rose from an occasional campfire, and the world smelled good.

It was good, too, for any moments spent in the company of a good friend are moments to be treasured, indeed.

A Tale of the Mexican War

PERSONAL LETTER
Commander Samuel F. Du Pont
NEVER DELIVERED

29 July, 1846

My Dearest Sophie,

San Diego is ours. As the sun rose this morning, we were positioned at the headland Point Loma just at the entrance to the harbor, ready to change this region's destiny once again. The day was crisp, and the smell of success was in the air. Lt. Stephen Rowan, my executive officer, led a small party of sailors ashore. Also, Lt. William Maddox, USMC, augmented Lt. Rowan's party with the ship's Marine guard. Together they were unopposed in their march into the town square. Immediately they raised the navel ensign, which I believe to be the first official raising of U.S. colors in this region.

While the San Diego settlement has been under rule of the Republic of Mexico for 24 years, it was from Spain that I wished to signify transfer. The locals had a time making a search for the Spanish medallion, but after a period of waiting, one was uncovered. We straightaway raised the Spanish standard, then let it drop once again. When it had done so, the Stars and Stripes immediately went up in its place.

Excitement reigns in my blood, for this is certainly a harbinger of quick success in this war against Mexico.

172

It has been a very long day, and the ship is quiet. It is time for me to douse my light. I am forever yours,

Your Loving Husband,

Commander Samuel F. Du Pont

Aboard the Sloop-of-War *Cyane*

PERSONAL LETTER
Mary Ann Hammond
CARRIED BY ARMY POST

July 30, 1846

My Dearest Husband Thomas,

You must think me silly, for even as I write, I long for you at my side once again. I knew you to be an officer when we married, and I have no excuses, but I wish the Army had not sent you away. I miss you greatly, and your son would surely be happy to spend at least some of his waking hours with you.

The garden, I fear, is a sad and wasted thing, for the soil has dried. Before the plants browned their leaves and wilted away, we had gathered nothing of value from our earlier labors. I am at Father's now, for town had grown close with the heat and the humidity. Sissy has come with me (for of course I have to have her at my side; I cannot do this raising

173

of an infant alone) and she has been a greater help than I could have imagined. I fear this thing of motherhood is a tiresome trial. It must be easier by far to have two parents managing a child than it is to go it alone.

In your letter, you expressed concern that our son would not know you when you return. I have read your letters to him repeatedly, and I do believe he has come to know your name. He laughs, sometimes, when I speak it. Your words lull him to sleep when I put him to his nap, and I am certain he will laugh for you the first time he hears you speak his name.

Mrs. Hartley-Buford (who runs the mercantile in Platte City, if you remember) came by before we left town for Father's. She brought little Tommie a pair of crocheted booties to keep his feet warm at night. They have a blue stripe across the toe, with a ribbon to tie them. I do hope he doesn't outgrow them before you return. I would like for you to see him wearing them.

We have a new tin measuring cup. Sissy brought it home one day with the sundry goods I had sent her for, and I didn't have the heart to send it back. She uses it daily, and it seems to give her a great deal of pleasure. When we arrived at Father's, she withdrew it from her bag, and I laughed. She is such a sweet girl. I do not mind overmuch when her thoughts run away from her, and she leaves a task undone. She never complains when I set her to it again, and for that I am grateful.

How does our brother-in-law fare? I know he fights with his demons, for my Dear Martha is gone, but I am certain you are the one to pull him through. I pray you have made it to the mountains of New Mexico, for if the Great Desert beats upon you with the same Fury our own Missouri Summer has used to scorch our fields, I fear you have had a very hard time of it. I feel certain the cattle you carried with you have been a boon to your stomachs, although from your stories, you feast nightly upon flamingo and baby quail. How I envy you your time together, you and our brother-in-law, although not your cot made up with its short sheets. Thank you, Dear Husband, but I will keep my linens and feather bed.

My father asks about you frequently, for he treasures you as a son. As you know, my brother Samuel has been a great disappointment to him, and he considers both you and Benjamin as the sons he should have had. I daresay, I hope my brother never reads the words I write, for he would rant at me, but they are true, none-the-less, and he knows it as much as anyone. However, I need have no real fear of that. He seldom comes out of his drunken moods, preferring to quell the blackness he carries inside with his worldly spirits.

Tell Benjamin that little Mattie is well and full of life. He plays officer with a wooden sabre, and when he falls down, he clambers right up. Yesterday I heard him cry, "I claim New Mexico as mine!" We laughed, until he ran off to get away from us.

Sissy is taking the carriage, for we ran short of flour yesterday, and I hear her calling me for this letter. I wish to get it in the post, for the sooner I send it off to you, the sooner you will know how much my heart goes out to you.

You are my First and Only Love, Dear Thomas, and I wait patiently (or impatiently, if I bare my truest feelings) for the return of My Other Half.

Please carry me next to your Heart, for I will always be

Yours Loving Wife,

Mary Ann Hammond

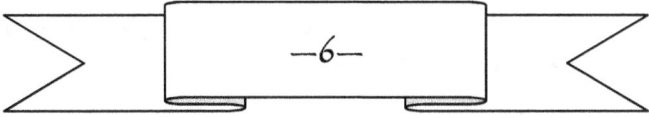

PERSONAL DIARY
Mary Todd Lincoln
SUNDAY EVENING

Aug. 2, 1846: We had a visitor today, one unexpected, but far from unwelcome. Dear Daniel Webster happened to be in town. He seems to have taken an open invitation to Sunday lunch on any week he is in residence, and I am glad for it. Sunday's repast is always a wonderful meal for unexpected guests, with a wide variety of meats, drink, and good conversation.

As we entered the dining room, he reminded me of a conversation we had one Winter's day, some half a decade before. I had not thought to remember it, but Mr. Webster brought it to my mind with a short story. Resting his China cup on his saucer and placing it on the table at his side, he cleared his throat noisily to garner the attention of everyone in the room, and he said, "When I campaigned for the Presidency in 1836, I did so wish for someone to come live with us in the White House. I thought of you, Mrs. Lincoln, although you were still Miss Todd at the time." He gave a short laugh, his cheeks flushing with his admission. "If you must know, Mrs. Webster has not a social bone in her body, and just like Dolly Madison did for Thomas Jefferson, you could have helped entertain the dignitaries. What a great help you would have been!" I reminded him of Emily Donelson, and he remarked, "Yes, she did serve as hostess, did she not? For Andrew Jackson. You would have certainly done as well for me." How I wish that could have come true! Yet, I am married now, and the White House may yet be mine. I wished for it once, and I still hope for it. I did not share that with Daniel Webster, however.

I do know a great deal about politics, and my male cousins respect my discussions. If only my sisters and female friends would cease calling such topics "unladylike." One day I will show them unladylike when I am in control of this country. Women need to be interested in these matters, and it is disappointing that they are not. It is sheer folly to have no sense of our country and how it operates. I mentioned my feelings on this to Mr. Webster, and he remarked that he has never met another woman like me. I asked him what he meant, and he looked at my husband with a smile. "You have a brilliant woman at your side, Abraham. If you should ever make President, I suggest you already have your Vice-President." I blushed, but I wish that could be true. It is a shame that women cannot hold political office, for we are American citizens, too. However, we also cannot be published under our own names, and none would dare to let us vote! It makes my teeth grind.

I asked Mr. Webster about this war now going on with Mexico. I explained that I have followed its progress, and I am in full agreement that Mexico has given the United States no cause for invasion. When he was noncommittal, I asked him if it was fair to the wives who are left behind, for no other reason than for the generals to have a few more medals attached to their chests. I know two good men, I told him, who rode off to this war at the end of June: Capt. Benjamin Moore, who was in the Black Hawk War with Mr. Lincoln, and Lt. Thomas Hammond, a friend of the family through our political connections. These two men left young children behind in order to go fight a politician's war.

Mr. Webster looked at Abraham and questioned him, "This is the Capt. Moore you told me about with the sextant?" Mr. Lincoln nodded, and Mr. Webster went on, "To be traded from the Navy! What a magnificent head he must have on his shoulders! I should have such a man on my side." I made it clear that he had missed my point altogether, but he changed the subject, and my meaning was lost.

It seems that politicians will always be politicians, and no woman's opinion will make a difference. I know this: If I am ever the President's wife, my opinion will make a difference. I will make my husband sit down and listen, even if I cannot vote!

Tomorrow may well tell if I am allowed to take another step along that road. Abraham has the Whig nomination for the House, and if all goes as we hope, one more day will put him in the United States Congress. Election day tomorrow! I find it painfully dreadful and extremely exciting at the same time. If Abraham is to rise in government, pray God that it goes well for him.

IRAQ
SPC Matthew McCreary
AUGUST 3, 2009

SPC Matthew McCreary screamed. The horrors that he had thought were too much to bear were as nothing to what he felt now.

Hot water poured over his testicles, and his skin vibrated with pain. His stomach welled up within his throat, and vomit spewed from his mouth. In that moment, he wished for death.

Death was not to be his, though. His captors had other plans.

MEXICO CITY
President José Mariano Salas
NATIONAL PALACE

National Palace, Federal District, Mexico City, 5 Aug, 1846.

To the Mexican People, the Mexican Government, and All Corresponding Bodies, Etc. Etc. Etc,

Sirs:

The Country of Mexico is a proud nation, one that must stand tall against foreign aggressors. Interlopers must be thrust from our shores, and the Honor of Mexico's Glorious Past remain unchallenged.

However, the Presidency has once again fallen into limbo, abandoned, with no clear transfer of power in place. It is a desperate hour when the Glorious Office must be turned over for a time to Nicolás Bravo, in order for former President Paredes to take his place in the field of battle against other rebels.

As the upcoming War with the United States now presses at our borders, the establishment of a firm government has to be foremost in our Nation's politics.

By unanimous approval of both the previous Senate and the previous Chamber of Deputies, and in light of the clear incompetence of the former Government of President Paredes, please be informed of the new State of Affairs under which the Mexican government will now march forward.

To that end, I have reestablished the Federalist Régime of the Mexican government, placing myself at the helm, and have invoked a new Congress to support that goal, Etc. Etc. Etc.

With Utmost Consideration for a Strong Mexico,

President José Mariano Salas

IRAQ
SPC Matthew McCreary
AUGUST 5, 2009

Matthew McCreary crawled on the stone floor to the crack of light he could see along the bottom of the door. It was truly dark in the room. He now knew that. The blindfold had been removed, but the darkness remained the same as always.

He felt for the food he had heard being slipped into the cell. Food? He wasn't sure he could call it that, but this was certainly a cell. He was imprisoned, and there was no getting out. He had lost track of the days, although he had dutifully tried to keep them straight, singing his way through the alphabet at first, only going to the letter that matched the day. Then, one day he had let himself slip, going through to the end, and he had lost track. Had he stopped on M or P? Maybe it had been S or T. He rolled to his back, moving gently to avoid the pain in his body.

A, B, C, D . . . he hummed . . . *E, F, G . . . All the world . . . has gone to Hell . . . and all that's left is me.* The words didn't seem exactly right, but they fit his life at the moment.

His hand felt slowly around him. Eventually it found the metal container of slops, and he pulled it closer. Without turning his head, he rummaged in the hodge-podge of bits until he found one his fingers could grasp. His thumbs were still useless for gripping, unless he wanted them to swell again, making his hands useless, also. He raised the morsel and slipped it into his mouth, pushing it to one side with his tongue. He pressed against it until it broke apart, ignoring the rancid taste that nearly overwhelmed his senses. He chewed slowly as he savored the fact that the bit of food in his mouth was sustenance, and that he might or might not get more before the next beating. When he finally gave in and let it slip down his throat, his hand reached to the metal container once again, gently searching for another piece he could put to his lips.

Matthew knew he would eventually have to roll over and drink the remains of the liquids that were left in the dish, for he didn't always get water. If the pan held dry bread, they might give him water, too. If it held this soup of a meal, then no. The water was in the soup. He'd tried once to lift it up to drink it like milk from a saucer, but he'd quickly found that was a mistake. With his useless thumbs, his fingers hadn't been able to control the shallow dish, and it had spilled down his chest. He'd been so thirsty that he'd turned and tried to lick the moisture from the floor. Later that night, the rats had come and nibbled the remains of the slops from his skin, inflicting numerous bites over his bare torso. Now, when the biggest bits were gone, he simply put his face in the pan and lapped up the dregs like a dog.

As he swallowed the second bite, he tried to remember that day at the lake. The sun had been bright in the sky, his mom and dad had been there, and Brittany . . . he had held her in the water. The words of the events were all he could recall. Yet, he knew he had been there that day, and he tried to visualize it in his mind. Even so, he only pictured darkness. He couldn't see any of it anymore.

His thoughts began to drift, and he hummed once again. *A, B, C, D . . . E, F, G . . .*

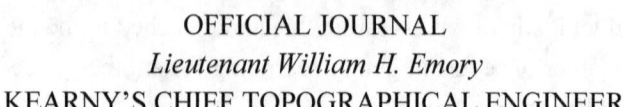

OFFICIAL JOURNAL
Lieutenant William H. Emory
KEARNY'S CHIEF TOPOGRAPHICAL ENGINEER

August 6 – It has been four days since leaving Bent's Fort. The rise in elevation has been considerable, averaging nearly 800 feet per day. Today, alone, we went from 5,896 feet in the morning to 7,169 feet by the time we ceased our travels. At first, water seemed to be hard to come by, until on the 4th, about 10, p.m., we found a "hole in the prairie" with water. Our horses had become attenuated, and the grass we found was a good thing for them. The night was delicious, and we slept in the open air. Our total distance that day was about 36 miles. About sunset, we had seen Pike's Peak, somewhat to the north, and the dim outline of the Rocky Mountain chain had begun to show itself.

We had descended into a considerable valley on the 5th, reaching the village of Purgatory. Much was blighted, and the hills were bare of vegetation. The horses of the infantry were almost worn out. Captain Cooke of the 1st Dragoons had been sent ahead several days previous to sound Armijo. A Mr. Liffendorfer was empowered to buy wheat if possible from the direction of Taos. He has a secondary mission, however. He is married to a Santa Fe lady, so he went with two Pueblo Indians to find the measure of the Pueblos and any Mexicans he could find, as well as to distribute the proclamations of the commanding colonel.

A spy guard of six men led by Wm. Bent went to reconnoitre [sic] the mountain passes. Today they returned reporting all clear. They only managed to reach the Canadian river. We commenced the ascent of the Raton, and after 17 miles halted with the infantry and the general staff just short of completing the pass. Parties had to be sent forward to repair the road, for it had fallen into disrepair.

Tonight our animals are refreshed with good grass and water.

August 10 – We have received news that Lieutenant Abert is much better. The news was received from a Mexican who came into camp from Bent's Fort. Colonel Kearny gave him permission to pass to Taos, provided he carried copies of his proclamation.

Five Mexicans sent to reconniotre [sic] our strength were captured. They had been directed to detain all persons passing through New Mexico. Bent's spy company brought them in, and, as they were riding on diminutive asses, even Fitzpatrick, who rarely laughs, convulsed with the comedy of the situation.

A Mr. Towle, who is an American citizen, showed up at headquarters, and reported himself to have been a captive from Taos. He says Governor Armijo has spread a proclamation calling citizens to arms, for the whole country is under martial law. By his words, it would seem the Mexicans are anxious for a fight, even to a man.

Rain has repeatedly passed to the north and west, but we have remained dry. Our height is 6,027 feet.

August 11 – Our travels today were long, leading to the Ocaté. There the river runs through a cañon. The grass is good, although the lakebed is now dry.

A matter of interest occurred today, for six or eight Mexicans were arrested, and in their possession, they carried the proclamation of the Prefect of Taos, calling for the citizens to repel all Americans, lest we destroy their land and their liberties. It orders all men to enlist. Then tonight two Mexicans came into camp. It was obvious they were spies, although they claimed to be searching for the Eutaws, reportedly in the neighborhood. The colonel ordered them detained for a day or two and released. Perhaps the news they carry back will be of benefit to us.

August 13 – We have had a false alarm. Several Americans have been encountered. At the Sapillo, nine and a half miles from our last encampment, a Mr. Spry came into camp, telling us he had escaped Santa Fe the previous night to inform the colonel he might likely expect some resistance. Armijo's forces had assembled, and he advised the colonel to skirt the city. Bent of the spy-guard procured four prisoners who claimed 600 men were positioned at the Vegas ready to engage battle. These two messages foreboded possible trouble ahead.

We had not gone far, when at the Santa Clara Pools, the colonel held up the glass and proclaimed, "The enemy at last!" It was to be a fight to the victory! Trot, trot, trot!

However, it was not to be. It was a mirage, and they were no more than harmless timbers standing against the sky; there was nothing there except the pine stakes of a corral. The Dragoons were greatly disappointed, for they wished either a fight or a chase.

August 14 – Armijo sent a message today with a Mexican lieutenant and several Mexican lancers. He said that he is completely prepared to defend his city. He wishes us to stop at the Vegas and allow him to meet for negotiations. A halt was called. Colonel Kearny called the Mexican lieutenant up and said, "I will soon meet General Armijo. I wish it to be as friends. Go. The road is as free to you as to myself." The Mexican embraced the Colonel and several others who happened to be standing nearby, myself included.

August 15 – At about 12 o'clock last night, it was reported that 600 men were collected at the pass into the Vegas. It was only two miles. At 7, we moved. As we made the road, Major Swords, quartermaster, Lieutenant Gilmer, engineer, and Captain Weightman joined us. They were very pleased to present Colonel Kearny with his new commission as brigadier general in the United States Army. It was quite a proud moment, though of necessity a brief one. Swords and his accompaniment had heard of our upcoming battle, and they had ridden hard to join us. It seemed that it would not do to miss the excitement.

Upon reaching the Vegas, the general made a speech from a rooftop, telling the people that General Armijo is no longer their governor, but that he is. It was quite good, for

he described how we come as protectors, and not con-
querors. His reception was very well received.

Then we went to meet our 600, only to find no one there.
For all our yells of "Trot!" "March!" and "Charge!" there
was no hostile force. How disappointing!

Excerpt from *International Encyclopedia, 2016 Edition:*

On August 16, 1846, General Antonio de Padua Maria
Severino López de Santa Anna y Pérez de Lebrón (b. Feb.
21, 1794 d. June 21, 1876), more commonly called Santa
Anna, entered Mexico once again at the Port of Vera Cruz.
He had been living in exile in Cuba at the time, having
attempted a failed endeavor to regain Texas in 1842. His
expedition had resulted in no positive benefits for Mexico,
rather serving to cement sentiments in Texas that annexation
by the more powerful United States was a necessary option.

At the declaration of war in 1846, Santa Anna made two
different proposals to two different governments. To the
United States, he promised that if he were returned to power,
he would sell all contested lands to the United States at a
reasonable price. To the Mexican government, he promised
to fight off all adversaries as he had done many times in the
past. Once back in Mexico, he reneged on both promises.

In his prime years, many in Mexico knew Santa Anna as a
hero. In Texas, he was more often called the Butcher of
Goliad for his execution of 350 prisoners after that battle. In

Mexico, Santa Anna held the office of President eleven times, none in succession. During the Mexican-American War, Santa Anna's prosthetic leg (made from cork) was captured by the Americans and never returned.

Santa Anna's most passionate hobby was cockfighting. He is known to have purchased prize roosters at the expense of tens of thousands of dollars.

By the end of Santa Anna's life, he was forgotten by his government and ignored by those around him. In 1876, he died in Mexico City, crippled and almost blind from cataracts.

Read the full article at www.interencyclopedia.com/2016/ Antonio_de_Santa_Anna/Mexican_War

CUIDAD DE LOS ANGELES, AUGUST 17, 1846
Commodore Robert F. Stockton
PROCLAMATION OF CALIFORNIA

I am Commodore Robert F. Stockton, commander-in-chief and governor of the Territory of California. I stand before you at Los Angeles, California, and make this proclamation for all the people of California to hear:

There is no more Mexican rule in California. The flag of the United States now flies over this Territory, and Mexican dominion is gone. The "City of the Angels" is now part of the United States of America.

When José Castro, the Mexican commandant general of California, fled at my approach on the 13th of August, Mexico opened its arms to welcome him back. Castro abandoned California, and the United States is now your protector.

Laws similar to those currently in force in the other Territories under the American Flag will soon be in place in California. However, until those who are to hold the offices of government are appointed, military law will be enforced. Until that time, I will fulfill the role of both governor and protector of California. All persons who follow the new government will be considered citizens of the new territory with all rights accorded therein. No person who does not support the government will be allowed to remain in the Territory.

Those with weapons found outside their dwellings or discovered to be thieves will be shipped out of the territory or put to hard labor. A curfew is in place while martial law prevails, and curfew is hereby established at 10 o'clock each night until sunrise.

Signed,

Comd. Robert F. Stockton

Best Friends and Brothers

SANTE FE
Army of the West
AUGUST 18, 1846

"Look at that, Ben." Lieutenant Thomas Hammond wearily dismounted from his horse, and he stepped forward to rub along its neck. The pace of many hard days could be heard in the lilt of his words, and his face was stained with dust. However, his eyes were on the scattered collection of brown buildings in the distance. The town of Santa Fe didn't look like much to his weary gaze.

"So, we have reached another milestone. General Kearny claimed we would find ourselves in Santa Fe by the eighteenth. Well, here we are." Captain Benjamin Moore gave a brief smile that faded almost as quickly as it had appeared. He sat astride his mount and held his reins gently in one hand. There was no need to be cautious of his animal doing anything sudden. It could barely do anything at all, even walk, such was the exhaustion the horses in their care exhibited. "How many mules do you think were shot today?"

"I'm afraid I've lost count." Thomas Hammond carelessly shrugged, too tired to care much about them. There was nothing to be done about it, anyway. Collapsing mules had been put out of their misery regularly over the past weeks, although the numbers had increased frightfully in the days just previous. Today had been the worst. It had been an especially long ride, for the general had pushed hard to reach Santa Fe before dusk descended. It was only about three o'clock in the afternoon, but it would be another three hours or so before the final troops could settle in. Even if Kearny wished it so, it was still in some doubt whether the sun would continue to shine upon the ragged tail of their weary army when it found its way into the camp.

"Come down, Ben. Let's find something to drink. Our horses will wait on us to return." Thomas absently tugged at one sleeve, straightening it a bit. After a moment he glanced at Ben, waiting on a reply.

There was little outward joviality between the two men. The ride had been long, and there had been no end to the difficulties. This was a harsh land. In addition, the inaction surrounding their military goal had proven almost as challenging an obstacle for the troops as the landscape. Now, it seemed even the conquest of Santa Fe would be no more than a handshake and a glass of wine.

"Did you see the two Mexicans who came trotting after the general?" Ben still hadn't dismounted, but he did smile again, this time holding it on his face. "The one, no more than a boy, came to us as the acting Secretary of State. I found that most amusing. All the grownups have seemed to flee at the first sign of trouble."

"I agree completely. Can you take into account that General Armijo simply ran away? He could have defended this city fifteen miles back with little effort. Remember the steepness of the valley? We could have never gotten in and would have had to go completely around. Come, Ben." Thomas walked to Benjamin, placing one hand on his horse's withers. With his other hand, he pointed to the various parts of the city. "There, a flag. I am certain we will see ours in its place, soon."

Footsteps fell at his side, and he turned, his brother-in-law finally standing.

"Where to, Thomas?" Ben's hand clapped Thomas' shoulder, sending ghostly remnants of their day's dusty travels into the air.

"Water. We'll feel better with a fresh supply. Thank goodness for one small measure of blessing. We no longer feel the excessive heat of Kansas on our backs."

"The heat I'm glad to see gone. With this coolness, I can exist for a time longer, but you are right. Water." Ben dropped the reins. The horse was well trained, even had exhaustion not claimed its ability to wander at will, and he would find it in this spot when he returned. "That way," he pointed, seeing a wagon with some various barrels.

Before they could start off, however, a voice called to them, and they turned as a mount and rider drew near. The steps of the animal were brisker, and its coat shinier, than their own had been for some weeks. The approaching horse raised its head at the men, snorting once before shaking its mane in a rippling shiver. This was no worn-out beast carrying an equally ragged soldier. The tailored uniform astride the animal was that of a major, a superior officer. The wearer seemed distinctly less bedraggled than the men who had drudged halfway across the continent with Ben and Thomas. Clearly his time in the saddle had been one of brevity, consisting of quickness, rather than the trudge of an army on the move across a dry and dusty landscape. Even his boots glistened with the shine of recent time spent in the East.

Then Ben remembered a group having arrived with the news of General Kearny's promotion just days before. He recalled this man as the one who had carried the satchel, although in the rush of the moment, he had glimpsed him only momentarily.

Ben saluted, and out of the corner of his eye, he saw Thomas do the same.

"Captain Moore? Lieutenant Hammond?" Major Swords' inquiry was brisk to the point of brusqueness. This was his first sighting of Hammond, and he felt the need to make his superior rank clear. Even so, he considered his manner to be well within the confines of a gentleman, for other less polite terms for the men had flashed through the major's thoughts, ones along the line of *Court-Martial* and *West Point.* He kept those names buried inside. He knew who Moore and Hammond were.

"Yes, sir," Thomas called the answer. "I'm Lieutenant Hammond, and this is Captain Moore. What can we do for you, sir?"

After a moment in the sun with no answer forthcoming, the seated officer raised his hand in a perfunctory salute and let it drop, freeing Hammond and Moore to do the same.

"Ah, Captain Moore, it seems we are well met on this field." With a sound of clipped superiority, Swords' words cut the air. He made to clear his throat, as if this was an attempt at a convivial conversation between equals, and he might continue with additional camaraderie. It was anything but, and no other words came to his mind, leaving the moment dead. Swords adjusted his position on his steed, idly toying with the reins he held in his hand. His animal took one nervous step backward but stopped immediately when Swords' knee pressed its side and his fingers twitched the reins the slightest amount. He snorted and remarked, "Poorly trained brute."

"Yes, sir," Benjamin agreed, unsure at the sluggishness

of the conversation, as well as at the identity of the man, clearly a superior officer, who had ridden up at such an inopportune moment. He and Thomas wished for water. However, until the major released them, it seemed they would remain thirsty. He licked his lips, realizing one had cracked, and he tasted blood. It was warm and coppery.

"Captain Moore, I venture to recall you were in this area once before. With Colonel Cooke, I might hazard." Swords' cumbersome attempt at familiarity was a blind stretch, the first part, anyway. Yet, his words were a neutral entreaty that would be deemed innocent enough if it turned out to be grossly inaccurate. The mention of Cooke was surely on the money, however, whether real or imagined, for he recalled a connection between the two.

"No, sir, my travels with Colonel Cooke didn't take me so far from Fort Scott as this." Ben frowned. The man's voice seemed very familiar, and he appeared to know Ben's military history to a degree. He tried to place him. He couldn't, however, not in a major's uniform.

Then, as though bored with the subject, Swords turned to Hammond with his next question. "Lieutenant Hammond, you know Mr. Lincoln, I understand." He had learned something of this young man during the time he had remained at Fort Leavenworth, and he wished to make his superior knowledge clear. His eyes turned from one man to the other as if evaluating the two closely.

"Yes, sir, socially," Thomas replied, "if you mean the congressman from Sangamon County, Illinois."

"I mean the same. Explain." Swords' eyes were shadowed under his cap, but there was no doubt they were now locked on Thomas Hammond's face. His abrupt demand was backed by his rank, and he expected a full and thorough reply.

"My father is Senator Robert Hammond from Pennsylvania. He's a brigadier general in the state militia and also has been appointed Paymaster, U.S. Army. You may have heard of him, sir. He currently serves aboard the steamship Orleans. He's the one with the connections to Mr. Lincoln. However, my wife and I dine with Mr. Lincoln's family from time to time."

"And, Captain Moore," Swords turned his gaze, "I believe you also have an acquaintance with the good congressman from Illinois. Did not your elder half-brother serve as governor of that fair state?" This was less presumptuous than his earlier remark, for it fit with what he knew from his time spent with Captain Duncan those many years ago. For Moore to make this confirmation would place another game piece firmly on the board.

"Yes, sir. Joseph Duncan, you mean, for he did once serve as governor of that fair state."

It began to dawn on Ben just who this man might be. He seemed to remember he had once been under Ben's own command at Fort Scott. If this were the same man, though, the rank of major sat newly upon his uniform.

The officer astride his horse let the moment languish as he glanced away to gaze on the dusty town of Santa Fe. A number of Indians carried what appeared to be sacks of some sort of grain down a street.

After a moment, Swords turned back to the two at his side, nodding to Ben. It seemed he wished to know still more.

"In what fashion are you familiar with the congressman,

if I may inquire? Are you also a family friend, or are your connections of the political bent?" Even carrying the rank of major, Swords knew he could go only so far to vent his frustrations at the old remembered wrong if this man indeed had the good connections suggested by Mrs. Kearny.

"Joseph, my brother, the governor, was involved with Mr. Lincoln through his politics, and came to know him in that fashion." Ben spoke openly, as the responsibility of a reply to a superior officer's inquiry could not be questioned. Besides, he saw no reason to feint from his revelations. Such well-known facts were no secret to be held closely to his chest. "In addition, another elder brother, James Duncan, knew him from his time as clerk of the Supreme Court in Illinois. As for myself, I had chance to spend some hours at Mr. Lincoln's side during the Black Hawk War."

"Governor Duncan." Swords' jaw tightened, and he made a reflexive verbal jab, his wish for a measure of vengeance causing his control to slip from his grasp. "Your *half*-brother, you mean."

"If you must, yes. My half-brother." Ben frowned and glanced at Thomas.

"I see." Swords growled the words, then looked away in a rather disgruntled fashion. His correction was a slap, a distancing of this man from the honor of such a highly placed office.

The remark seemed unnecessary to Benjamin, even offensive, as there was no cause for such ill-held rancor.

Yet, still, Swords did not have the verbal confirmation for which he had come, and he wanted this man to confirm his relation to Captain Matthew Duncan with his own words. He pressed him, "Captain Moore, I understand you have yet another brother." Swords' glance was still diverted, and a muscle in his jaw twitched uncontrollably.

With the major's latest parry, a new level of hardness set itself around his eyes. Clearly this was the pivotal question, even if the captain and the lieutenant at his side were blind to its hidden meaning. The officer sitting so formally on his mount, his manner calculated and cold, continued to look across the land. What he really saw was a court-martial from a decade before, and he was absolutely certain Captain Moore had served as a witness against him in that debacle. He needed to hear it from Moore's own mouth, though.

"Several brothers, sir," Benjamin confirmed, "although not all still walk this earth." He cleared his throat, his tongue rapidly growing dry with all the answering. He felt he was facing something much like a tribunal, and it caused him a certain amount of unease. The cracked lip had begun to irritate him, also. Still, the man was superior in rank to both Ben and his brother-in-law, and he responded evenly, "Joseph, former governor, and another elder brother, Matthew, died just one day apart two and a half years ago. It was in January, I believe."

"Captain Matthew Duncan? Of the United States Army?" *Say it, sir!*

"You know of him?" Ben had the officer's full attention once again. Now that he watched the man's face, he remembered the expression he saw there, one that could quickly go hard when crossed. Not only had this man been a lieutenant under Ben's command at Fort Scott, the officer sitting so proudly before him on his horse had been acting quartermaster at Fort Leavenworth when Ben and his elder brother had served together under Henry Dodge, post commander. They hadn't been in the same company, but Ben now remembered a few severely butted heads.

"Possibly, if your Captain Duncan is the man I think." Swords' face tightened again. He felt he was pulling teeth to get a clean response. He pressed forward with a clarifying prompt, "From Fort Leavenworth?"

"Yes, sir. I do believe he served there, recruitment at one time, I think. It has been a decade or more, however. I was also with him at Jefferson Barracks in '33-'34."

"With a man named Jefferson Davis, also?" The officer didn't care about Jefferson Davis, there being no relation between the man's name and that of Jefferson Barracks, other than the similarity of the words. The question was more to give a sense of superior knowledge.

"Yes, sir, I believe so. Why?"

"No reason. I am sorry for the loss of your brothers." He said it with an indifferent tone, though. He had his confirmation. Still, there was one more duty he must perform. He took a deep breath and continued with a superior lilt in his voice, "And your nephew, Lieutenant Thomas Duncan, is he well?" He had now satisfied Mrs. Kearny's request to inquire after the man.

"You know of him? I've not heard from my brother's family in several months, sir."

Swords looked away disinterestedly. He had confirmed his suspicions beyond doubt, as well as done his duty to Mrs. Kearny. There was no cause for further discussion. As though fatigued, he turned aside and pulled on the reins of his horse. "Carry on, men." He spurred his mount, and he galloped away, the dust kicking up under his animal's hooves.

"Ben, do you know him?" Thomas laughed in spite of his tiredness and his earlier proclaimed need for water. "He certainly seemed to be interested in us, but you especially. He is a dour-faced old man."

Benjamin chuckled. "Old? Be careful to whom you speak those words. His asking about my brother seemed to put me in mind that I do know him. Major Swords, I now remember. Fancies himself a bit the ladies' man. However, I'm certain he cannot have many years on me." He saw no occasion to mention the old tensions that had been evident between his brother and Major Swords so many years ago. Such things were ancient news that couldn't matter now that Matthew was gone.

However, Thomas grasped onto the mention of the man's name, a moment of his normal good humor bursting forth. "Ah, the infamous Major Swords! I knew of him but had yet to make his acquaintance. So, you are an old man now, as this Major Swords appears to be? Shall we wrestle to see? You put me off by cheating last time."

"No, I'm only tired. Saddle sore, thirsty, and tired. I'll feel much younger when I've had something to drink." Benjamin remembered his friend's offer from earlier, and he had twisted his arm to make him relent. He would not do so again.

"As will I." Thomas slapped Ben on the shoulder, and he jumped back when dust flew everywhere. "Then perhaps we will find a good drinking trough in which to douse that coat."

That brought a real laugh from Ben. Every officer's coat was just the same. There was hardly enough water in this entire territory to dunk them all.

"Thank you, Thomas. I think I'll do better to simply wear it, instead."

"It's your coat." When Thomas reached to brush his sleeve, a cloud of dust arose from it, also. He coughed, then shook his head to clear the debris from his eyes.

"Need to dunk your own coat?" Ben asked.

"I need to dunk my body." Thomas coughed once more. "You're right about that. I think we both do. However, water for our lips, first."

"Water first, Ben. I'm with you. For our throats, I mean." And that was exactly what he intended, his steps starting off across the dry ground, his boots kicking up puffs of dry earth as he trudged along.

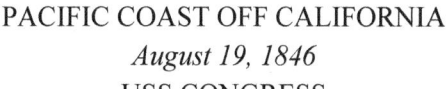

PACIFIC COAST OFF CALIFORNIA
August 19, 1846
USS CONGRESS

"Fremont, I want you to look at this." Deep in the bowels of the ship *USS Congress* off California's Pacific coast, having transferred from the *Savannah*, Commodore Robert F. Stockton leaned over his desk, an oil lamp burning at his elbow. Through the rippled glass in the small windows at his back, the dark smudge of the coastline a half-mile away erupted violently from a green-black ocean. Stars punctuated the heavens above, their pinpoint brilliance a crown of diamonds cast across the darkening sky.

The men sitting with Commodore Stockton were

unaware of the vast beauty of the California night drawing across the landscape. Their interests lay upon Stockton's heavy, wooden desk.

Stockton slid a piece of paper across. The texture was thick, a linen weave of good quality. It was filled with words that were hard to make out with it lying flat on the desktop. At that angle, the text was a tangle of loops and swirls, words written in a generous hand with ink that had pushed the lines into a mixture of spider silk and bulbous black knobs.

Across from him was Brevet Captain John C. Fremont, a man who seemed extraordinarily pleased with himself. Fremont had the broad forehead and prominent cheekbones of a working class man. A rampant bush of dark hair exploded from his head, and his eyes seemed to be constantly looking for something. A full beard shadowed his jaw, albeit it would be a rather hollow compliment for anyone to call it attractive. At Stockton's side rested Lieutenant Archibald Gillespie, a spit and polish Marine who had come further in his career in a shorter time than anyone had the right to expect.

The light in Stockton's cabin on the *USS Congress* was dim, but it was adequate for the task. The beams overhead were low, and while a tall man might have had to nod his head to pass under them, they posed no problem for the seated trio. The ship made creaking noises as the water in the bay pressed its mass one way, then another. None of the men sitting there noticed, however. Other things were on their minds.

Stockton continued, "I will head the territorial government. Does anyone have a question about that?" His eyes searched the other two men. He had come in and taken this wild land, wrested it directly from the hand of Mexico, and he deserved the respect his new position would bring.

"Tell me, Commodore," Fremont began, "about what you have in your plans for us." He motioned to Gillespie sitting at Stockton's side. Fremont was used to reaching out and grabbing what he could get. Having been born illegitimate—his parents had shocked Richmond by having an affair, then had run off together when his mother's elderly husband had refused to grant her a divorce—he had pulled himself up by his bootstraps. He had no qualms asking what his due was in all this.

"How does Military Commander of the Territory sound?" Stockton smiled. He'd known just what would rub Fremont's mongrel fur the right way. After all, the man was only a brevet captain, and anyone who knew anything understood that much of his success was due to his wife's father, Senator Thomas Hart Benton. Such information could be useful in the right hands, and Stockton was no slacker in getting things done, or in passing out rewards when results were to his liking.

"It sounds very officious. I like it very much." Fremont bobbed his head in a quick nod, and even in the dim light, his anticipation brightened his face.

"And for you, Mr. Gillespie, I would think Commandant of the Southern Department will do nicely. Will that be acceptable to you?"

"I would like to see it as you have listed it on the paper." Gillespie tried to suppress a smile, and he reached for the longhand discourse on Stockton's desk, the motion a barely disguised effort to hide his extreme pleasure. His response was spoken very casually, but his hand shook as he lifted the written words.

"Is it agreed that we have California firmly in our possession?" Stockton knew it was. His question was just a precursor. "If so, I would like to send Mr. Carson overland to carry the news of our success to President Polk. Does anyone have an objection to this?"

"How soon do we wish him to leave?" Fremont's eyes gleamed with anticipation. Despite his extreme eagerness, he understood it wasn't possible to assemble the makings of such a journey in a single day, or even in a handful of them. He had planned and carried out numerous expeditions of his own, and it would be fraught with myriad details. Be that as it may, this was glory in his socks, and he wanted word of his military achievement out. He wanted to gloat before his detractors Back East. He began to calculate the time it might take to put together Carson's expedition.

"Mr. Carson has spoken to me of this." Gillespie put his fingertips together in an inverted V and continued, "We have become friends, of a sort, in our common military endeavors. He speaks to me from time to time, and he suggests he can make it to Washington in less than sixty days. He could be at the President's ear before the first of November, if he could leave within the week."

"I do not see that as possible," Fremont cautioned with a quick interjection. He had thought this out, and to leave in less than a month for a trip across the continent would be cutting it very closely. Three weeks. It could perhaps be done in that length of time, if all went well. "Provisioning would be difficult in such a short span as a week. Certainly by the end of the first week in September, though, should be possible."

The other two men nodded their acceptance of the provisional time frame.

"I have one more thing I need to discuss among us." Stockton shifted position, and the gloom cast by the light of the oil lamp darkened his eyes. They became deep pools of blackness in a room filled with flickering shadows. His lips were clearly visible as he spoke, though, catching in the flames' gleam. "I am in preparations for a blockade of Mexico's western coast, and I wish to make everything clear before I leave. My plans for California have divided the new territory into three districts."

He pulled a second, rolled sheet of paper from a narrow shelf, and he flattened it on his desk, preparing to expand on what he'd mentioned to them earlier. A silver letter opener across the top held it flat. His fingers traced the lines drawn there. "This northern district is designated as your section, Fremont. I, of course, will have the central district, and the southern is to be yours, Gillespie." He looked at the second man hard. "I do ask that you not unduly antagonize the citizens of Los Angeles, Mr. Gillespie. I know how you enjoy discipline. Be patient with these people. They are already ours, and I see no need to create ill will where there is none already."

"I understand." Gillespie still held the first sheet, and he slid it back to Stockton's desk. With one finger, he touched his left eyebrow, smoothing the hairs there, the action telling more than he knew. "I may insist on strict discipline among my men, however. Correct?"

Stockton smiled. "Certainly. Now, one final thing. Have either of you heard of this new Indian uprising near Sutter's

Fort?" When the answer was negative from both men, he went on, "It may be nothing, but if it is, I may have to deal with it. I will make sure I'm prepared, in any case. We would not want to leave this new land open to any foreign aggressors, now would we?"

Stockton didn't realize how patronizing he sounded. He wouldn't. Patronizing wasn't his style. He was aggressive, bold, and decisive, and if others couldn't see that, he didn't care. They'd best simply get out of his way.

SANTA FE, NEW MEXICO
Jon and Mary Ann McCreary
AUGUST 24, 2009

Mary Ann McCreary held an ice cream in her hand as she sat on the narrow bench. The sun was bright, and its warmth felt good. She was surprised at how much she was enjoying Santa Fe. She saw Jon coming down the sidewalk and raised her arm to wave. When he got to her, she held her hand up to him as he sat, catching his neck and letting her hand trail him down.

"What was that for?" He smiled. It was something she used to do, and he had missed it.

"I know this place." She motioned to the town around her, the old part of the city, the one with the buildings that had been there a century or more, some much longer.

He laughed. "How can that be? You've never been to Santa Fe, and neither have I."

"Oh, yes, I have. In my research." She crossed one leg

over the other, and she let her foot bounce as she took a bite of her ice cream. When it began to drip, trailing down the corner of her mouth, she laughed, then quickly reached her thumb to catch it on her chin. When she saw Jon fighting a grin, she poked him with her elbow. "You can laugh, you know. I really feel I've been here. Kearny crossed those hills just there, and Thomas Hammond and Benjamin Moore were at his side. They were thick as thieves." She crossed her first two fingers and held them up for Jon to see.

"Thick as thieves, huh?" He reached for her ice cream. "You ready to let me have a bite?"

He was glad to see her talking. She didn't always anymore, not about anything except Matthew, anyway. They didn't always agree on the best way to approach that topic. Jon wanted to let it go, to grieve quietly. Mary Ann didn't want to grieve at all. She wanted to hang on to something that wasn't theirs to have and hold any longer.

"You know, if you half close your eyes, ignoring the cell phones and air conditioners, it could be 1846 all over again." She squinted and aimed her face skyward as if she could really see it. Just then they heard the bleat of a car horn.

Jon grinned. "And ignore the cars, power lines, and all the palefaces, then maybe it could really be 1846."

"You bully." She slapped his arm but not hard. "I felt I was there for a moment. You know, I dreamed of Matthew last night." She looked up to see him wince. She sighed. "What, Jon?"

"You know what. For a few minutes, you stepped out of all we've waded through the past months, and I saw the sun in your face once again. Now, you bring it back up." His mouth had gone suddenly tight, and the day felt hotter than before. The cars were noisier, a baby was crying, and the sky had lost some of its blue. The smell of pollution was in the air where there had been none before. "I miss the old you."

"I do too, sometimes." Her voice was quiet, but the dream had been real. She wouldn't let him convince her otherwise. "Matt is alive."

"Oh, come on, Mary Ann. We've been through this." He stood, dropping the ice cream into a waste bin. "I want him back just as much as you do. God, I'd give anything to have him back home." His face was twisted by then, and he turned away.

"He's alive, Jon. I know. We can go on to California and pick up his things. Sure. We're halfway there, so let's go ahead. I've always wanted to see where my cousins traveled when they made their last journey into battle." She tugged at his hand. "Let's do it together, Jon. Please?"

He sat and put his arm around her. "We have to do it together. We're all we've got."

"We'll be a family again, Jon. Just you wait and see."

"We're a family now. Can you see that?" He hoped they still were, anyway.

She just stood and pulled him up, and as they walked down the street, she began to hum an old song. It was the first one Matthew had ever learned, and she'd forgotten how he used to sing it under his breath anytime he looked up information in the phone book or in the dictionary. It had come back to her in her dream the night before, and it had been like a token of reassurance, one she had desperately needed.

"*A, B, C, D . . . E, F, G . . . H, I, J, K—*"

"What's that tune? It sounds familiar." Jon was no longer upset, and he almost sounded cheery. The song had caught his attention, and he was intrigued.

"That old alphabet song."

"That's right. I should have recognized it. I haven't heard it in years."

"Do you remember how Matt used to sing it as a boy?"

He laughed. "How could I forget? He sang it constantly. I would wind up humming it at work, and my employees got to where they would walk up behind me and begin singing it to me."

"It is a pretty tune, isn't it? Simple and easy to sing. I like that. Anyone could sing it, no matter what else was on their mind. Did I ever tell you I used to sing it as a girl when I was lonely? You know, when my folks had to be out of town, and I was at my grandparents' house."

"You never did!" Jon was grinning now, and it looked real.

"I did. I haven't thought of it in years, though."

"What made you think of it now?" His arm was around her, and it seemed her dream was forgotten, or at least put aside.

"I don't know. I just did." She did know, however. It had been her dream. She had woken, and the song had been in her head. She'd imagined Matthew singing it at night in the dark, and it had made her somehow feel better.

Jon gave her a kiss on the forehead. "I'm glad you did. I like that tune."

She smiled, and she wrapped her arm around his waist. She was happy for the first time in a long time.

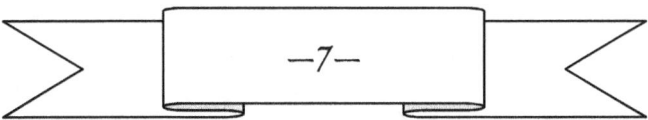

—7—

PERSONAL DIARY
Susan Shelby Magoffin
SEPTEMBER 1846

Wednesday 2nd. I am most delighted to finally be in Santa
Fe. Samuel has found a fine house for us to live in. I have a
household of *my* own, now, one of which *I* can touch the
walls and claim them for *mine*. It is with great delight that I
walk through these rooms, for they are a testament to how
far I have come in my life. I also find myself exceptionally
pleased to see that there are no gardens outside my door. I
shall not be asked to weed a one. Oh, that my family should
see me now!

The hired men have set up our bed in one of the rooms
of the house. With the bed clothing made up, it is a pretty
sight, much more so than when it resided simply in our tent.
It is strange to put my feet on a dirt floor each morning, but
it is hard packed, and not much of it comes off. I shall insist

to Samuel that he spread a heavy cloth across the floor each evening. I do not wish to soil the fabrics. He is most accommodating, and for that I am grateful. However, I would not have chosen a husband who was otherwise.

I am looking forward to meeting some officers soon. I expect on the Sabbath, there shall be occasion to converse with one or two, for surely they do not all abandon their faithful leanings, as soon as they are on the March. Until then, I suppose I shall read the Bible or other pious books, reflecting on the austerity of living in a city in which I know no one. I must find opportunity to entertain, and soon. Otherwise, I shall go quite insane.

PERSONAL DIARY
Kit Carson
AMERICAN FRONTIERSMAN

Saturday, September 5, 1846. Today, we have begun our journey. At Fremont's instigation and request, I carry news of our successful Conquest of California to President Polk.

It is good that I have been made a Lt. in the Navy, for without it, I would have a difficult time enforcing my authority on this Difficult Endeavor, for to travel across the continent in only 2 months is to be quite a challenge. I am certain I am up to it. Those who are with me will be forced to travel hard if they are to match my pace.

I have assembled 15 good men of European descent, Ned Beale among them, and in addition, I also have 6

Delaware Natives to accompany us. We have muskets and powder, and we carry any other necessities we need, including 10 lbs. of bacon and a sack of coffee. We will keep fit by our quick pace, and we will fill our stomicks [sic] by our keen eye and skill with the musket. I have no doubt that we will all eat much more than we should, at least while there is game to be found.

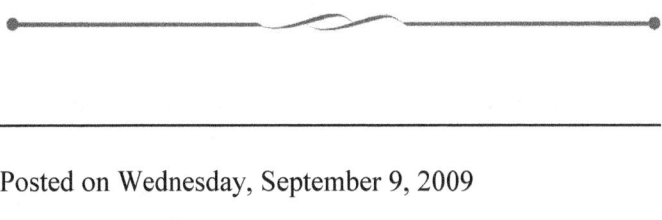

Posted on Wednesday, September 9, 2009

MEMORIAL SERVICE STILL ON TRACK FOR
SOLDIERS KILLED IN IRAQ
The Associated Press

FORT PIERCE, Fla. – A planned memorial service for five soldiers killed in Iraq has been postponed once again. However, authorities have insisted that the event will take place in Washington, once the President returns to the country.

Families say they wish all soldiers killed to have a representative present, and as individual funeral services for the deceased involved have already taken place, the families insist the timing of the memorial service is less important than to have everyone involved.

Clayton Strugger, the father of Army Spc. Jeff Strugger, one of the soldiers killed, described his son as caring and loyal. He said his son had written home about a childhood friend who was stationed with him in Iraq, describing the other soldier as the best friend a man could have at his side in war.

As Mr. Strugger broke down, he identified the childhood friend as Spc. Matthew McCreary, a soldier previously identified as Duty Status Whereabouts Unknown. Spc. McCreary was the sixth man in the convoy in which the five soldiers were killed. Mr. Strugger made a plea for the parents of Spc. McCreary to plan to attend the memorial service, to give closure to all involved.

Information from: The Palm Beach Herald,
http://www.pbherald.com

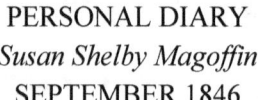

PERSONAL DIARY
Susan Shelby Magoffin
SEPTEMBER 1846

Monday, 14th. What a manner of man it takes to be a soldier! They make noise from the first light until the final rays of the sun have faded from the sky. There are things being thrown, Indian war-whoops, and the playing of musical instruments, the trumpet of which is most offensive. To my female ears, *it is quite the abhorrent noise.* The Sabbath was yesterday, and I took a most delightful discourse with Gen. Kearny. He is a wonderful man, most pious. During our discourse, his Episcopalian nature came to be evident, and I do feel it is most fortunate, for it doubles his elevation in my esteem. There can be no better leader of the American forces than Gen. Kearny.

During the course of the day, I had two soldiers come to call. One was a Lieut. Warner, and the other was the aide-de-camp to the Gen. I expressed my dismay at the dereliction of the Christian duties that seem to be so easily exercised by the general soldier. I was delighted later in the day when the men returned, bringing with them a present for me. Four enormous clusters of grapes were placed in my hand, and I ate one, finding them to be very good, for all that they are smaller than our American grapes. Still, all in all, I was quite pleased with my gift.

We had a little dance the other night. I did enjoy myself so very much. Cpt. Moore of the Dragoons illustrated to all the joys of the intemperate drink, which he called with some amusement on his face, "the ingredient." He pointed to the man at his side, telling me his brother-in-law, Lieut. Hammond, was the aide-de-camp who had so kindly brought me my grapes. "Alas," I told him, "they are all gone. Shall I ever get some more?" He laughed and said he would prod his brother-in-law until he acquiesced.

Shortly afterward, Maj. Swords stepped to my side. I

have heard talk of his reputation, for he is alleged to be quite the lady's man, and I had looked forward to meeting him very much. He was tall, and of a striking stature, but my, he had a dark look upon his face, as he peered in the direction of the retreating Cpt. Moore and his charming brother-in-law. The good Maj. questioned me, "Madam, did they treat you well?" I laughed and assured him they did, at which time, the darkness about his features brightened, and the Maj. excused his presence for a time. I wondered what it was about, deciding perhaps that these men had developed some sort of contention with one another. Perchance we will yet see a duel in this little town. How exciting!

After a time, when I had finished a light meal, I happened upon the Maj. just outside the door. His comportment seemed to be much improved, and he laughed at my unexpected company. Then, with a little flourish, he pulled a cigarete [sic] paper from one pocket, and a horn of tobacco from another. "Do you mind if I have a little smoke, Madam?" He gave me a little bow, as if this were a very familiar action to him. I had no doubt of his wit and quick perception, from that moment on, for he had charmed me. When I assured him his little smoke was of no concern to me, he bowed once again, and called to me, "Will you have a cigarita [sic] with me, then?" He reached inside, and pulled a handful of papers from his pocket, waving them about, and the whole thing became a burlesque. The Maj.'s sarcasm and irony made the time pass quickly, and he gave me no lack of attention.

Best Friends and Brothers

The Gen., with his aides, Cpt. Johnson and Cpt. Turner, called this evening, sitting and talking for some time. They have agreed to call to take me to Fort Marcey [sic]. I should expect them at 10 o'clock in the morning, they assured me. It is only newly built, for Lieut. Emory and Lieut. Gilmer of the Corps of Engineers (such an official sounding name!) chose the location, an auspicious one, I feel confident, only within the past weeks.

During the Gen.'s visit, a beating thunderstorm accosted my house, and rain came through the ceiling, pelting the Gen. He jumped, and we attempted to find the source of the flow, but within a short time, water was flooding through all the weak spaces in the mud roof. Except that the storm passed, we would soon have known only the sky above for a ceiling, for it would have all washed down upon us.

I so look forward to my ride to Fort Marcey [sic]. On days when no one calls (and they do happen from time to time), I grow most despondent, for what else is there to do in this place except entertain those around me, or read pious books? I do tire of reading when it is all I have to do. Ring has been good company, and of course I speak with Jane each day. However, good conversation with new people is what makes my spirit burn most brightly, and I long for it when it does not come my way.

Still, even in all, Santa Fe is more than I ever thought it would be, and the officers in the Army are pleasant, good company. I would spend more time with them, and I shall, on the morrow.

El Siglo XIX, Wednesday, September 16, 1846

ANTONIO DE SANTA ANNA
RETURNS!

Yesterday, Mexico City rejoiced. In a great procession that wound throughout the city, crowds cheered as our great leader, General Antonio de Santa Anna, brought Mexico hope once again. Paper streamers hung from the buildings, and a band marched before the great leader, with loud trumpets playing. People clapped, and no one was unhappy.

Rejoice, Citizens of Mexico. Soon, you will feel pride in your country once again! The Americans will no longer be thorns in our side!

Long reign General Santa Anna!

MILITARY JOURNAL
Brigadier General Stephen W. Kearny
COMMANDER, ARMY OF THE WEST

25 Sept. 1846. In little more than a month, all that needs done here in Santa Fe has been settled. I believe it is time to move on, for I am certain this war has many more battles, not a few of which will be bloody, costing my army dearly. Even so, it has been an opportunity for my men to have a few weeks of rest (if the occasional yelling and shooting of firearms can be called rest), and I believe we are thoroughly provisioned once again.

I have chosen to divide my troops into four commands as follows: First, Col. Sterling Price is to be the military governor, and with 600 men, is given title to occupy and maintain order in this region. Second, Col. Alexander Doniphan is assigned 800 men and given express orders to capture El Paso, at which time he is to join up with General John Wool. Third, under my direct command, 300 dragoons mounted on mules will follow me to California along the Gila River trail. Fourth, under Lt. Col. Philip St. George Cooke, the Mormon Battalion will follow my dragoons to blaze a new southern wagon route to California.

Over this New Mexico Territory, I have established Charles Bent as acting civil governor, for he has lived in Taos for quite some time as a notable Santa Fe Trail trader. His authority will be accepted and respected by those in this region.

God be with us, for California must be secured. I trust that with 300 good men at my disposal, there shall be nothing that comes in my way, for if I cannot do this, then I fear that no man can.

PAINTED DESERT
Motel Room Just Off I40
SEPTEMBER 28, 2009

Matthew:

Mary Ann:

From: Matthew Duncan
McCreary, SPC
Date: Sept. 28, 2008
To: Mary Ann McCreary
Subject: Thanks!

The guys here pulled a
good one on me, Mom. I
guess with the promotion,
and all . . . well, anyway,
you remember Jeff's with
me, and I guess he knew
my birthday was coming. I
didn't think much about it,
because, you know, well,
it's Iraq, and what do you
do for your birthday?
Nothing, really, unless . . .
well, I won't talk about
that, and no, don't worry, I
didn't do that. Um, you
don't need to mention
anything about that to

Mary Ann reached and
touched the screen, and
just for a moment, she
closed her eyes. She
remembered this e-mail
word for word. It had been
one of Matthew's first
after his promotion. He'd
been so proud. She held
her breath tightly inside
her chest, afraid she would
cry. She hadn't been able
to imagine anyone could
be so cruel to men who
served alongside them
every single day.

Yet, she knew such
behaviors weren't isolated
to desolate Army
compounds somewhere in
Iraq. People drove down
the freeway every day,
cutting other drivers off,

Brittany, either.

I pulled latrine duty, and trust me, no one wants to be on latrine duty. It's hot, and it smells, and the waste has to be hauled out. Like I said, trust me, no one wants to be on latrine duty.

Well, I was prepared (even though I didn't want to, but "want to" or "don't want to" are not phrases in Army vocabulary), and this morning when I got there, the guys had gotten some spray paint somewhere, and they had spray painted a giant birthday cake on the side of the latrine with my name under it.

You may think it was funny, but the latrine is made out of canvas, and I got to clean all that up. Yeah, scrub it with soap and water until it was

honking their horns at them, and even flashing rude hand signs to people they'd never think to insult if they spoke to them over their fence.

What makes us not care? she wondered. Is it that we don't know how the other person feels inside? Or is it the brutality of the overall situation that makes the small cruelties seem less horrible, somehow, that they're okay because they are less terrible in comparison?

She and Jon had almost not made the cake and sent the picture. It had been a hard day for them, what with Matthew gone on his birthday, and Matt's favorite cake not theirs. It wouldn't get eaten, not unless they gave it away. So, what was the point, just to take a picture and throw the cake in the completely gone. That didn't excuse me from my other duties, either. I still got to empty the latrines.

It was nice when I got back to camp and checked my e-mail. You'd sent me a picture, and there you and Dad were with a cake and candles and everything. That made it all ok. I was pretty down after cleaning the latrines all day, and what you sent helped me a lot.

Jeff caught up with me on the way back from the latrines, and he told me he tried to get the other guys to not do that to me. I guess with nothing else to do out here, pranks can get out of hand.

I did get a Frisbee, though, and Jeff has a football. Tomorrow, we're going to

trash? Jon had pushed her, though, reminding her of how much Matt always loved blowing out the candles. They could afford to bake the cake and then throw it out, but they could also invite some friends over the next day. When she was exhausted emotionally? she'd asked him. He'd just given her a hug and pulled the eggs from the refrigerator.

They'd made the cake, she and Jon, and her smile had been bright on her face to disguise her longing for her son to be at her side. Jon had set up the tripod, and once the camera had flashed, her tears had burst from her, and she'd gone to bed and cried for hours. Jon had gone online and sent the picture for her. Now she was ashamed that she hadn't been able to do that herself.

get some of the guys together and make a day of it.

Love,
Matthew

"I love you, Matt," she whispered, and she pressed the lid of her computer closed. She didn't have to read her son's words. She knew exactly what he'd said.

That made it all ok.

They'd done that for him, made his horrible day okay. What else were parents for, if they couldn't be there when their children needed them?

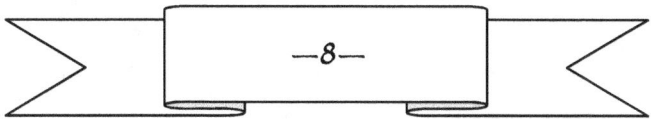

PERSONAL DIARY
Kit Carson
AMERICAN FRONTIERSMAN

Tuesday, October 6, 1846. I am in a moment of Fury, and my hand shakes as I put my pen to this paper. My party of 15 men, not including my Delaware Indians, have made the best of time, for we have been Diligent and Determined in our Passage. On this afternoon, when our group saw the Colors of the United States upon the trail before us, I turned to Ned, exclaiming, "They are too late. I should ask them if they wish me to lead them back to Washington, except that we are in too much of a hurry. Such a large group would only serve to slow us down," for the assemblage of men was not inconsiderable. I now know I looked across 300 soldiers when my eyes chanced upon them. Ned laughed at my words, but they have been twisted back upon me.

Gen. Kearny leads this company of Dragoons. I told him of our Victory in California, stressing my sworn promise to be at Pres. Polk's side in no more than one addl. month. He was quite determined, telling me, "I am a Gen., Mr. Carson, and you must take your orders from me. I insist you accompany me to California at once. Another man may carry your news East just as well." It seems the Gen. has no small opinion of himself. I wished to argue with him, but thought better of it when he reminded me I only hold the rank of Lt.

I did encourage him that the best time would be made with fewer men, for the trip over the mountains is quite rigorous. Cpt. Moore interjected his support of my suggestion, and I am glad he did, for only then did the Gen. seem to consider my idea. I think this Cpt. Moore is a good man, and I will make a point to speak with him to some length. His opinion seems to matter to Gen. Kearny, and as I have no choice but to return to California, I may as well make the best of it.

Gen. Kearny, with the help of Maj. Swords, chose 200 of his Dragoons to return to accompany the Mormon Battalion, which is following the trail this way. I happened to overhear their discussions, and I suspect there are raw wounds within this group. Maj. Swords spoke very strongly that he wished Cpt. Moore and Lt. Hammond to accompany the 200, claiming Cpt. Moore "does not have the fortitude to stand to a challenge." The Gen. did not listen, for which I am glad, for I feel that Cpt. Moore might well be the best of those who are to travel with me, and if Lt. Hammond is anything like him, I shall not regret such a man standing at my side.

In any case, I am now to return to California. We had used up the lbs. of bacon already, and the coffee was nearly gone, so there may be a bright spot in this, if I wish to call it that. It would seem that our new companions have a substantial supply.

I am sorry that I did not make it to Pres. Polk with the news of our Victory over the Mexicans, but another will have that Honor. I am now a Soldier in the United States Military, and such dictates my movements.

OFFICIAL JOURNAL
Lieutenant William H. Emory
KEARNY'S CHIEF TOPOGRAPHICAL ENGINEER

October 13 – Four days we have waited, for General Kearny wishes to abandon the wagons and take only the mules. We can thank Mr. Carson for this, for he has only recently traveled this route, having been instructed by Commodore Stockton to carry a packet of information to President Polk. Mr. Carson says the deteriorated road ahead will not allow our wagons to pass without certain damage. We have had to idle ourselves to await the mules' arrival, for they have not traveled as quickly as we. This is the most awful news, for my instruments have not been outfitted to ride upon the back of a mule. One small hole in the road, and a mule might trip, destroying all it carries. I must admit, I feel I am the only one who regrets the use of the mules as our sole mode of transportation. I shall have to grit my teeth and bear it, I am afraid, for there is nothing much I can say in the matter.

From the measurements I have taken, the distance from Santa Fe has been 203 miles. I feared I would have to estimate our travels from this point, but we have managed to mount the viameter to the wheel of one of the small towed howitzers. I regret I did not have time while in Washington to obtain a pocket chronometer, for the large ones are unsuitable for carrying either on foot or by mule.

The nights have turned quite cool, and we may soon wish for additional blankets. 56° at 10 p.m.

SANTA RITA de COBRE
Army of the West
OCTOBER 20, 1846

"How do you think it goes out there, Ben?" Thomas Hammond stepped up to stand beside his brother-in-law. They had left the Rio Grande and turned west to the Black Mountains. Now they stood at the deserted copper mine known as the Santa Rita de Cobre. Some time ago, the inhabitants had been driven off, it was learned, by the notorious Indian chief, Magnus Colorado.

"It's hard to tell. You can see Kearny, and the man next to him is Colorado. The others are various Apache chiefs." Ben paused. Then he turned to Thomas with a grin. "I had expected the general's aide-de-camp to be at his side. Without you, he will certainly falter. Do you not agree?"

There was the barest thread of tension in the words, for Ben had been at some odds with the general, although not grievously, by any military measure. Ben felt undue pressure was being put on the troops to travel too quickly, despite the general exhaustion of the men and animals. He had privately expressed such and been roundly set on his ear. It seemed Thomas remained in the general's inner sanctum, though, privy to Kearny's every whispered secret. "The general and I are not married, Ben. I have a wife, already, as does he." Thomas had felt the thread of intimation, and he wished it wasn't there. "He's a good man. See how far he's brought us, and he has done our men only good. Look out there. Who would have thought to see such glorious designs paraded about by savages?"

His final words were no more than to divert the subject. Even so, the Indians were beautifully attired with helmets, short skirts, bare legs, and buckskins. Black feathers bedecked their helmets, and belts gathered their waists. They seemed ancient Greek warriors. Thomas grinned as he made attempts to further smooth the waters, "Peaceful Indian negotiations. Carson doesn't trust a one of them, but what does he know?"

"Afraid of a few Indians, Captain Moore?"

Ben and Thomas turned, surprised that someone had come upon them afoot, catching them unawares. It was Major Swords, and he had a cigarette in his mouth. The breeze carried the smoke away from them, but now they could smell it easily enough.

"Major Swords." The lesser-ranked officers made to salute, answering as one, and even as they raised their hands, Swords had his up and let it drop.

"Carson is a smart man, well-versed in matters such as these, even if he does rankle me. He is most good at what he does, but that only means he is simply good at being a scout, does it not?" Swords took a drag on his cigarette, then dropped the butt, twisting it under one heel. "I hope my tobacco holds out. We are hardly half there yet, I daresay. A quarter is more like it, if we wish to trust Emory's measurements."

"Yes, sir," Ben replied. He glanced at Thomas. Major Swords hadn't exactly been friendly with either of them.

"How's the new baby, Lieutenant?" Swords turned to Thomas. "Barely more than three weeks old when we left. What now, five months?"

"Yes, sir. Five months. I shared with the general about little Tommie just the other day. My wife writes, and she tells me stories. Her letters are carried in on the express."

"The general spoke of it to me. And you, Captain. How is your nephew? I hear he may soon be headed to Vera Cruz." That was closer to the meat of why Swords had come to stand beside the two men.

"If you say so, sir." Ben pursed his lips. "Matthew's son, you mean, I presume."

Swords laughed, but it was excessively bright, a sound that spoke of glittering shards of jagged glass. "Of course, Matthew's son. Need I remind you we were all together at Leavenworth?" His tone was calmly casual in spite of the laughter.

"No, sir." He also recalled a few tense times between his brother and Swords, but Ben left that alone, reminded of his part in the matter.

"And was court-martialed because of him." Swords' words were still light and fresh, belying the dark tone of his casual comment.

"Court-martialed, sir?" Thomas Hammond turned, surprised. He knew of a soreness between the men, but a court-martial was another matter entirely.

Ben took a deep breath. He'd in fact testified for his

brother, but he'd not supposed that Swords would hold to his rancor for so long. His eyes found his brother-in-law's, and he jerked his eyebrows up as if to suggest this was news to him, also. He hoped Swords would quickly segue to another topic, and this one could be left undisturbed. No good could come of this old wound if it still rankled the man who had brought it up so unexpectedly.

"Yes, sir, court-martialed." Swords' tone abruptly changed, and his words were tight. "He was a coward, refusing a duel when it was presented him. Are you a coward, Captain?" Swords' eyes locked on Ben, and they drilled into him, demanding an answer.

"Sir, I don't understand the point of the question." Ben felt blindsided by the depth of this unanticipated animosity. It seemed the matter of the court-martial would not be left alone. Major Swords had been distant, perhaps even cold, but now it felt the Indians weren't the only ones involved in negotiations of a sort.

"The question is a simple one, Captain. Are you a coward?"

"No, sir." Benjamin drew a deep breath and framed his words carefully. "I am certain my record in the service of the United States Navy, as well as my years with the United States Army, speak of my dedication and willingness to move forward into any dangerous situation that should arise."

Swords took a deep breath, and he watched his general and the Indians for a time. After a moment, he released the breath with a sharp huff. The sun was overhead, and while it wasn't hot, it was intense in its brightness. The scene seemed surreal, as if out of a painting where only the purest of colors were slashed upon the canvas.

"This nephew on the way to Vera Cruz. Remind me of his name and rank." Swords glanced down and dug with his toe at the remains of his cigarette butt on the ground, intentionally feigning a lack of thorough knowledge of the man. It was a familiar tactic to disarm and create a sense of unconcern.

"Thomas Duncan, sir, a lieutenant, I recollect you referenced, when you spoke to me last about him. I'm unsure if he's received an increase in rank in the intervening time." Ben found irritation in the request. He was certain the major had recalled Thomas' name and rank without hesitation when they spoke previously. He could not have forgotten it so soon. The man was toying with his words.

"Is he his father's son?" Swords' eyes remained downcast, but the skin around his mouth grew taut. His foot was still, and his hands were clinched in tight fists.

His question was a jab, and Ben understood it as such. This man intimated his nephew Thomas was a coward, as his accusations had done many years ago with his brother Matthew, when the truth was vastly different in both instances. Ben stood firm in his reply.

"Neither my half-brother, Matthew, now deceased, was a coward, sir, nor my half-nephew, Thomas. Both can only be spoken of as courageous individuals, filled with moral fortitude. I am sorry for your difference of opinion, but I cannot change mine. Will there be anything else, sir?" His heart pounded, whether with defiance or concern that he had been too forward, he couldn't have said.

Swords replied brusquely, "Good day, men." He stomped a boot on the cigarette butt, grinding it roughly, and walked away, his steps hard.

After a safe time had passed, Thomas turned. "Ben, did you understand that? Calling your family cowards, I cannot believe he did that."

"I cannot believe I called Matthew and Thomas half-brother and half-nephew." Ben's face was tight.

"They are, Ben. In any case, I was glad to hear you as I did."

"I should have claimed them as closer, not distanced myself from them. I had thought Major Swords to be restrained with me on several previous occasions. It seems the reason chooses to reveal itself. He has not forgiven an old wound."

"Not just with you, Ben. He has been the same with me."

"I wonder if there shall be further confrontations between the two of us."

However, the answer was not to come in that moment. General Kearny and the Indian chiefs had concluded their talks, and the parties were separating. Turning back to their weathered group of just over one hundred men, it seemed hard to imagine that they were an invading army, the Army of the West. No one who saw them would think so, in any case.

A whistle sounded, and the men began to move. It seemed they would be covering more ground before the day was ended. The general wished it, and what the general wished, the general generally got.

MILITARY JOURNAL
Commodore Robert F. Stockton
UNITED STATES PACIFIC SQUADRON

26 October, 1846. Gillespie has been driven from Los Angeles, and the Californians are once again in control of that city. It was with some relief that I learned he was allowed to exit the place with his men, arms, and some $2,500 that had been designated for setting up a new city government.

Yet, matters grew worse, even as Capt. Mervine of the *Savannah* offered his support. In his moment of defeat, Gillespie could find no kind words for the assistance of Capt. Mervine. Perhaps the prospect of help from a Navy officer at such a time rankled Gillespie's wounded pride more than he could bear.

When he heard of the revolt, having just reached San Pedro, Mervine marshaled with Gillespie's force and marched immediately for Los Angeles with about 300 men, together with the ship's Marine guard, commanded by Captain Marston. The Californians began firing at the column as it entered a steeply sided area. Gillespie and his men charged ahead, firing their weapons, and the enemy scattered.

However, Mervine later raised his voice to Gillespie, telling him the troops could not spare the caps, and other such discouraging comments. In a later confrontation with the Californians, a 4-pound gun fired upon the Americans, and Mervine called a retreat, breaking contact with the enemy. 4 were killed and several wounded. Gillespie felt the victory could have been his, and he firmly blames Mervine.

I fear the men are now bitter enemies, but if it is so, it cannot be avoided.

Today I ordered a detachment of seamen and Marines ashore. The Marines have managed to retake the summit of the hill at San Pedro. As the Californians beat a hasty retreat at their advance, there was no loss of life, and the flag of the United States once again flies over San Pedro.

I do not have the men nor the supplies to make the necessary preparations for another attempt on Los Angeles, and I must abandon the effort until a later time. I have invited Gillespie's men aboard the *Congress,* and we shall sail soon for San Diego. It is hoped that provisions will be plentiful there, and once we are resupplied, another attempt on Los Angeles may be made.

OFFICIAL JOURNAL
Lieutenant William H. Emory
KEARNY'S CHIEF TOPOGRAPHICAL ENGINEER

October 28. Found more Indian pottery this morning, scattered pieces with patterns, and one pot nearly complete. I have collected a number to carry along with me, marking on the back of one the location in which they were found. I wished to explore ruined Indian pueblos off to the north, but am reminded that this is a military expedition, not one designed for exploring all things interesting. I was most fascinated by the appearance of what seemed to be the remains of aqueducts off in the distance. I had heard reports of such in this region, but who would have thought the reports were true? There are history books that tell of the great Roman builds of centuries ago, but here we are in the wild North American west finding the same extravagant structures.

Today we have cleared the Black Mountains and have reached the valley of the Gila. We cannot be far from Mount Graham. All around I find fragments of obsidian and quantities of agate. I have remembered the writings of William Prescott. He once described the stone in this area as appearing to be the same as the stones the Aztecs used to cut the hearts of their sacrifices from their victims' chests. The scouts tell us Mount Turnbull is just ahead, not more than three days' travel.

I sketch what I see each day, when I have the time. At a later date, I will have Stanley prepare more detailed sketches for use in my final report. In the evenings, occasionally I find time to go through my pottery shards, trying to piece several together. Earlier I found two I thought were a match, and I called excitedly to several of the men nearby, but it was all for nothing. The pattern was close, but the grains of the two pieces ran differently. It sometimes seems they will fit, yet they never do. I will not give up, though. I may find a match yet.

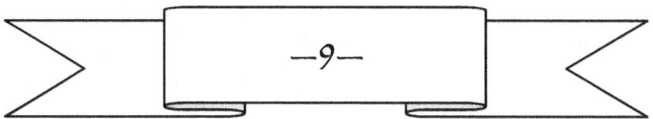

PERSONAL DIARY
Kit Carson
AMERICAN FRONTIERSMAN

Sunday, November 1, 1846. During our travels this day, we have left the Gila river, and are now upon my old trail. I have taken it upon myself to speak with Gen. Kearny, and I have informed him that we will see nothing except rough terrain for the next 60 miles or so. He seemed intent on other matters, though, and I thought he barely paid my words any mind.

I have approached Cpt. Moore about his strained relationship with Maj. Swords. He expressed that he had been unfamiliar with the cause until the Maj. brought it up between them, but that there is nothing he can do in any case. It is Old Blood that had gone bad between the Maj. and the Cpt.'s elder half-brother. I thought whether to tell him that Maj. Swords had attempted to return both the Cpt. and his brother-in-law along with the Dragoons back to Santa

Fe, but after considering it for a time, I decided it would be better for the incident to be left alone. Cpt. Moore and Lt. Hammond are with us, and further dissention will be ill for our Company's Morale.

In my comparisons of Maj. Swords and Cpt. Moore, I do feel that Cpt. Moore is the better of the men, for his answers have been considered and without rancor. As for his brother-in-law, Lt. Hammond, he seems less practical, and as I understand he has never seen battle, I fear he may act in an untoward manner once the event is upon us. They seem to be devoted to each other, however, and if I am to choose Cpt. Moore as a confidant, I have no doubt Lt. Hammond will place himself directly in the midst of our company.

If Maj. Swords acts irresponsibly toward Cpt. Moore, I sincerely hope Gen. Kearny will be forward enough to take action. We have too few men to warrant Discord within our Company.

NEAR FLAGSTAFF, ARIZONA
Jon and Mary Ann McCreary
NOVEMBER 3, 2009

"Jon, how well do you think Matthew really got along with all those other boys he was with?" Mary Ann rested her head on her pillow and turned to her husband at her side.

"Huh?" He looked up from the book he was reading, and he adjusted his glasses farther up on his nose. He didn't often read in bed, but Mary Ann had become more restless than ever before. California was growing close, and she wasn't sleeping well at night. Besides, they had finally been reached by the group responsible for the memorial service commemorating the soldiers who had been killed in the bombing in Iraq. "Now?" Mary Ann had exclaimed. "It's been months. They want to have the memorial service now?" That had wrecked what little self-control she had managed to construct around her days.

"With all those other boys. Do you think they were really friends, or just buddies, you know, like the kid who sits beside you in civics, and you're friendly to him, but outside of class, you'd never think to call him up to do something. Like that." She pursed her lips, her paperwork bundled up in her notebook, closed and in her lap. She seemed to be in serious thought over the matter.

"Well," he pondered, placing his book on the bed beside him and sliding his glasses up onto the top of his head. He turned to look to her, then frowned for a moment, his mind considering.

"Jon," Mary Ann pressed on his leg, "it's not that difficult. Matt got along with everyone at home. How about there? Over there in the desert?" She remembered the latrine incident.

"There's a reason for this question, isn't there?" Jon turned his face fully to her and looked into her eyes. "What is it, sweetheart?"

"Something I found in my research." She didn't dare tell him she was still rereading the e-mails. "Our cousin, the one in the Mexican War. Benjamin Moore. He was court-martialed once, rather his brother was. His older half-brother." She pulled a copy of the military court-martial from her folder, holding it out for him to see.

"A bad seed?" Jon chuckled. "I didn't know you had any bad seeds in the family tree."

"We have some bad seeds, like William Linn. He married into the family and wasted his wife's fortune." She smiled at that. "No, the court-martial wasn't Benjamin's brother's fault. Another officer challenged him to a duel, and he refused. They were both locked up for a time, however."

"Together?" He said it with a smile. He meant his expression of mirth as a tease and was relieved when Mary Ann let it go as such. It was something he could have trusted a year ago. Now her moods were raggedly uneven, and he wasn't always sure whether to trust the old ways he used to get through to her.

"Well, the issue is this man." She pointed to the paper where it showed the name of Thomas Swords. "He was cashiered, whatever that means. He was one of three instigators, and he apparently called out Captain Matthew Duncan as a coward. See? Read this."

"Let me get my glasses." He felt on his head. "Now, here. I see. This little sentence?"

"Yes, Jon. Read it aloud." She waited, wanting to hear it spoken in his voice.

"Can I paraphrase it slightly?"

"Just read it, Jon."

"All right. Here goes." He looked at her for a moment

over his glasses, then he started reading, his voice deep and excessively dramatic. "I have challenged you to a duel, Captain Duncan. You have refused me. Are you a coward? Why, this just shows what sort of a captain Colonel Dodge has to depend on to go out against the Indians." He looked up and smiled.

"It did not say all that." She glared at him, then let the look gradually melt into a smile. "But it was very good."

"So, and the reason I read that?"

"This." She pulled out another sheet of paper, a list of officers who had traveled the final stage of the trip to California that fateful fall in 1846. "Look at this list. You'll find Thomas Swords there. He was a major by this time, a quartermaster, I believe. Then look, there's Captain Benjamin Moore, Matthew Duncan's younger half-brother. Do you think Thomas Swords knew? Then, what about Thomas Hammond?" She pulled the paper back to study it.

"Hammond?" He sometimes had trouble following all the names and relationships his wife continually rattled off, and this time was no different.

"Benjamin Moore's brother-in-law. They married sisters, remember. Benjamin's wife had died several years before, but they still considered themselves as close as brothers. Thomas Hammond tried to save Benjamin at the end, you know. Gave up his life for him, I guess, although things were so bad by that time that I suppose it wouldn't have mattered. People were dying right and left."

"Mary Ann," Jon began. "I hear what you're saying, but I don't know where you're going yet. What's this about?"

"It's this Thomas Swords. You know, he received his commission as major just weeks before the war started." She paused, her eyes tense, and she looked off.

"That's when he became Major Swords?" When she didn't respond immediately, Jon prompted her, "When he gained his new rank?"

"April 21st of that year. For the first time, it would have given him an edge in authority over Benjamin Moore. If he knew that Benjamin and Matthew Duncan were related, do you think he would have taken it out on him?" She looked at Jon. "People hold grudges, you know."

"I saw the date on that court-martial. It happened in 1835. This war began in 1846. I think after eleven years, it would have been a moot point."

"And," it was as if she hadn't heard a word, "if he did, do you think Thomas Hammond would have stood up for his brother-in-law? They were friends, you know. Closer, according to all I've read about them."

"I see now," Jon said, setting his book on the bedside table and pulling his glasses off. He slid closer to his wife and slipped his arm around her. "This isn't about these dusty cousins at all, is it? This is about Matthew. The real question is did he die trying to save someone else, someone who was a good friend, like Jeff, maybe?" He looked down to see tears running down her face.

Mary Ann didn't reply. That wasn't exactly it, but she couldn't tell Jon. The real question was whether someone else could be helping their son, that maybe someone out there was risking his or her life for Matthew, and this unknown person could help him come home to them safely. That was what she really wanted to ask, but she knew how Jon felt, and she didn't think she could bear to hear his answer. The question was too big a risk for her to take.

BAGHDAD, IRAQ
A Life Is Worth Saving
NOVEMBER 4, 2009

Nestled on a dusty, sun-parched side street, in the desolation of a shattered Iraqi home, the walls cracked with the explosions that had rocked the city for months on end, a ragged electrical cord snaked along a wall. It was attached with metal clips, and multiple layers of paint helped it blend with its surroundings. The paint was peeling in places, showing layers of faded colors underneath, and it was clear that the cord occupied a familiar place against the wall.

Just before it turned and entered a rough hole that led into a closed-off and secured room, it joined with a slender, equally ragged phone cord that somehow had escaped the devastation the city had been forced to endure. Many of Baghdad's inhabitants hadn't been so fortunate. They had died while this one slender lifeline remained alive.

Deep within the room, heavy curtains shrouded the interior with darkness, keeping the activities hidden from prying eyes, as a woman's slender fingers reached from within her burka. They rested at an old laptop computer. The gentle song of a phone modem hummed as it reached its electronic fingers out to the far side of the globe, the Internet it accessed unfamiliar with the barriers of country or battle-field.

The woman hesitated. She had so wanted to help the downed American soldier when the bombs had gone off. The blood had already begun to soak through his clothing, but he had still been alive. She had reached with her hand to staunch the wound, hoping to help until his companions could reach him. His face was so young, and for a second she had seen her brother, the way his trusting eyes had sparkled in the sun before Al Qaeda had stolen his life away. In that moment of heartfelt empathy, she hadn't been able to bear leaving the American soldier to die alone in the wreck-age. Then the bullets had come, and she had been forced to run, looking back to see her countrymen rush to drag the boy into the shadows. Only when she had reached the inside of one of the buildings had she looked at the blood on her hand. There had been the stiff slip of paper, the end fluttering free, the rest adhered to the thick red fluid painting her skin. Peeling the card loose, she remembered she had rested her blood-soaked palm on his chest as she had searched for a place to hide. This card had been sticking out from his pocket. It was in Western script, but it contained an e-mail address. She recognized that with no doubt in her mind. Standing with her back against a wall, her heart pounding in her chest, she had closed her eyes in a gestalt of under-standing. It was as if Allah was giving her divine direction.

She hadn't been able to do more than wad the rectangle of paper into her pocket. Even Allah could not expect her to do what this card insisted she must. Her sons. They were just small boys. She could not risk their lives. And she hadn't been sure the American still lived. Should she risk her family for a dead man? So, she had hidden the paper and done nothing.

Late in the evenings, in the dimness of an oil lamp, she had memorized the letters on the card. Then, after many troubled nights, she had seen the television, the chanting, and the name tag. It had been Allah speaking to her, telling her what she must do. She had made discreet inquiries, and her trusted uncle had told her the man was the same. Her path was clear.

The style of the letters she typed into the e-mail program address bar was an unfamiliar one, although she recognized it well enough to enter the letters on the computer keyboard. Then, swiftly, and with nervous motions, she adjusted the language on her computer and moved to her message. There her fingers typed swiftly and without hesitation. Soon finished, she noticed how much prettier the swirls and loops of her native script were against the blocky ones in the address bar. She just hoped whoever received this message would find a way to read what she had written.

At a noise on the other side of the door, she gasped in a surge of frightened apprehension. *The children have returned!* With a jerk of a nervous finger, she tapped the send button. A window popped up, a bar sliding across to show the status of the task. She held her breath, wishing for it to hurry. When it reached the end, telling her the delivery was complete, her hand shook with an overwhelming rush of adrenalin as she gently and quietly closed the top of the computer and unplugged both the phone and power cords from the back. Then she slipped the small machine behind a broken bit of plaster in the wall and drew a panel of cloth to cover it. If the message she sent was tracked by those of her countrymen who despised the Americans, it would be a disaster worse than death, for herself as well as her children.

Taking a deep breath, she stepped to the door and paused, hoping to give her heart a chance to settle. Then, with a smile on her face and a lilt to her voice, she pulled the door wide.

"It is you, my little one. And where has your brother gotten to?" Her three-year-old had come to find his dinner, and his brother was surely not far behind. She suddenly knelt and grabbed him to her. She knew what she risked to send the message she had just typed. She risked everything, including the lives of her two children. Even so, how could she not? Al Qaeda had taken her brother, a boy with ideas for freedom and equality, and now he lived no more. The American soldier who had been captured and hidden away was little more than a boy, and he was a mother's son. Would she not want another mother somewhere else in the world to do the same for her own, to help create a safe world in which her children could grow?

Another boy, maybe six years old, came running into the shattered ruin of the home in which the three lived, and she pulled him to her also. When she felt her eyes would no longer reveal what she had dared risk, she released them from her arms and brushed her slender hands against their smooth faces.

"And now, my sons, I have something very special for you. It is my birthday, and I have made a cake to share with the two of you."

As they cheered and jumped up and down in excitement, she stood and gently guided them into the kitchen. It was the one room in the house that still worked properly. There on a narrow table was a small cake lightly dusted with powdered sugar, one just large enough to be shared by two. Pulling a knife from a cabinet, she pressed it into the sweet, giving half to each of her sons. If the bad men came, then they would have this final happiness. They had little else. This was the least she could do.

TEXAS-MEXICO BORDER
Murder of a Mexican Boy
NOVEMBER 5, 1846

Dust flew from the base of the cacti outgrowth as a bullet impacted the soil, and drunken laughter rang through the air. It was November, General Zachary Taylor's 1st Kentucky Volunteer regiment was far from home, and occupation duty was distressingly boring. Some activity had to be pulled together to keep the men stable.

Organized and meaningful responsibilities were not initiated soon enough to retain everyone's sanity, however, for the current set of events reflected what civilized and moral American citizens might consider to be woefully immoral senselessness.

In the distance, the Rio Grande River sparkled in the harshness of the late fall sun. Stands of trees stood grouped in pockets along its banks. Those from the eastern shores of the United States might have called the vegetation scrub, for even the tallest of the trees paled in comparison to the mighty forests that still filled great swatches of that rich, well-watered land. Still, life inhabited this rough landscape, if one knew where to look.

The drunken volunteers from the 1st Kentucky regiment had found life, albeit of the two-legged variety, and they were having great sport in the chase.

"Ya' missed 'im," slurred one roughly-dressed, blond-haired man in contempt, the butt of his musket in the dirt at his feet. His words suggested that he wouldn't have, if he'd been the one firing the gun. His name was Ollie D. Holder, and he had a jug of hooch at his side. A patchy blond beard partially concealed his chin, and acne scabs covered what the beard couldn't. His elbow rested on the live end of the weapon, and with his free hand, he mopped sweat from his brow. Even in November, it could be very hot along the Rio Grande, and the day had been a scorcher. The sweat stains covering the man's shirt were testament to that.

"Won' a secon' time," the man at his side growled in a distinctive slur of his own. Cooper Crampton was tall and skinny, with oily black hair, and a scar that ran down one side of his face. He'd treed a coon once, and when he'd climbed the tree to pull it down, it'd taken a piece of his cheek off before escaping back to the woods. Since then, Cooper didn't like things to escape. He tamped powder and ball into his barrel, keeping a narrowed eye on the stand of cacti. He didn't intend to allow his prey to get away again.

The Mexican boy they hunted couldn't be more than ten or twelve, but Cooper'd found he could run like greased lightning. Rather, he had been able to run before that shot that caught him in one foot about an hour back. Now the chase was more manageable. He and Ollie didn't have to scramble so fast to keep up. With the liquid fortifications they had consumed, they didn't have all that much run left in them, anyway.

"I see 'im," Ollie hissed, picking up his musket, and stumbling in the process. Alcohol made up a sizable percentage of his blood volume at this stage in the game, and he nearly dropped his weapon. He cursed when he realized it wasn't loaded.

Behind the stand of cacti, a small boy's dark face could be seen peering out. Looking closely, it might be observed that he had on no shirt, and the flayed remains of rough, home-woven pants were tied with a thin rope at his waist. His feet were bare, and one had been bleeding. A mixture of blood and dirt had formed a crust, and each time the boy put pressure on it, his face twisted in torment. His life was at stake, though, and he must run or die. The Americans who had come to occupy his village, proclaiming freedom from the oppressive Mexican soldiers who had been there before, were offering no quarter. The boy's only hope was to keep alive until the men were drunk enough to forget he still lived.

"Blast it, Coop, 'e's gonna ge' away agin." Ollie grabbed at Cooper's loaded weapon and raised it to aim. Before he could fire, Cooper lunged for it, knocking it askew. The weapon went off, and a cactus pad just above the boy exploded, showering his back with its spiny detritus.

In the distance, the child involuntarily cried out, falling to the ground. His foot had been a torment to walk on, but he had managed to tune out the regular jarring sensations of pain. The cactus spines were unexpected and caught him off guard. Now he was in the open, and he made to scramble to his feet, his heart pounding in fear. He had only gone out to hunt for wild animal chips to burn for his family's midday meal. He was certain now that he would never venture from his family's small rancho again, if he could just make it home.

Ollie and Cooper didn't consider that the boy might have a family that loved and cared for him, one that might miss him if he never returned. They were bored, the Rio Grande was Hell on Earth next to their verdant and fondly remembered Kentucky hills, and the Mexican boy was simply one more vermin to rid from the face of the land. He was sport for the day, and they hunted him for no other reason.

"Here, Ollie. Got th' gun loaded agin." Cooper had his patches and powder out, and he pulled his rod from the muzzle as he handed the gun over. He sniggered, "Get 'im while 'e's down." He nudged Ollie with his elbow. His comment was a clear and intentional slur aimed at the boy. No respecting Kentuckian would shoot a man fair and square if he was down. However, a Mexican? That was a different matter.

"Coop!" Ollie spat, slamming the butt of the gun into the ground. "Whad'ya goin' say that for? Spoil my fun, will ya'. No fun, if'n's easy." He called to the boy, "Run, scum!" Then he reached to the jug at his feet, popping the lid to take a swig.

"Doan bother me, none," Cooper sneered. He leaned in and grabbed the gun. With a sure motion, he raised it to his shoulder, and let a drunken wild shot fly. As a youth in far-distant Kentucky, while running with Ollie, he'd been the best rabbit hunter in the hills, and even drunk as a fox chewing on wild grapes, he knew he had more skill in his soused little finger than a sober man had in his whole body.

A wild shot for Cooper was as good as a tediously aimed round for most men.

With the shot already in transit, it must be noted that musket balls are not high-velocity bullets. Some say that when death by musket comes your way, time freezes, and you can see the ball tearing through the air right at you. The sun glints off the imperfections in the metal, and the wind from the moving ball spreads out like the ripples around a stone that's thrown in still water. A spider's web of magnificent proportions weaves itself through the air, shimmering in the light. It's said to be beautiful, a glimpse of exquisite artistry given as a final gift to the one doomed to die.

It must be so, for as drunk as Cooper was, his teen hunting skills served him well. His wild shot flew straight and true to its target. The boy looked up just as the gun fired, and his dark, perceptive eyes froze. He saw the path of the shot as it flew directly toward him, and mesmerized, he didn't flinch or try to get out of the way. The sun sparkled off the shard of death boring his direction like the morning light shimmers on a dew-covered spider's web, shattering the rays of the sun into a thousand colors. The fractured air undulated out from the ball as it sliced the sky, making the rainbow of colors sparkle in the sultry heat of the afternoon. The small boy knew he was going to die, and he found the manner of his death beautiful and most welcome.

Anyway, that's the way Cooper told it that evening around the fire. Ollie backed his story up, too. Ollie knew the tale well, for he'd listened to it after every rabbit ol' Coop had taken out when they'd hunted together back in the Kentucky hills.

The other volunteers in the 1st Kentucky regiment

laughed at the story. Knowing Cooper and Ollie, they were pretty sure it was true, and if so, that was one less Mexican to grow up and make their lives a living hell. Good riddance, they said to one another. Good riddance, and no regrets.

When he would hear of the incident, sadly to say, General Zachary Taylor would voice exactly the same sentiments. His words would sound different, but they would mean the same.

"It is war, and soldiers will be soldiers. Tell them not to do it again."

Not everyone killed in the war deserved to die, and all who deserved to die were not killed. Such was the war, and the battles went on.

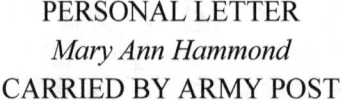

PERSONAL LETTER
Mary Ann Hammond
CARRIED BY ARMY POST

November 8, 1846

My Dearest Husband Thomas,

There are no words to express my longing for you. It has been five months since I have held you in my arms. In my mind, I count the days one by one, and each looms as an empty hole without you. I have missed you dearly each of those days.

Our son looks around when I reread your letters to him,

and I am now convinced he knows when I call your name. "Thomas," I say, and his expression lights up. When you return, I know he will do the same for you. I wish for you to look forward to his small arms around your neck, for he loves to hug me in return when I pull him to me and hold him tight.

I spoke to Father about returning to town for the Winter, and he pushed the thought from my mind. He thinks it silly to build two fires, when one can heat two families just as well. Mother agrees with him, and I fear I will never sway her from her line of thinking. It will be three families, in any case, for Mattie and his sister Molly count as one in themselves. We cannot help but count them, for they are underfoot all the time.

The trees have long since begun to change. Most have lost their leaves already, and the rest will be down in the next storm. Benjamin's little Mattie asked if he could run in them just the other day, and I told him he could. He seemed to enjoy it so, falling into piles where the wind had swooped them into great bunches, and screaming in delight. I remember such pleasures as a girl, and sometimes I miss those times. Even so, I did not run and fall into the leaves. I stood at the side and laughed, for part of the enjoyment lies in watching the pleasure of those who are children now, as they take new joy in those events we once claimed as ours. One day, you will see our son run and jump in the leaves, and you will find in him the same happiness I have seen in little Matthew.

I have spent some time helping Sissy with the canning

this year, as I have had little else to do. We packed all manner of vegetables in the salty brine you dislike so, and those that could not be jellied or candied, we baked, or hung in the cellar to dry. I have never known the Summer kitchen to be so warm. This Winter, we will be glad to use the kitchen in the main house, for it will keep many rooms toasty and warm. Yet, I was most glad each evening for the canning to be pursued in the kitchen away from the main dwelling. Mercifully, the coolness of the house felt wonderfully refreshing each evening when we returned.

Father convinced Mother to host a gathering for the officers from Leavenworth a week past. Many men came, although with the War in progress, there were not as many as there might have been. Still, all in all, I played the part of Hostess, and it was quite agreeable, indeed. It was not the same without you here, Dear Thomas. I wish for your return.

I have not had many letters from you recently. I hope you are well, and that all my letters reach you. I wish to know that you carry them, even still, next to your heart, and should something untoward come your way, I trust that my love (which is bound up in my letters to you) will be there to protect you, keeping you safe from all harm.

You are in my Heart, and I will be

Your Loving Wife Always,

Mary Ann Hammond

OFFICIAL JOURNAL
Lieutenant William H. Emory
KEARNY'S CHIEF TOPOGRAPHICAL ENGINEER

November 10. This has been a day of most considerable reward. We reached Casa Grande, and as we arrived long before sunset, I was given all the time I wished to explore the famed buildings. We explored room after room, finding shards in various places, and with undisguised delight, we made judgments telling the uses of each place we came upon. Of course, there can be no true way to know the use of some of the spaces, but a few seemed clearly to be designed for sleeping, and others were plentiful with shards, suggesting a storage facility or something similar. The structures are of mud-baked clay, and it seems they must eventually return to the earth sometime in the future. Stanley has been instructed to provide sketches acceptable for presentation in his final report.

Barrel cacti are plentiful, as are the Brittle Bush and the Ocotillo. Several instances of the Soaptree Yucca have been sighted, and even the Velvet Mesquite, or velutina.

Elevation is approximately 4,976 feet.

November 12. Have seen well-cultivated fields of both the Pimas and Maricopas Indians. These people live well without the effects of white-man's spirits, and I feel grateful that they do not yet know the evils of drink. They are a peaceful people, prone to a religious nature. However, they are well able to defend themselves, as instanced by the appearance of a band of warriors just returned with many Apache scalps and prisoners. Have seen numerous Saguaro Cacti, species gigantean. They are a wondrous sight, for nowhere else in the world does such a plant grow.

November 15. Our mules have traveled some 1,800 miles, and I do not see how they still stand. Each day at sunset, they seem as if they will fall over, yet each morning, they have revived, and are ready to carry our supplies once again.

Boulders came into view today, and they were covered with hieroglyphic symbols. Also seen, often on the same surfaces, were modern inscriptions. Several American names were among them.

Signs are visible from time to time of Indian habitations, all deserted. Although, as we approach the Colorado river, there are fewer and fewer settlements to be seen.

Temperatures remain in the 90s each day, but it is cooler at night. Last night, it was approximately 58°.

November 22. Came upon a recently occupied camp of probably 1,000 Mexicans. Kearny prepared to order an attack. At Kearny's orders I set off with a 15-man reconnaissance party. Soon, we reached the intersection of the Gila and Colorado, and encountered a number of Mexicans driving 500 horses. The horses appeared wild, and the Mexicans were not detained.

Returning to camp, we intercepted a Mexican courier with dispatches detailing the uprisings in California. The dates they showed were 15 October. Kearny feels we must make the best time possible, and he is certain our company can inspire a victory once we are there. He wishes to leave as quickly as possible. Tomorrow we set off for the trek across the California desert.

Even so, I have been pondering whether the lower Colorado is navigable by steamboat, or whether flatboats could navigate up the Gila, eventually reaching the Pima villages. It does seem it might indeed be possible, and of good benefit, if it is.

November 25. We have crossed into California. The sand is overly soft for the animals, but we hope to cover fifty miles in two days. Thorns abound, cutting all who walk too closely.

The land is barren, and one of the officers found one of the best pack mules slaughtered, the choice parts cut from the shoulders and flank. Rations have run low, and soon, many more of our animals may fall to such ends.

Under cover of darkness, wolves can be heard fighting over depleted animals that have been abandoned along the way.

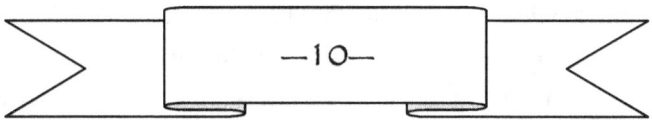

—10—

NEAR WARNER'S RANCH, CALIFORNIA
Army of the West
DECEMBER 2, 1846

Lieutenant Thomas Hammond no longer retained the spit and shine of his West Point days, nor was he the dapper man from Fort Leavenworth. The leather inside one boot had separated, he was exhausted and trail worn, and he was hungry, too. The Army had been on half bread rations for some weeks already.

His mule was even worse, and most of the horses had already been eaten. He walked alongside his mount for fear it would collapse if it had to bear his weight.

"The next divide will be the one, Thomas. We're there. We must be." Captain Benjamin Moore laughed, but it came across as weak and ineffectual. The march had taken an equal toll on his constitution. "The California we have all heard about, with golden fields and fruit ripe for the picking, will be ours. Just one more divide, I'm certain."

"Why do you not just walk without speaking?" Thomas shot a look at him. "Your words tire me more than my plodding feet." The jesting had brought the crinkle of a smile to his eyes, though.

"My thirst tires me, that and the empty pit that I claim for a stomach. I may soon fall by the wayside, but your youth should do you for another hundred miles, my friend." Benjamin paused for a moment, leaning over and pressing his hands to his knees. He was afoot, also, for his mount was hardly in better shape than the one Thomas guided.

"And your experience yours." Thomas paused beside his friend, and in his stance, there was tiredness for two. "If the Mexicans should come upon us now, I should have to remove my sabre and lay it at their feet. I couldn't fight if I wished it."

"At least you could remove your sabre. I would need to let the Mexican general remove mine for me." Ben tried to laugh again, but it sounded more a snort of derision. "I would that the Indians hadn't abandoned San Felipe when we rode through yesterday. It would have been more gracious to leave us a fine meal for our enjoyment. Still, I believe the next crossing will show us the lushness of California."

"Shush, Ben. I cannot look for listening. Now, if I had my Mary Ann here, I would walk on stronger legs, for she would encourage me with her beauty."

"She would run from the smell."

"From the both of us."

It was true. Bathing had been in short supply, and the

men smelled just about the same as the animals. However, the next "divide" would indeed bring them to the first large stands of evergreens they had seen in weeks, and the next after that would open to their imagined picture of a verdant California.

It would also lead them into the valley of the Agua Caliente, and from there onto Warner's ranch, where they would have two days to recuperate, and the officers would feast upon an entire fat sheep.

The Army of the West had finally arrived.

The Weekly Tribune
Liberty, Clay County, Saturday, December 5, 1846

CALIFORNIA IS OURS!

Well-known scout, Kit Carson, was dispatched from San Diego by Commodore Robert F. Stockton to hand deliver news to President Polk telling him that California is now ours. Carson, recently given the rank of lieutenant in the United States Army, met Brigadier General Steven W. Kearny on his way to California, telling him that he was too late. Captain John C. Fremont of the Topographical Engineers, along with Commodore Stockton and Lieutenant Archibald Gillespie, had already made California secure from the Mexicans. "Please send your army home," Carson is claimed to have said, "and since you are here, kindly take the news to President Polk for me." With those words, it is supposed he turned and disappeared back into the mists, returning to the wilds of California, from which he had so recently journeyed.

———————————————⟨⟩———————————————

PLATTE CITY, MISSOURI
Home of Judge Matthew Hughes
DECEMBER 5, 1846

"Father, you must come see." Mary Ann Hammond's voice rang with excitement. "Sissy has just come from town. Mrs. Hartley-Buford's *Liberty Tribune* came by early delivery today, and look! The war's over."

Judge Hughes stepped into the house, pulling the door firmly behind. At the thought of the suffering he knew the war must have already brought to the soldiers within the Army's ranks, a chill ran down his back. However, Mary Ann's words stirred a quickened moment of hope in his chest. He dared not put overmuch confidence in his daughter's enthusiastic exclamation without fair justification, though, although an end to the country's current hostilities was what he wished most dearly.

He stamped his feet before moving his hands to undo the fasteners on his coat.

At a quick kiss on his cheek, one that surprised him, and a whispered, "Thank God. The boys are coming home," he looked to see his wife disappearing into another part of the house. He smiled understandingly at her retreating back. She continually felt cold in the winters, and to be in the kitchen was her way of staying warm.

"The *Liberty Tribune*, you say." Hanging his thick tent of a coat on a peg protruding from the wall, the judge chuckled at his wife's whispered sentiments as opposed to his daughter's raucous excitement. Their responses revealed them as different as two women could be. "I believe you should look at the paper again, daughter. It's called *The Weekly Tribune*. Mrs. Hartley-Buford let Sissy bring her copy home?"

"Yes! Sissy said Mrs. Hartley-Buford thought of me and sent her personal copy for me to read. Look! Thomas is coming home." Mary Ann spun in a circle, her skirts billowing out around her. "Thomas is coming home."

"Let me see, my child. I wish to read the words." Judge Hughes reached for the paper. He waited until his daughter had quit spinning, then gently took it from her grasp. It was not his, after all, and there were few enough copies to go around. Over the course of the next week, this very one would certainly be read by many dozens of eyes. "It doesn't say the Army is returning home, my dear. It says this Lieutenant Carson is claimed to have said that." He laid the paper aside. "Be patient, my girl, and your Thomas will arrive shortly."

"Father, I must return to town and get our little house ready. Thomas will expect to find me there with our Tommie."

"You haven't written him to say you're staying with

your mother and me?" He was certain she had. He made a pouty expression, knowing it would amuse her.

"Oh, Father," she cried. "What if he doesn't remember? I cannot have him show his face there, only to discover an empty and cold dwelling. I must locate Sissy."

Judge Hughes laughed and pulled his daughter to him, giving her a hug. "This news did not happen yesterday, my child. This story is surely two months old, if it came from California. Another day or even a week won't matter over-much. Your young man can sweep you off your feet then just as easily as he can carry you away today. Your mother has read this?" He turned and tapped the paper.

"Yes. She says the same as you."

"Then we must listen to her words."

"I know, Father." Mary Ann's face glowed, despite the admonitions. "I have missed him, and little Tommie has missed him also, even though he doesn't know him."

"He will know his father in due time, my girl. Can you wait a few more days?"

Mary Ann rested against her father, happy and serene in her news, certain she would only have a short time before she should see her husband once more. She looked up at her father and smiled.

"A few more days, Father. I can wait a few more."

"Good, my dear." He patted her shoulder with a smile on his face. He, too, was glad his son-in-law was coming home.

SPRINGFIELD, ILLINOIS
Abraham and Mrs. Lincoln
DECEMEBR 5, 1846

"Mary, are you up and about?"

It was Saturday, and Abraham Lincoln had been busy for some time. His dark hair was a wild nest where it had found freedom from underneath the brim of his hat, although he had run his knotted fingers through it numerous times since waking. The day before, three cases for which he had been for the plaintiff had been decided, and later he had written court orders for three more. Today wasn't for immersion in law, for concern over Mexico, or for considering how the war might benefit him in the political arena. Today was his day for rest, but rest was relative. He didn't mean to laze around from dawn to dusk. He removed his hat and coat, hanging them by the door, letting his mop of unruly tresses remain in a state of unattended disarray.

"Mary? I believe I shall have a bit of that cake from dinner last evening, if you don't mind. The small morsel you allowed me was quite good." It hadn't been enough, he intimated, with no small amount of humor in his voice.

When there was no answer, he stepped into the kitchen and lifted the tin that covered the remains of the delicacy. Looking though a cabinet, he found a knife and sliced a section of the cake free. Without a moment's hesitation, he lifted it in his large hand and brought it to his mouth. Just before he sank his teeth in, his wife cleared her throat.

"Mr. Lincoln!"

Abraham turned slowly, the sweet still to his lips. He caught his wife's eyes. She wore a dark dress, and her hair was in its usual knot at the nape of her neck. A white lace collar graced her throat. A twinkle was in her eye.

"Is it not still acceptable, husband?"

"I don't know, wife. I haven't taken a bite." As he spoke, his lips brushed the surface, however, knocking small crumbs to the floor, and the smell that broke free was intense. He licked his bulbous lower lip for the merest morsel of crumb. Then he smiled.

"Did you get a taste?" Her eyes crinkled in mirth.

"A bit. May I have the rest?" He made as if to continue his endeavors. His eyes glittered in amusement, the lines that had formed around them even in youth crinkling in anticipatory humor.

"If you are to be a congressman, and the people have spoken it so, then you will have decisions to make. If you cannot make this one now without my help, how will you ever get anything done in office?" She walked up to him and pushed on his arm, forcing the cake to his mouth. "Eat, Abraham. Tell me if you truly like it still, as you claimed last evening."

He bit into the moistness, and he chewed slowly as he closed his eyes. He had the slice finished before he spoke, and his words told it all.

"I have never had better, Mary. Never better in my entire life."

She nodded decisively. "I thought so, Abraham."

"You did, did you?" He put one arm across her shoulders and gave a hearty laugh.

Abraham Lincoln felt good today. There was no hint of the shadow that often haunted his moods; the War with Mexico was far away; and he was glad to be alive.

MILITARY JOURNAL
Brigadier General Stephen W. Kearny
COMMANDER, ARMY OF THE WEST

5 Dec. 1846. Help from Stockton has finally arrived. 37 volunteer riflemen commanded by Lt. Archibald Gillespie have joined our ranks. With them they bring one field gun, which will not be unwelcome. I am most glad for Gillespie's presence, for he brings news of the country ahead, as well as fresh mules for our use.

In spite of Lt. Gillespie's welcome presence, the torrential rains of the past days have left the troops demoralized. We have traveled some thousand and more miles, never to fire a shot. Now we must also endure mud and dreary skies. At least the rain has abated for a span, although the skies threaten to drench us once again.

Yet, if we trust the new information we have recently received from Lt. Gillespie, we have been given the opportunity for which my troops have been anxious. It seems the solution to our low spirits lies just ahead at the Indian village of San Pasqual. Gillespie has been given warning that Captain Andrés Pico, brother of Mexican Governor Pio

Pico, lies in wait with 100 Californios. I am sending my aide-de-camp, Lt. Hammond, with a number of dragoons, accompanied by Rafael Machado, to scout the enemy position. Although a Californio deserter, Machado knows the area as well as anyone, and pleads desperately to help. I have assigned him to accompany Lt. Hammond as guide.

I have put Lt. Gillespie's offer to use his "mountain men" for reconnaissance aside, for I feel it is important that this mission be carried out by my regulars. Lt. Hammond is preparing to leave as I write, and I anxiously await his return, for with God willing, we will attack at first light.

I am certain that against the prospect of a rousing fight, the morale of my men will soon be restored. I also trust this damnable rain to hold off, for I fear it will dampen our powder, and it would be disastrous if our carbines should misfire.

NEAR SAN PASQUEL, CALIFORNIA
Army of the West
DECEMBER 5, 1846

"I told Kearny this is stupidity." Captain Benjamin Moore sat at Lieutenant Thomas Hammond's side, watching him as he pulled on his boots.

"You did not tell him, Ben. You shouted at him." Thomas chuckled, then quietly, but with dramatic overtones, repeated Benjamin's words spoken so recently in General Kearny's emergency Council of War. "Take them by surprise! Strike while they are dismounted! The Californios are fresh, and once on their horses, will prove our masters!"

"I sounded so pompous?"

"And worse, Ben. However, I consider you my brother, and I was not offended."

"You wish to do this, then, reconnoiter the enemy in the dark of night? I do not trust this deserter, Machado."

"Nor I, Ben, but I am sick and tired of doing nothing. If Kearny had been swayed with your argument, I would gladly attack under the element of surprise, for I also feel a quick jab without warning to be the much better tactic. However, you are not the general, and neither am I. We are officers in the United States Army, and there is a chain of command. We must follow orders." He also remembered Swords' suggestion that Ben's family were cowards. The man would be proved wrong, and he would see the fortitude Ben had claimed. It was Thomas' as well.

"He wishes to attack in the morning. First light. We should attack now." Benjamin's jaw was firmly set. He could not believe this mistake was about to be made, and there was nothing he could do to prevent it. "At the least, attack in the morning without risking revealing ourselves now."

Thomas stood, and he slapped Benjamin on the shoulder. "I know where your Major Swords will be when the attack begins." He grinned.

"You are now privy to General Kearny's plans?" Ben looked up to catch the grin.

"When a man accuses another of being a coward, what

is the reason for that?" The grin was broader.

"You tell me. I'm too consumed with this mistake that is sending you into unwarranted danger."

"A man calls another a coward because inside he feels himself to be one. When we attack, I wager to find Major Swords at the back of the charge." Thomas made ready to exit the tent.

"He's quartermaster." Ben watched Thomas turn to face him. "Of course he'll be at the back of the charge."

"He feels a coward, and that is why he will be at the back of the charge." Thomas winked. "I'm reluctant to take this mission, although I have accepted my general's command. Am I a coward, Ben?"

With those words, Benjamin leaped to his feet and threw his arms around his brother-in-law. "You are an officer of honor and distinction, one who will be first to step into battle. I am proud to claim you as friend." He released his friend and stepped back, his eyes gritty with unexpected and very intense emotion.

"That's the Benjamin Moore I know. We shall win this battle. Keep your chin up."

Thomas threw his brother-in-law a sharp but clearly mocking salute, and when it was returned, he laughed. Within moments he was outside the tent, and his voice could be heard calling for Machado.

The enemy had been found at last, and five months of fruitless overland travel were now at an end. Battle was soon to be engaged.

Best Friends and Brothers

NEAR SAN PASQUEL, CALIFORNIA
Mexican Californios
DECEMBER 5, 1846

"I heard the words of that Indian, and I do not trust him." Captain Andrés Pico reached into a wooden bowl at his side and pulled out a tight bunch of freshly picked grapes, still damp with moisture from the evening's spattering rain. They were small and purple, but the taste was sweet. He pulled one off and sucked on it. Not an old man at 36, the captain's hair had already begun to recede, and he had the beginnings of circles under his eyes. A carefully trimmed moustache swooped down his jowls, giving his face a dark cast.

The rough room he was in was shadowed, lit only by an oil lamp. The Indians who had occupied the village had left dried vegetables hanging from the crudely dressed logs that formed the rafters, and there was a supply of sticks to burn in the earthen oven. The roof kept out much of the fitful rain, and it was relatively cozy inside.

"But if the Americans have come this close, they may attack." An unexpected stab of nervousness gave the second man's tone a frightened quality. The American troops were known to carry within their ranks large swaths of untrained volunteers. Atrocities had been committed: innocent families ravished, cattle butchered, and homesteads burned. News of the boy hunted and killed for sport by the Kentucky regiment had yet to filter this far west, but rape, pillage, and plunder were not unknown when untrained troops comprised an army. The man at Pico's side had reason to be of

271

a timorous mind. He offered a suggestion cautiously, "Perhaps we should send a scout."

"Pah! There will be no attack. Let the men rest. My brother, the governor, will not let the Americans claim our land again. It is over and done with. They are defeated. Pah!" His repetition of the dismissive word was enough for him. He had no fear of the American interlopers. They were dung, to be trampled on and left behind for another to also ignore.

As his subordinate exited the meager room, the captain reached for another grape. Anyway, tomorrow would be time enough to send out a party to check on this story, but it was probably not even a story at all, just spiteful words from a disgruntled Indian in order to make his men restless in their sleep. Andrés was not worried. He was a brave man, and his brother was governor of Alto California. It was dark, anyway, and the skies were heavy with rain. This was a good time to enjoy his bowl of grapes. He pulled another one free and popped it into his mouth, soon adding one more seed to the small pile he had assembled on the table at his side.

SAN PASQUEL, CALIFORNIA
Army of the West
DECEMBER 5, 1846

Rafael Machado knelt in the dark, pulling his collar around his face. His black hair swept back from receding temples, ending in damp curls at his neck. His brows were thick, lending him a heavy, ponderous look. When he began to talk, his eyes unconsciously narrowed, giving his words a shifting quality. He looked up, his features betraying his readiness to speak.

"There," Machado pointed. This was familiar terrain to him in the daylight. It was nearing midnight, though, and the clouds overhead blocked any light from the landscape. He blew into his hands. It was indeed cold outside. "We must go that way."

"You wish us to travel such a hopeless path?" Lieutenant Thomas Hammond, kneeling at Machado's side, was finally out of patience. Machado had led them through the darkness, stopping at every tree and wash. It was now late, and General Kearny was waiting on a report. There had been too many months of loitering, traversing unfamiliar ground, and then loitering once again. He felt he would burst if he didn't take action.

"Yes," Machado agreed. "We will find the Californians a half mile that way. If you wish to see their encampment, you need only to search for them there. It is an old Indian village." He used the Anglo term for the Californios, certain its usage would substantiate his claims to be on the American's side. In the presence of his Mexican brothers, he would have called Pico's men by the regional and more accurate Californio, for they had all been born in California, worshipped in the Catholic Church, and spoke Spanish as their primary tongue.

When Hammond's sabre clanked in the darkness, Machado put his fingers to his lips. "Shh!"

"Do not shush me!" Thomas Hammond stood abruptly,

cursing softly when a tree branch caught his face in the darkness. He pushed it roughly aside. "I see nothing there."

"I know," Machado whispered. "Yet, it is there."

He hoped his message to Pico had gotten through. The Indians were two-faced, however. They would say one thing and do another. He was uncertain whether the communication he'd sent warning Captain Pico had been delivered or simply forgotten. He could help ensure its success, perhaps, if he could take the Americans closer. Perhaps then he could find a way to warn Captain Pico of the size of the invading American forces, and all would be forgiven. He would surely be welcomed back if he were instrumental in revealing the presence of the approaching army.

"You're a fool, Machado." Thomas Hammond found his mount's reins, and he pulled himself into the saddle. "There is no one there, and if there is, they will certainly flee when they hear us coming."

It was a valid conclusion. The Army of the West had traveled from the Kansas-Missouri border all the way to California, even taking possession of Santa Fe and the surrounding territory, and not a shot had been fired. At each turn of the trail, the Mexican forces had fled in apparent terror when the Americans had approached. There was no obvious reason why this should be any different. Besides, Hammond had been an officer for three years, and he had idled his boots the entire time. He had not seen one day of battle. He felt he would explode if he didn't take this moment, and with that, he began to move.

Lieutenant Hammond called to the men's outlines he

could barely see, black against the blackness of the hills, "Gentleman, our guide has shown us the enemy. I say to pursue them now is to scatter them thoroughly. On your mounts, men, and after me." He dug his spurs in, and his mule darted ahead, his sword clanking at his side.

Lieutenant Hammond did get what he wanted, at least the part of making his presence known, for with the clanking of the swords, and the general noise of the party riding directly into the Indian village, dogs soon began barking. A number of Californios leaped to their feet, shouting, "Viva California, abajo los Americanos!"

In the darkness, both forces seemed more formidable to the other side than they actually were, and the Americans began a hasty retreat.

Yet, in the U.S. Army's mad scramble to exit the suddenly tumultuous situation, Andrés Pico was given certain evidence that meant he could no longer doubt that he was side-to-side with his enemy. Hammond's party left a blanket lying on the ground, one emblazoned with the letters "U.S." Even a dragoon jacket had fallen and not been retrieved. The evidence was damning, convincing Pico that behind the small force that had so quickly run away, there was a much larger American contingent, and he prepared to abandon camp. He only had seventy-six men. He could not take on the vast American army. It was time to leave the field to the larger, invading force.

"Vamos!" Captain Pico waved a hand in the darkness toward where he knew his men were, uncaring that he couldn't be seen. "Vamos, muchachos! Vamos!"

NEAR SAN PASQUEL, CALIFORNIA
Army of the West
DECEMBER 5-6, 1846

"Confound it, Hammond. You say the Californios are preparing to attack? It's well past midnight, and colder than a dry dog's teats." General Kearny shivered. "Has anyone checked the firearms since that drenching several hours ago?" He stepped to the door of the tent and moved the flap aside. The night seemed coated with a blue-black glimmer, for the sheen of moisture had attached itself to everything. He thought of Captain Moore's earlier warning and entreaty. Turning, he questioned, "Did you see their mounts?"

"Sir," Hammond insisted, "They have good horses. Well fed and fit, it seemed. We glimpsed a number of them."

"Then we must attack now. If we could procure replacement horses for ourselves, it would only do us good. To wait would be folly."

In his assessment of the facts, Kearny misread the situation entirely, for he would need to capture the horses to use them as his own. He failed to consider that the Californios might already be upon their well-fed brutes, the masters of the field in any ensuing conflict of opponents. Instead, he looked to Lieutenant Gillespie standing quietly at one side. Next to him was Kit Carson.

"Gillespie! Will you back me up, Gillespie?" His men, Kearny meant. He had no doubt Gillespie as an officer would.

"General, there is one thing I have seen repeatedly in

my time in California. Any Californian of Spanish blood is predisposed to a holy terror of the American carbine." He nodded his head sharply as if that settled the matter. "My sailors and Marines will be at your back, and we will not let you down, sir."

"Carson, your men?"

Kit Carson stepped forward. "It is my belief that all Mexicans are cowards, General."

The general understood his words. The Californios had been Mexicans for generations. They were Mexicans, still.

"It is decided, then. Lieutenant Hammond, notify Captain Moore, and let us get this organized. Gillespie, Carson, gather your forces. We attack now."

SAN DIEGO, CALIFORNIA
Jon and Mary Ann McCreary
DECEMBER 6, 2009

"Jon, can you read this?" Mary Ann McCreary squinted her eyes at her computer screen. She glanced to find him across the room. He was in bed already, and he had his book out again. He hadn't made much progress in it since he'd started, although he'd been tackling it for months. Reading wasn't his thing, and he had found no compulsion to press forward into the story.

He looked up over his glasses. "From this distance? Hardly, Mary Ann. I can barely read this book." He held it up, then closed it and set it to the side. "What do you have there?" He remembered his rendition of Major Swords' tirade against Captain Duncan, and he wondered if he was about to have the opportunity to do another.

"I don't know." She reached to the keyboard, tapping it several times. "I'm not even sure where this came from. I mean, I *know*, because I'm in my e-mail program, but this is like a foreign language."

"What?" Jon chuckled. "Let me look at it. Are you sure it's not one of those virus messages?" He threw the covers aside and sat his feet on the floor.

"A virus? Oh, Jon!" She looked up, horrified, remembering all Matthew's stored e-mail messages. What if they were lost? "I didn't even think. Oh, I hope not."

He walked up beside her and frowned, his eyes on her screen. A window was open, and the words it contained seemed gibberish.

"Where did you get that?" He dropped to sit at her side. "That looks Arabic. This came in an e-mail, and you opened it?"

"Well, I was looking at some of Matthew's old e-mails." She knew Jon wouldn't like hearing this, and she looked at him in apology. "I'm sorry, Jon. I know you tell me not to, but I just can't help myself."

"Okay, sweetheart. You were looking at Matt's old e-mails." He nodded his head, his thoughts turning. The past few months had been hard on their relationship, but they were still there for each other. He intended it to remain that way, and he framed his words with care. "But this. How did you get this?"

"That's just it, Jon. I was looking at Matthew's e-mails. I know them all, and I was scrolling through them. Suddenly, a new one popped up." She pointed to the heading of the e-mail.

"A new one?" Jon looked closely. "Mary Ann, this isn't to you. This was sent to Matt. It was forwarded to you."

"Sent to Matt?" She pursed her lips, then nodded. "Yes, that could be. I called up months ago, and they told me how to go in and have the program do that. You know, just in case there were any bills he had set up through his e-mail account. Several things came in months ago, but nothing since. Do you think this is something like that?"

"In Arabic?" Jon chewed his lips, his thoughts of taking care to avoid emotional landmines set aside. This could be bigger than that, it seemed, and it worried him.

"Should I delete it? I don't want a virus."

He pulled the computer from her hands. "It's too late for that, if this is a virus. When did you get it?"

"Just now. I told you that. There, it says it was received today, December 6th."

"Well, it was sent weeks ago. See? There's the original date. I want to see what this says."

"You can read Arabic?" Mary Ann laughed, her nervousness brushing her voice with a quaver not normally there. "You never have before."

"There are programs that can. Watch." He looked at her, an uncomfortable twitch in his stomach. "By the way, are we on the Internet here?"

"The motel's Wi-Fi, I think. See, the green light's there on the keyboard. I think that must be why the message appeared. I haven't been hooked to the Internet in quite a while."

"Good, because I have to have Internet access to do this." He opened a search engine and typed in a request for a translation program. Almost immediately, a list of possible choices appeared. He clicked on one that looked promising, and it opened, filling the screen. He went to the opened e-mail message and copied the Arabic text, deftly pasting it into the translation program. Then he looked at Mary Ann.

"Ready?" His voice was light, but the twitch was still there, buried in his gut.

She had been watching his face, though. She smiled, her earlier tensions eased by his attentive help, unaware of his inner warnings. "I didn't know you knew how to do that." She glanced at the screen then back to her husband. "When, I mean, how—"

"All Army fathers can do this. Now, are you ready? It might be one of Matt's Arabic girlfriends leaving him a smutty message." He tried to keep his words light and playful.

She chortled, playfully pushing on her husband's arm. "He did not have an Arabic girlfriend. It's probably an advertisement for a weight-building drink. Matthew never could keep extra pounds on. He was always trying the latest thing to build muscle."

"Let's see." He moved his finger on the touch pad, and then he clicked the translate button. After a moment he frowned when nothing happened. "It didn't work." He sounded almost relieved.

"Oh!" Mary Ann laughed. "See? It still says English to English. See if you can change that first box to Arabic."

She followed as he clicked on an arrow, and a list of languages pulled up. He clicked on the word Arabic, and still nothing happened.

"Click again to translate, Jon."

When the translated text appeared, the words didn't reveal a smutty message from an unknown girlfriend, and they didn't offer to sell them body-building power drinks. Instead, the words gave Jon the revelation he had hoped not to see, one that filled him with anger, and he quickly turned the computer so his wife couldn't readily see the insult on the screen.

For Mary Ann, the words would be her first glimmer of real hope, once she got to read them, and he knew that. It would be a false hope, too, Jon was certain. These things always were.

"This is a prank." Jon made to roughly close the computer, jerking his head to the side and looking away. "Some fool somewhere needs to be shot."

"What, Jon?"

"Did you read it?" For a moment he hoped she had. Maybe she would see the truth in spite of his doubts.

"Well, I tried, but I can't very well with the lid in the way." She reached for the computer, but it was tight in his hands. "Jon?"

"I need to send this to the State Department. Harassment. This is harassment, Mary Ann. Here. Let me deal with it. I'll get on the phone and call someone right this minute. They'll know how to deal with this." He made as if to stand up, but she grabbed his arm.

"Jon, give me the computer. I want to read the message." She placed her hand on it and looked at him.

"You don't, Mary Ann." He felt relief she didn't know the words. He knew she would see them as positive, and they were anything but.

"Jon." Her grip was firm with intent. When he released

the computer, she opened the lid all the way and let her eyes scan the translated words. Finally, she read them aloud. "I am friend to Americans. American soldier on television lives. I help you find him. Please send reply." She felt her breath quicken, and she looked at her husband. "Jon?"

"See, Mary Ann? I warned you." He sat at her side again, worry and love for her swelling up inside, the two mixed into a stream of confusion that he didn't always know how to manage. "I tried to warn you. If we reply to that e-mail, they will probably ask us to wire them money to buy Matt a plane ticket." He touched her cheek and found they were wet with tears. "These people are not our friends."

"You thought I would believe this was a real message?" She turned to look at him, her eyes rough and gritty. "I'm not a fool, Jon."

"I didn't say you were." He put his arm around her. "You're a mother, and you loved Matt very much."

"I love him, Jon." Her reply was sharp, as if it contained newly found shards of motherly iron. "You do what you suggested, though. Call. Do it now. You're right. This is harassment, and it needs to stop."

"Now?" When he had seen the words, he had been abruptly angry, but he knew this could wait until morning. It probably should, too. It was late to get someone at the State Department. His threat earlier had been to get the computer away from his wife before she saw the message. Now that she recognized it for the mean-spirited phishing attempt it was, there was no point in rushing.

"Now, Jon. Either you call, or I will." She narrowed her eyes at him. "I mean it."

She would, too. In spite of what she'd said, she couldn't

deny the thought that any shred of hope was better than none. If this really did concern Matthew, and it sounded that way, then it needed to be passed on quickly to someone who could pursue it. They couldn't. Jon wouldn't. Someone had to.

Matthew might still be alive.

Tears once again filled her eyes. Jon looked at her as he dialed the number, but he thought the tears were for the harassing message. What he couldn't see was the hope that she didn't want dashed. She so much needed this to be true, more than anything in the world.

NEAR SAN PASQUEL, CALIFORNIA
Army of the West
DECEMBER 6, 1846

"Your country expects much of you, men." General Kearny stood on a ridge between Santa Maria and San Pasqual. His troops were in good order, still, and he wished to keep them that way. This would be the last time he would be able to communicate easily until the battle was done, and he wished to make his instructions clear. "Charge with the point of your sabres. Surround the enemy camp and take as many alive as you can."

The general turned to his best men. "Captain Moore, I expect you to lead the attack, along with your dragoons. Lieutenant Gillespie, join Captain Moore and assist in surrounding the village. Note this, Lieutenant Gillespie, we are here to capture the enemy, not shoot them to death. That is a strict order."

Gillespie nodded but quickly looked away. He would rather shoot them all, and capturing the Californians be damned. They were a sorry bunch. If they proved true to form, they would all run as soon as they heard the clanking of the soldiers' arms and the sounds of horses' hooves, anyway. He would not have a chance to shoot a one.

Gillespie didn't consider one very obvious fact. His evaluation of the opposing forces' spinelessness might have been true when the Californians had been unprepared, but thanks to Lieutenant Hammond, such was no longer the case.

Kearny remained stationary on his mount as the company began to trail forward. Turning his animal, he nudged it with his leg, starting it on the trek down into the valley. It concerned him that the men bringing up the rear had the poorest of the mounts, for in the heat of a charge, his officers, more passably mounted, could easily pull too far ahead. There was little help for that, though.

He paused his descent to turn to the back of the company. He could see only shadows moving in the darkness, but he knew Major Swords and his supply column brought up the rear. All points of attack were thoroughly covered, and victory would be theirs.

However, even as General Kearny paused, his force was unavoidably scattering. The path into the valley was littered with brush, small trees, and pitfalls each step of the way. In the darkness, tired mounts and exhausted men had difficulty finding their footing.

When the last of the soldiers had begun to clear the ridge, the general called an order, "Trot, men!"

In the scramble under the cover of darkness, Captain Abraham Johnson misheard the order, and he called to those forward of him, "Charge!" It was an honest mistake in the cold and damp, yet one that could easily spell disaster.

Realizing the mistake, Kearny voiced to several men nearby, as if in apology, "Heavens! He surely misunderstood!" It was too late, though.

In a matter of moments, Captain Johnson's better mount, along with twelve dragoons, had passed Captain Moore's struggling mule, and Johnson was quickly at the forefront of the column. He was—as were all the Americans—spoiling for action. This was his moment, and the rush of adrenalin in his blood made unlikely chances worth the taking. He would trust in his weapons and his skills, and when those were no longer enough, others would step in to support his efforts. It was the way a battle was won.

Any further help he might require from General Kearny, Lieutenant Emory, or the engineer, William Warner, would be out of the question, however, for they struggled far behind. Even farther behind were the additional fifty dragoons who might have provided crucial support, riding the worst of the Army's mules. Captain Johnson and his twelve men were on their own.

A party of Pico's men, covering for those preparing for retreat, opened fire on the closing enemy troops. The first volley caught Captain Johnson in the head, killing him instantly. Seeing additional Americans in the distance, the Californios turned to run, causing Captain Moore to cry out, "Continue the charge!"

With those words, Captain Andrés Pico and his men stopped their retreat and turned reluctantly to fight. They surely had no other choice. In that moment of perceived desperation, they could only hope the victory might be theirs.

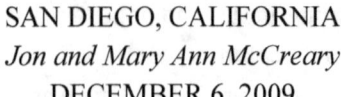

SAN DIEGO, CALIFORNIA
Jon and Mary Ann McCreary
DECEMBER 6, 2009

"So, Jon. What's the verdict? Are we no more than crazy civilians crying wolf at nonexistent trauma?" Mary Ann McCreary laughed nervously. "You see, I have copies of the newspaper articles from 1846. Mary Ann Hammond, my namesake, you will remember, held the proof that her husband was alive. It was in the *Liberty Tribune*. The war was over, and the Army was coming home. She held that paper in her hand on December 5, not knowing that her husband had not returned to Santa Fe as the story claimed. He had gone on to California, and he would never see the light of another day. You see, Jon, I don't know whom to trust." She looked at him from across the room, her eyes filling with impending tears.

"They gave me a forwarding address. They didn't say

anything except that they want the e-mail sent to them immediately. It seemed to make a difference when I told them it had been forwarded from Matt's old account." He walked to her, handing her a piece of paper with an unfamiliar e-mail address scribbled across one edge.

"A difference?" Mary Ann held the paper in her hand for a moment, her eyes tracing the inscription jotted down in Jon's firm script. Then she looked to her husband. "What do you mean, a difference?"

"The sergeant's words were noncommittal, but his voice sounded more urgent than I would have expected. It's possible, I guess, that they think there could be something to it. Do you want to be the one to send it?"

"Something to this? Mary Ann Hammond had proof her husband was alive, and she never saw him again. I can't let myself hope, Jon." She did, though. She twisted the paper, simply holding it and looking at it once again. Not entering it into the computer meant hope was still possible, because as long as the unusual e-mail was only on her computer, anything could happen. Once she forwarded it, though, it could be so easily dismissed by the State Department, and then all hope would be gone.

"Now, Mary Ann, would be a good time to send it." Jon remembered how surprised he'd been at the urgency in the voice on the other end of the line. Forward it immediately, the man had said. Jon chided his wife's reluctance gently, "I didn't put anything to this when I first called them, but you should have heard that man's voice. This might indeed be something. He was very clear that we were not to wait."

"Here goes nothing." She set the paper beside the keyboard and began to type in the address. Then she clicked send and watched the message zoom away through cyber-space. She murmured, "There goes everything."

It was everything, too. Every hope and dream of her Matthew coming home once again was in that message, and it had better come back to her with very good news. It had just better.

SAN PASQUEL, CALIFORNIA
Army of the West
DECEMBER 6, 1846

Underneath the banks of clouds, the sodden sky had started to lighten, and the field of battle was beginning to show itself. A cold rain had begun to pelt the ground, and Lieutenant Thomas Hammond gloated as he watched the defending Californios flee. Thomas had hated to see Captain Johnson go down, but any man who misinterpreted com-mands had botched his own powder. This was a battle, after all, and no officer was guaranteed to come out on the other side.

Prodding his mount on, he wrestled with his exhausted, travel-weary mule. The animal struggled forward against the unyielding terrain, at times refusing to plod ahead. Resounding off the splatting sounds of the cold, falling raindrops, the echoes of the occasional musket or carbine reverberated in the dim morning light. The yelling of men's voices told that the height of the skirmish had now been engaged. This was the fight Thomas had waited three years to engage, and he would not be left out now.

Up ahead was Benjamin, and a fierce resolve steeled itself in Thomas' chest. He must be at his friend's side. He no longer noticed the dampness of unaccustomed nerves soaking down his back, or the rough spot inside his boot that had plagued him the past weeks. All around, the dense battering of the cold rain continued to scour the landscape, but there was nothing in Thomas' thoughts except the missed chance for glory playing itself out just beyond arms' reach, and the fool animal that was the cause of it. If he could not force it to push itself ahead more quickly, Ben would catch the best of the fight. This was Thomas' time to join the fray, and the opportunity would not avail itself forever.

With effort, Thomas tore his attention from his floundering mount and focused on the battle scene before him. His heart caught in his throat, for there was Benjamin with his pistol in his hand, and several of the Californio lancers were coming directly at him.

"Fire, Ben," he yelled, and he reached for his own weapon. He was appalled to see his brother-in-law unaccountably cast his gun aside without firing and grab for his sabre.

At that moment, Thomas' mule went to its side, rolling with a braying bleat into a pan of thick mud, barely allowing him time to jump wide as it fell. Stumbling, the pounding rain making a soupy slurry of the surrounding earth, Thomas made for his friend's side, using his downed animal to stabilize his footing as he struggled by.

He soon found why Captain Moore had thrown his weapon aside, for when Thomas raised his own and pulled it to fire, there was only a spark and no resulting blast from the barrel.

"No," he cried, realizing the powder had surely become soaked.

Ahead of him waved the wet spears of the Californio lancers, and it seemed they were everywhere. They glistened in the rain, all fourteen feet of each one. The Californios yelled to one another in their rough-sounding Spanish, and each time a lancer called out, the glittering shafts of willow wood flashed through the air as a single entity. The terrifying sight reminded Hammond of his early days in the classroom as one of his Academy professors had described the African veldt. In that far away classroom, tribal warriors had gathered to resolve a long-standing conflict, and terror had reigned in the gathering gloom. Thomas blinked his eyes rapidly as he looked to the left and right. This was real, not some graphic demonstration of fierce warfare learned in his schooling. With a surge of preordained determination, he felt his blood course hotly through his veins.

Thomas turned to see others were in the same predicament as he found himself. Officers cast aside pistols and carbines alike with impunity. With certainty in his heart, Thomas pulled his sabre. He would fight with what he had, and he would be at Benjamin's side. They would know victory together. When the battle was won, they would gather around a fire, dry their clothes, and tell stories that would follow them into the history books, tales that school children would read about for decades to come.

The nearest charging lancer changed all that, for with a sweep of hooves, the larger, more maneuverable horse ridden by the solitary Californio swooped down, and with a ferocious scream of anger, the lancer drove his sharpened willow pole into Captain Moore's chest, where it came cleanly through his jacket in the back. Thomas ran toward his cherished friend and confidant, his adrenalin blinding him to the sea of approaching lances flashing through the air. He was now desperate to save his companion and brother-in-law. He saw Benjamin drowning in a flood, the scene from the river flashing through his mind. Thomas saw himself as his friend's only lifeline, and to leap into the churning maelstrom to rescue his best friend and brother was not a choice he could simply cast aside. He must move, even if it meant jumping directly into an unknown torrent of danger.

Just then, Benjamin, refusing to be defeated so easily, lashed out valiantly with his sword, only to have it catch on another lance, as it, too, pierced his chest in a second terrifying thrust. The sword's blade twisted in the tangle of lances until it snapped at the hilt, catching the early morning light as it skittered away into the rain.

Thomas fought forward, his eyes seeing his friend sinking beneath the waves. His upraised sabre flashed in the crystalline dampness of the leaden morning sky, a hero in his intentions, but he only ran into death himself.

Before the deed was done, Captain Benjamin D. Moore

had taken sixteen lances, and Lieutenant Thomas C. Hammond lay mortally wounded at his side, the letters he had faithfully carried against his heart no match for the plunge of the lancers' thrusts.

More valiant men died that morning. Almost every dragoon at the forefront of the attack suffered at least some damage from the lancers' lunging weapons. What had been especially deadly was the reata, the lasso with which Pico's men had so unerringly roped the dragoons, pulling them from their horses, and spearing them as they fell.

Chaos reigned on the field by the time General Kearny arrived. As Kearny was flustered by the ensuing disaster and unable to give any clear commands, for some long moments, it was every man for himself. Then a lance caught the general in the back, wounding him, although not fatally. Several of the Californios recognized Gillespie from his fighting in Los Angeles, and he was singled out, receiving multiple wounds, including a lance over the heart. Bleeding profusely but undaunted, he fought his way to one of the artillery pieces, but by that time, Pico's men had begun to retreat down the valley. Of the fifty Americans who had actually engaged the enemy, twenty-one had died, and another seventeen were left critically wounded.

In addition, it was later learned that the dragoons had taken Gillespie's mountain men for the enemy and mistakenly attacked them, having only met them the day before.

The Americans had been defeated in a bare span of minutes by a fresher and better-prepared force. Gillespie made one of the few brilliant moves in the melee. Having seen Johnson's charge fail, he moved his men to the south rim to realign with Moore's men. He was able to wipe out a number of Californians waiting to make a side attack and also captured Pico's second-in-command, Pablo Vejar.

Major Swords did, as predicted by Thomas Hammond, bring up the rear with the supply column, and thereby escaped the battle uninjured.

Due to General Kearny's injuries, Captain Turner took temporary command of the Army and immediately wrote a letter to Commodore Stockton requesting reinforcements, sending Antoine Godey and three men from Gillespie's command with him.

It wasn't until December 10th that the final shots of the battle would be fired. The Army of the West, with General Kearny once again in command, would reach San Diego the next day, seventy-eight days after having left Santa Fe.

It would be another fourteen months before the War with Mexico would draw to a close on February 2, 1848. The Treaty of Guadalupe Hidalgo would acknowledge the U.S. ownership of Texas, draw the U.S.-Mexican border along the Rio Grande River, and give the United States land which would one day comprise states stretching across much of the western half of the great country that was to come.

With that treaty, the Manifest Destiny of the United States of America would have finally expanded her borders from sea to shining sea, opening up opportunities for a growing nation in the century ahead.

REPUBLIC OF MEXICO
Chamber of Senators
THE HONORABLE CONGRESS OF THE UNION

Vote for Presidential Offering
December 6, 1846

A vote has been taken, and in spite of much dissention and argument, a decision has been reached, 11-9 in favor, determining that the Presidency of the Republic of Mexico be offered unconditionally to General Antonio de Santa Anna. The Vice-Presidency will be offered to Gómez Farías. Inauguration Ceremonies are set to be December 23.

Senate Members Voting:

Juan Jósef Ríncon	POR	Esteban Moncada	POR
Carlos Maria Junipero	CONTRA	Gregória Tapia	POR
Felipe Santiago Garcia	POR	Jose Cuadra	CONTRA
Pascual Antonio	POR	Juan Bódega y Tapia	POR
Jose Antonio Inocencio	CONTRA	Pedros Vallejo	POR
Josef Julian	CONTRA	Ygnacio Espinosa	POR
Antonio Rosalia	POR	Diego Bóríca	CONTRA
Jóse de Jesus	CONTRA	Joaquin Arguello	CONTRA
Manuel Esteban	POR	Jose Arrillaga	CONTRA
Diego Rívera y Martinez	POR	Miguel Fages	CONTRA

Best Friends and Brothers

PLATTE CITY, MISSOURI
Methodist Congregation
DECEMBER 6, 1846

"The Lord stand by your side." The minister paused at his pulpit and intoned his words. A majestic figure, the town's religious leader carried a halo of white hair, although his clerical robes seemed bulkier than usual. He wore them over his coat and heavy pants. Each breath brought a cloud of moisture in the chilled room. It was cold in the building, for it was early December, and winter had come with a vengeance to the Missouri hills.

He paused for his small congregation to respond.

"And at your side, also." The words were murmured in reply, puffs of condensation escaping lips with each syllable.

"Let your hearts be lifted." The minister's hands soared like doves into the air.

"To the Lord we lift them." The sound of voices spoken in common filled the small space.

"We give thanks to the One who made us."

"Our thanks to the Lord God above."

The attendees at the Sunday morning service seated themselves without being told. The small wooden building was the only church yet organized in Platte City, and for anyone who wished to attend, it had been offering a Sunday service each week since 1842. Nominally it was Methodist, although several of the attendees were of a less specific denominational background. It didn't matter, though. The Lord's House was the Lord's House, and there He could be found, no matter the denomination written across its charter.

Many pulled collars tighter, and several members of the small congregation readjusted gloves on their hands. The building was indeed little warmer than being outside, but that was only as expected. Even the fire in the small stove at the back did little more than knock the worst of winter's frost from the people's skin, for it would be impossible to heat the building to a comfortable temperature. In wintertime it was only used a few hours each week. For that reason, those present were still bundled in their heaviest coats this December 6th, even though they were firmly and decisively indoors.

"We thank everyone for their attendance this cold morning," the minister began. "We have a special reason to rejoice." He smiled and looked directly at Mary Ann Hammond.

She was bundled in a snug coat of bright burgundy, and a coordinating hat adorned her head. Her cheeks were flushed with the cold, but then so were those of most of the women present. She sat beside her father, Judge Hughes. The children, Mattie and little Tommie, and Mattie's younger sister, Molly, were at home with Sissy, as it had been deemed too cold to risk the children just for the morning's services. The judge's wife had been chilled, and had also remained behind, warming by the kitchen fire. Judge Hughes would have preferred to stay in, but Mary Ann had wanted to attend the service desperately, feeling a strong desire to offer her thanks for her husband's safe return.

"Miss Mary Ann? You desire a moment of our time?"

The minister called her by an outdated pet name, even though she was long since married. His reference to her spousal status, although incorrect, was a measure of their many years of association together. She was unoffended, for he had spoken with her earlier that morning, calling her by the virginal Miss even then. He knew she wished to speak to those present, and in a gentle voice, he had agreed to allow it. The congregation was small, and the services were often very informal.

"I wish to offer a prayer of thanks." She stood as she began to share. "My husband, Thomas, went to war this summer past, and news arrived just yesterday that he will soon safely return to me once more. It is only by the Grace of God that he is given back to me, and I wish to express my thankfulness for all to hear." She had tears in her eyes by then, and she reached with a handkerchief to pat them dry. Her father, smiling, extended a hand to her arm for reassurance.

"Thank you, Miss Mary Ann." The minister nodded and then spoke to the rest of the congregation, "It will be wise for each of us to remember God's goodness during the upcoming week. For the Scriptures tell us that when we pass through the Valley of the Shadow of Death, it shall not steal our comfort from us, for our hope is in the Lord. Our God is always at our side, and if we place our trust in Him, He will guide our footsteps and lead us home."

"Amen," came the murmured responses from several of the attendees.

"Miss Mary Ann," the minister turned, "we all look

forward to Lieutenant Hammond's return, and Judge Hughes, to the return of Captain Moore, also. I know little Matthew must look forward to seeing his father once again. We trust God will watch over them on their journey home."

The minister's words were truer than he knew, for even as he spoke, the two men, brothers in their hearts if not by blood, lay side by side in the cold California rain. They were indeed on their journey home, but this time, their passage would not lead their footsteps to their families in the beloved Missouri hills where they'd chosen to build good lives far from the lands of their births. No, they had begun a journey of a far different kind, that long crossing from which no mortal man can return.

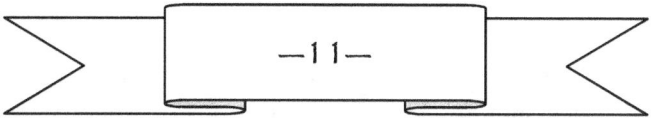

—11—

WASHINGTON, D.C.
The Reunion
WINTER 2010

The sound of a distant helicopter beat against the brilliant blue sky. The winter sun had come through with a day of mild temperatures, and the early morning breezes were gone with yesterday's snowfall. A band could be heard tuning up in the distance, and on a raised podium surrounded with bunting, several military officials could be seen searching for a seat. One important-looking official, surrounded by numerous black-suited men in dark glasses, appeared suspiciously like one who had exited the White House just that morning.

Other people, regular Joes, ones who hailed from Florida and Texas and Missouri, could be seen taking seats on the ground level. Their chairs were lined up in an orderly fashion directly in front of the Washington Monument, and where it thrust high into the sky over their heads, it cast a finger of a shadow in their midst. Some people were visiting, holding cups of steaming coffee against what chill remained in the air. Others huddled together, arms encircling weary shoulders, the pain of the freshened memories cutting them deep. All had been bonded, although most had never met before this day. By the time they left the Mall, they would become a family, a common grief threading them together for all time.

Mary Ann McCreary and her husband, Jon, were two of those regular Joes. They had finally consented to join the planned memorial celebration for the soldiers killed all those months ago in Iraq, but theirs was a special reason for being there. They didn't stand with the others near the podium and all its bunting. A distinct area had been occasioned for them.

Mary Ann removed her sunglasses and peered at the 'copter growing steadily closer. "Is that him, Jon?" She could barely breathe for her anticipation.

"Maybe. It's certainly someone." He smiled. He was sure it was. His eyes trailed the big machine as it drew closer, then settled slowly to the ground.

Television crews were poised and ready, for one of America's own was returning to the shores of his homeland. The arriving soldier might be battered and bruised, but he *was* coming home, and all America wanted to watch. They needed to see and rejoice in a perceived slap against the tyranny of terrorism. They craved a connection with something bigger than their everyday lives. This was their chance.

The scene hit closer to home for the two most involved people watching. Jon's eyes never left the door of the machine, for he needed this as much as his wife did.

When the side of the 'copter opened, out first stepped

one of the men in the dark suits and black sunglasses. Then another.

"Jon, where is he?" Mary Ann already felt tears building in her eyes.

"There." Jon nodded. "He's right there." They watched as a young man, his head cleanly cropped, leaned out of the machine and slipped a cap onto his head. Then he took the hand of one of the dark-suited men, and he stepped gingerly to the ground. He looked around as if searching for someone, his gaze moving across the podium and through the crowd. Then the man who had helped him exit pointed to Mary Ann and Jon. The young man smiled and raised a hand. However, before he moved, a gloved hand reached from inside the helicopter and handed out a cane. SPC Matthew McCreary took it and placed the end on the ground. Only then did he begin to make his way toward his parents, his steps slow, his limp pronounced.

"Can I go to him, Jon?" Mary Ann looked at her husband with tears streaming down her face.

"You'd better." He pushed on her shoulder, and she was off running.

On the way, her glasses fell to the ground, but she didn't care. Nor did she notice the television cameras panning her sprint across the roped off area that connected her to her boy who'd come back to life once again. Only one thing mattered at that point. When she reached her son, she threw her arms around him, heedless of what anyone might say.

"Oh, Matthew. You're safe and home." She ran her hands around his neck, relishing the touch of his skin. "You're safe."

"Mom," he said, holding his arms wide at first, and only

slowly closing them around her. "Careful. They had to reset some bones, and I've got to be cautious for a few more weeks."

"I'm sorry, Matthew. They told us all that, and I should have remembered." She lowered her arms, resting them gently on his shoulders, and looked into his face. "We just thought—"

She paused, blinking away an additional flood of tears. She saw a maturity in her son's face that she hadn't expected to find, the remnants of shadows under his eyes, new lines creasing his cheeks. She and Jon had been told he was captured, but what terrors would change him this way?

"That I was dead," he finished for her. "I wondered, too. I see Dad's here."

"Not dead," she stumbled, for a moment acutely aware of how perceptive his comment had been. "Lost to us for a time, perhaps . . . your father . . ." She quickly switched gears, unwilling to navigate such horrific memories. Today was to be a time for reunions and lives mended once again. "Oh, he missed you, Matthew. Just wait until after the ceremony. Your father has a big shindig planned. Everyone who wants to come has been invited."

"Mom, did anyone else come with you and Dad?" He began walking his father's direction, his steps measured and deliberate. However, his eyes were back to the crowd, scanning the unknown faces. Two years ago he would have seen the gathering throng as a fresh opportunity for potential friendship, and before the day was over, he would have invited one or more out to eat that evening. Today, though, his eyes held an indifference to the scene. He could no longer identify with these people, for they had no concept of the depths of depravity that one side could inflict upon another during the degeneracy of war. There was only one face he needed to find.

When Mary Ann didn't answer, he pressed her, "Mom? Did she come?"

"I'm looking, honey." Finally she pointed to the chairs grouped in their orderly rows near the podium. "There, Matthew. See?"

She looked up to his face, and it was clear he did, for he broke into a smile that spread from ear-to-ear. In that look, she caught a glimpse of the little boy who had once ridden his bicycle home from school and come bouncing into her kitchen, grabbing a cookie, saying, "I can't wait until dinner. I'm starving." She smiled, and with a motion of her hand, a very pretty girl came running their way.

"Mom, she's even more beautiful than I remember." Matthew stood as if frozen, his eyes glistening with his emotions, and he bit his bottom lip, determined to maintain control.

"Who, Matthew?" Mary Ann's question was bright, but it was just to tease. It was clear who had this boy's heart. "Had you forgotten Brittany's face so soon?"

"Not for a minute, Mom." Then he had his arms around his girl, and it was as if he'd never been away from her at all.

Did you enjoy this book?

Find more by this author at:

 THREE SKILLET

www.ThreeSkilletPublishing.com

www.ingramcontent.com/pod-product-compliance
Lightning Source LLC
Chambersburg PA
CBHW071059250626
47159CB00002B/522